"I was reading in a magazine," he begins softly, leaning a bit towards me, "about this new thing the CIA or somebody invented. It looks like this…"

He pulls a ballpoint pen – the kind you click — from his breast pocket.

"Inside the barrel is a small charge. It's loaded with a tiny projectile. If you wanna kill somebody and make it look like nothin' but a heart attack, you just…"

I turn towards him and he clicks the pen at my chest.

HEADLOCK

A Jeff Reynolds Mystery

by

Burl Barer

A Deadly Alibi Press Ltd. Mystery

Deadly Alibi Press Ltd.
An Imprint of
Madison Publishing Company
PO Box 5947
Vancouver, WA 98668-5947
madison@teleport.com

Library of Congress Catalog Card Number: 00-104532

ISBN: 1-886199-09-4 (Acid free trade paper)

To the Class of '65

Acknowledgments

I wish to extend special thanks to Robert Fazzari of the Pastime Café, and his uncle, Art Fazzari of McFeely's Tavern, for their kind cooperation, friendship, and sense of humor. Gratitude to Supii for insights into wrestling; G.M. Ford for his positive encouragement; Lawrence Block and Tony Fennelly for their sense of humor; Jane Gelfman for her representation; Margo Power for her publication; my family for being patient, and Richard for being prudent.

I

"His brains exploded."

"Really?"

"Yeah, that's what killed him. His brains exploded right in his skull. I demanded an autopsy, but before I could do anything, they donated his brain to science."

"Not for a transplant."

"No, right. Not for a transplant."

***

Anyone who says they've heard it all, hasn't.

Everybody's got a story.

Out of courtesy or curiosity, I'll listen to anything — tragic family histories, details of financial deception, implications of insurance fraud, and steamy escapades of erotic sexual infidelity.

I'm Jeff Reynolds, a private investigator who also writes books. That's not my real name, and I've been other things in my life – radio DJ, professional psychic, show-biz promoter, and producer of irritating television commercials. I invented the name "Jeff Reynolds" because folks are always asking, "What name do you write under?" and "Have I ever read anything you've written?" Either way, the fake name lets them off the hook. It sounds vaguely familiar, and it's easy for them to say, "Oh, yes. I'm sure I've heard of you."

Being a crime-cracking private eye author is really an easy gig. You can do it too, in your spare time. I'll share the basic trick right off the bat: tell everyone you're an author. When people find out that you write books, they want to talk.

Everybody's got a story, and you can always use a plot, a motive, culprit, or victim. Victims and plots are plentiful because victims never stop calling. That's why I became a P.I. – make a few bucks; find a few plots.

Here's another piece of advice: always meet clients in public and record the conversations. You'll erase most of them, but some are keepers. Particular tales border on madness – private hells acted out in public places, delusions born of desperation or undiagnosed chemical imbalances. Like I said, everybody's got a story.

And then you have guys like Richard Tibbit.

"His brains exploded, you understand. Okay?"

"Okay."

I met Richard mid-morning in the Red Apple, a coffee shop in Walla Walla, Washington.

Don't laugh.

Walla Walla, the town so nice they named it twice, is a real place, the oldest town in the state, and I live here. So does Richard Tibbit. I brought my small cassette recorder and a yellow legal pad with me to the Red Apple. When I pulled out my recorder, he pulled out his.

He's late-fifties, husky, careful, edgy, pale, and smokes Bel-Airs with heartfelt dedication. The guy is sly — the kind who checks his rear-view mirror too often, packs heat, and considers it prudent.

He's ready to talk.

"I've kept my mouth shut, okay? I can do that, keep my mouth shut, I mean."

He's not here to keep his mouth shut.

"Did you ask the cops about me," asks Richard.

"Never occurred to me."

"Good. I have no credibility in this town, not with the cops. She took care of that. She was smart, real smart. Remember, we're talking murder here, okay?"

HEADLOCK

I browse the menu, sneaking a quick glance at my watch. The Red Apple has one hell of a taco omelet, and a dandy chicken fried steak. I order two eggs, basted, with bacon and hashbrowns.

"My wife said to call you," he admits, "it wasn't my idea. She saw your picture in the paper, read about your books. True crime, right? Fiction, too. You won some award, okay? She showed me your picture, said you looked honest and likeable."

I also looked ten years younger. As for likeable, no doubt about it. Being likeable is not a character defect, and I'm not ashamed to say that people gravitate towards me like soup stains to a silk tie.

"I just want to know it's over," says Richard, "that I can stop looking over my shoulder because of what I know. If I tell the story, get it out, maybe there'll be some closure."

Maybe he listens to Dr. Laura. Middle-aged toughs don't seek "closure," they seek vindication or cash.

"Of course, if you turn this into a book, I want money."

Bingo. His Zippo clicks, the flame wavers, and another Bel-Air begins a slow burn. His narration is an unintentional imitation of Jack Nicholson so accurate it's uncanny.

He says his life was normal once, but not now, not since that first night in Walla Walla's Dacres Saloon over fifteen years ago, before the murders, before the brains exploded.

"Ya know," says Tibbit seriously, "this is the first time I've been out."

"Out?"

"Out in public."

He shifts his weight.

"Meeting with you today is very important to me. This is the first time in fifteen years I've been out of the house."

I reach in through the top of my shirt and slowly peel the Nicoderm patch off my shoulder, toss it in the ashtray, and fish the Old Golds out of my jacket. This story's a keeper.

Go ahead, Richard. I'm dying to hear everything.

We both roll tape.

"I would go downtown and play the punchboards," he begins, "well, I figured out the punchboards, I'll tell ya right now. I would make money, but on this particular evening I wasn't into punchboards at all. I'd had trouble with my oldest son, so I went downtown to drink. I found it relaxing."

He stretches out "relaxing" as if five beers were seven days in the Bahamas.

"People leave me alone when I drink, and I never had any trouble in years. So, there I am, walking into the Dacres Saloon..."

Nice place, the Dacres. It's just around the corner from the County Courthouse. The lunch crowd is lawyers, judges, and businessmen; the nighttime crowd is peppered with undercover drug cops pretending they don't know each other. The Dacres was the first luxury hotel in Washington State. It had a fancy balcony, upscale clientele, and a whorehouse across the street. The hotel lobby is now a furniture store, upstairs is empty, the whorehouse finally vanished a few decades back, but the saloon remains.

As you walk in, there are tables on your left and a long bar awaiting you up front. Tibbit says friends were at a table when he walked in, but he didn't join them.

"I was in a foul mood," he made "foul" a two-syllable word, " I wasn't good company. The bar was empty, I could sit on any stool and it wouldn't matter. So, there I am, alone at the bar, drinking beer when this guy come up and sits down next to me. Never saw him before in my life. He calls me every name in the book. I tell him, `Get the hell away from me, man.'"

Tibbit pauses, smiles, and leans forward as if sharing a secret scientific discovery.

"Well, I knew something was wrong. I mean this guy just flat wouldn't leave me alone. Damned if I'm gonna get up and move. The last thing I remember, he called me a son of a bitch. Later in the story you might understand that's a word I will not take from anybody."

Note: Never call Tibbit a son of a bitch.

"I used to laugh at people who said `I lost it. I don't remember.' What a bunch of shit, right? You're up for murder and you don't remember? Well, I lost it."

He forces a laugh, flicks ash, and involuntarily flexes massive biceps. I see them moving beneath his windbreaker. I also see another bulge just under his right arm. Like I said, prudent.

I lean back, as if relaxing, measuring his reach.

"WHAM! I mean I decked that guy but good," says Richard, "I came to on top of him, pummeling his face into pulp. They had to tear me off of him, drag me to the door, and toss me out. They had me for assault, pure and simple. There were lawyers and judges sittin' back there while I'm beatin' the guy's face in, for Christ's sake. Hell, it might have a prosecutor who pulled me off, and a public defender who slammed the door behind me."

"So, what happened?"

Tibbit extends his hands in an expansive, inclusive gesture.

"Nothin' happened. No charges were pressed. Nothin' was ever said about it again."

"What did you do?"

"What do you think I did? There was only one thing to do – I changed bars."

Oh. Hell of a story. I check my watch. I've only been here a few minutes; he's been in his house for fifteen years. I can afford to keep listening.

"I switched taverns, and went into McFeely's one evening to play the boards – the punchboards, right? There are three big Indians in there. I mean good size Indians."

"Not Hindus."

"No, Native Americans they call 'em now. Big Indians. I walked up and gave the bartender a twenty, ya know. Before he got the money, this Indian grabs it and rips it in half. Throws it down. And I'm going, `Jeeesus'."

"What did the bartender think of that?"

"He never said a goddam word. Not a word. So I got my beer, got my change, and went to sit down. There's this woman, I don't know her last name, but her name is Verna. She's been a prostitute in this town for years. I'd always been polite to her, Okay? If she chose to do what she wants in her life, I'm not gonna judge her. She knows me and I sit down. We're chattin' and the three big sons of bitches walked up. I took off my glasses, and one of em grabbed my arm. He says, `c'mon, let's go outside.'

Verna said "Dick, don't do it."

"Down at the end of the bar was a lady I had never seen in my life. She's doing one of those long French inhales with her smoke, ya know, up her nose. I'm thinking maybe I can handle this. I can handle two of these guys anyway. And the lady I don't know looks right at this one big Indian, and I mean this guy was huge, and she says `He used to be a professional wrestler.' Well, this giant guy turns around and look at me, right? It was like she was meant to be there. Freaky. Things changed. That was like hitting a switch. He backed off right then, and so did his buddies. Hell, they practically climbed over themselves to get away from me. Tell you the truth, I was glad, real glad."

"That's it?"

11

"Well, then I knew. I knew right then, or at least I suspected, who was behind it, but I didn't know why. But I knew something was going on."

"Was this after....?"

"No, this is way before. Before the murder. See, I'm telling you this in order, but I'm not telling you everything. It was all a set up. Everything – the first guy, the Indians..."

"Richard, paranoid is when you think the person in front of you is following you."

A pained expression crinkles his face, the waitress brings my breakfast, and he holds his response until she's out of earshot.

"I'm not paranoid, and I know what you're thinking. Ya see, I played my own shrink. I put myself through the wringer on this whole deal, right? I examined myself very carefully. I'm not paranoid, at least not without reason. You should be careful too."

A cop car drives slowly by the coffee shop. Big deal. They do that all the time. I usually don't notice.

"Two weeks later, I go back and there're two guys sittin' there. One turns and suddenly grabs for me. Wrong move. I had him in a headlock so fast he didn't know which way was up. I pressed his head down against the bar, and said, `What's your problem?' He just says he thought I was somebody else. I'm so sure. I let him go, bought a beer, played the punchboards. Believe me, I got the message."

He smiles as if everything is now obvious. I may be slow on the uptake, but I'm not ashamed to ask questions.

"Tell me, Richard, exactly what message did you decode from these experiences?"

"Well, I figured someone was trying to put me in jail or something. At least discredit me, play me as a troublemaker, marginalize me, right?"

Exciting stuff. I'm mopping up egg yolk with white toast.

"And there's more."

"There better be, Richard, I don't see the plot."

"Oh, there was more than a plot, there was...."

"Let me guess – a conspiracy?"

He sucks hard on that poor Bel-Air. I wonder if he saves the coupons. He has a wonderful smile.

"An anti-credibility conspiracy," he laughs, but it's more from irony than humor, "I have no credibility in this town, and even less with my family. Hell, even my dad wouldn't listen to me. I tried to warn him. He thought I was just paranoid. By the time he was murdered, there was no one left to believe me."

"Your father was murdered?"

"Yeah, that's what I'm trying to tell you," Richard says emphatically, "my father was murdered. His brains exploded. I tried to warn him, I could see it comin' and I knew that's what was behind all this weird shit."

Weird shit. Sure is.

"And I mean real weird shit. For example, about this same time, someone kept trying to pick the lock on my house. This would happen every few days or so, some guy sneaking around, peering in the windows."

Figures.

"Well, I just had a hunch he was comin' 'cause I hadn't had any trouble for a day or two. I took my .38 and hid out in the car and waited for sundown. Sure enough, some character comes right up to the house. Well, I collared him, shook him like a rag. Oh, he almost wet himself, claimed he was only delivering my newspaper."

"Was he?"

"Delivering the newspaper? Yeah, he was delivering the paper, and he went to the cops and claimed I shoved my gun up in his face, which I didn't. Little liar."

"Wait a second. He wasn't doing anything wrong, right?"

"No, he was later arrested for being a peeping Tom. I wasn't paranoid, I was absolutely right. If you don't believe me, check it out yourself."

"All this happened at the same time?"

"Yeah, that's the point. My life up 'till that first guy in the bar was *normal*, at least for me. I never had weird shit happen, except for maybe when the wrestlers had it in for me, but that was just a minor incident back in '74. They ripped me to shit, I sued, but I later dropped the whole thing. They didn't trust me…"

Wrestlers will do that. They have to trust you. Wrestling is all about trust. You don't let three hundred pounds of sweat-drenched muscle jump on you from the top rope without trust. No man is more despised than an untrustworthy wrestler. In my adventurous youth, I worked the old Pacific Northwest wrestling circuit as the flamboyant lawyer of the Hell's Demons tag-team. You don't need a law degree for that kind of gig – you just need a gift of gab, a vivid imagination, and the ability to keep a straight face.

I met all the qualifications.

Wrestlers.

Personally, I always liked them. They work hard, have a strong internal code of ethics, and a flair for the dramatic. We always got along. Then again, they trusted me. Apparently, they didn't trust Richard.

It's off topic, but I have to know where he wrestled.

"Seattle, but only in '74 back when Dean Goldblatt was booking matches. I did some `curtain pullers' at the Masonic Temple..."

"...just off Broadway on Capitol Hill," I complete his sentence.

"Yeah. That's the place. I was trained by the Irish Rogue."

I was there in '74. If I close my eyes, I can almost smell the stale popcorn, cold cement, and old women.

"Hell, that was over twenty years ago," he says, "the promoter gave me a stupid name — Larry Large"

My, my, my. Larry Large.

I watched him get pinned by a big Indian back in '74. It was a one-fall match warm up before Killer Kowalski took on Pretty Boy Pat Paterson or Chris Colt for the Championship Belt. Never saw him wrestle again. Neither did anybody else. They carried him out of the ring on a stretcher. I thought it was part of the act. I remind him of the incident, and mention my brief, tangential relationship to professional wrestling.

"They messed up all my ribs, muscles, tendons," says Richard. "They can do that if they want to, okay?"

"Okay, but the wrestlers didn't have anything to do with your father's murder, right?"

"No, no. They never knew my dad, my brother, my stepmother, or anything like that. Dad wasn't murdered 'till five years later, you understand."

No, I don't, but the breakfast is good.

His eyes narrow as if looking at me for the first time.

"I'm using up too much of your time, okay? I mean you probably think I'm crazy hiding out in my house for fifteen years. The time was I would have just gone after the bastards, all of 'em. But I don't do that anymore, right? I gave my life to God, I think about spiritual things, and I don't try to get even, snitch on a snitch, ya know?"

"I think about spiritual things too, Richard."

His squint tells me he doesn't perceive my radiant spirituality.

"Maybe you're not being straight with me, Jeff," murmurs Tibbit menacingly, "I mean, isn't it peculiar that you were on the wrestling circuit the one year I was?"

"It's called a coincidence, Richard."

He reaches under his jacket, going for the bulge.

The damn guy's a hermit for fifteen years and comes out of hiding just long enough to shoot me? Had I known this was my last meal, I would have ordered the chicken fried steak.

It's not a gun, it's money – a stack of bills bound together with an old rubber band. He slaps it on the table and shoves to towards me.

"Here's a thousand bucks. Find out."

"Find out what?"

"Find out what went on, who was involved – find out everyone who got away with murder. I have my suspicions, my beliefs – I'm sure it way my stepmom and her dickhead friend – but there could be others. Most of all, find out if it's over. My wife can't take it anymore, me just pacing around the house all these years. Hell, they could get me on the way home. Maybe they will."

He snuffs his last Bel-Air, tosses seventy-five cents down on the table, and makes movements to leave. I pocket the grand. The bills looked older than both of us.

"That loot should get you started, maybe even finished, right? If you make a book out of this, I'll get it back."

He's sure there's a book.

"Oh, before I forget." he reaches into his jacket's opposing inside pocket and pulls out a folded manila envelope, "here're some photocopies – dad's death certificate, insurance stuff, tax returns, newspaper stories, things I figured you'd need, ya know. You'll find all primary players' names, and I'll tell ya more as we go along, I mean, if you're on the case. Here, take this stuff."

Swell. The more paper they give you, the more obligated you feel to follow through.

"Don't bother checking with the police," insists Richard, "They'll just fuck with you. You're a smart guy, I can tell. I want to know if they're still after me."

"Who are `they?'"

"I won't say. After all, you could be one of them"

"That's what you're paying me to find out, right? If I'm one of them, you'll be the first to know."

15

"Yeah, I guess so. Don't worry, I won't call and bug ya. You call me anytime. My number's in the book. I gave it to you over the phone, remember?"

I remember.

"Think it over, Jeff. Hell, you can always give the money back, okay?"

Not likely.

I wrote a check for my breakfast and followed him out. He had a perfectly restored 1961 Borgward Isabella.

"Do all the work yourself?"

"No. Had it done. Funny that I would have a car restored when I don't go anywhere, right?"

"Right. Being a hermit keeps the mileage down for resale."

"Well, to tell the truth," admits Tibbit, "I'm not a *complete* hermit. I mean, I go to the store, drive my wife to work, and visit my son in prison. But that's it, okay? I don't go out, I don't play the punchboards, I don't do nothin'."

Except, perhaps, exaggerate.

I drove home, positive no one followed me. For some reason, I kept checking the rearview mirror. I also check my mailbox. Bills, a K-Mart flyer, and two more museums informing me it's time to renew my membership.

Museums are one of my weaknesses. I don't care if they're spectacular or tacky; a museum is a museum. I once drove out of my way to visit the Leno Prestini Memorial Museum in Clayton, Washington, not far from Loon Lake where my daughter and I go fishing. Batista Prestini built the museum in memory of his deceased artist brother, Leno.

Batista told me that Leno was a happy, good-natured man right up until the day he died. I asked how his brother passed away, and he didn't hesitate a moment before saying, "He blew his brains out right here in this room." I'm not making this up. Leno's last pack of Salem cigarettes is still there on the dresser.

Two cats, the feline kind, were waiting in the kitchen when I got home. There's only one hill in Walla Walla. I live on it. Snob Hill, some call it. In honor of my cats, probably. Both are spoiled, pampered, and ill tempered. Angel, the female fur ball was meowing; Pooter, the arthritic asthmatic male, wheezed a rattling command.

I fed them and they shut up.

Cats.

HEADLOCK

A dog will love you forever, but take a dump on the kitchen floor. Cats couldn't care less if you live or die as long as you pop the top of a Friskies can. I love 'em both. If there is life after death, I'm among the millions who anticipate finding their pets in Paradise.

Seriously.

Life after death and other spiritual topics are my hobby, and don't tell me that doesn't make sense. I always did love a mystery. I'll curl up on the big, red, art-deco chair in my bookshelf-lined living room, and contemplate serious matters, unresolved issues, and eternal questions – conundrums such as "are there dogs in heaven?"

If there are dogs in heaven, I doubt they're real. I don't buy the "pet soul" theory. When Fido drops his last bone, his bones will never roll to Canine Jerusalem for the Great Resurrection. So, what does the All-Loving God do for all dog lovers to make life-after-death more pleasant?

Simple. The All Merciful allows them to have their beloved pets in the next world just as long as they think they need them.

How long is that? How transcendent is the desire to hug a pooch, be licked by Lassie, or rescued by Rin Tin Tin?

If you fall down a well in the next world, who will run and bark to Gramps?

In the realms beyond, dogs may seemingly run through waving astral planes of wheat, barking amongst the barley and romping mud-pawed in alternative reality rice paddies. Pet lovers, delighting in the antics of these etheric dog-equivalents, find heaven in compassionate illusion.

Mom says I should have been a Rabbi.

Right.

Rabbi Reynolds.

The phone rings. I stand to answer it and Pooter plops from my lap like a sack of onions. The poor thing can't land on its feet.

"Yes, hello?"

It's Richard.

"Hey, I know I said I wouldn't call, but I thought I should let you know I was followed home. All the way, okay?"

Okay. Now he sounds *exactly* like Jack Nicholson.

"What did you want to tell me about, Richard?"

He coughs out an unexpected answer.

"About the dead body in the park."

I don't enjoy dead bodies in the park. Never have; never will.

I've found them myself, but only from a distance. That's back when I was a professional psychic. They have a fancy media name for folks who do now what I did then – "profilers," or "distance readers" – but it's the same mind numbing, gut wrenching experience.

I'm no coroner. One too many dismembered bodies, and a killer who's identity eluded my otherwise accurate mental impressions prompted me to hang up my psychic hat for good.

To hell with it.

Those were not good times.

If my mind were a metropolitan area, there's one district I'd stringently avoid – the area where "the gift" is.

The gift.

What a stupid name for it. It's neither gift nor curse, but a craft or talent you can develop or ignore. I've done more than ignore it; I've banished it.

"What park, Richard?"

"Rooks park, by Mill Creek."

I know Rooks Park. Great place to make out. My teenage flame and I go would go to the Liberty Theater, then dine on Chinese at the Modern Restaurant. When I wheeled my dad's powder blue Bonneville into Rooks Park, she was already undoing her pants. My ego attributes her eagerness to arousal, but dispassionate common sense tells me it was internal pressure from all that almond-fried chicken.

"Hold on a second, let me get this on tape."

I transfer to the hand-held phone, and press the answering machine's record button. He's probably doing the same thing.

"Go ahead, Richard, I'm here. What's the deal?"

"Even after the Indians and the bar fights and all that, I decided to take walks by Mill Creek. For my health, okay? The doctor said it was for my heart. This was back then, right? And it was always in my head that Rooks Park was perfect if you wanna `do somebody.' So, I always take my gun, okay? This one-day we start out by the college…"

He means Walla Walla Community College, it's built right along side Mill Creek and near Rooks park.

"If you keep walking up, then there's a place to sit, and a young man is sittin' there, he's wrestlin' with himself. He's having a tug of war. I mean, if you've studied people, if you know people, it was weird. As I'm walking up, I pass him on the walkway there, and I flashed on the gun — a German 9mm Luger. I mean, c'mon, right? Where's he gonna get that? So, I made sure she was on the outside, and I was here..."

I can't see "here" over the telephone, but I get the picture.

"I watched him out of the corner of my eye. I said `hi` to him and he said `hi' back, but he's fightin' with himself. I told my wife. I even told her what kind of gun he had. Okay, three or four days later they find him dead up there. I mean he'd been dead for a few days before they found him."

"He killed himself?"

"Oh, they *say* he killed himself – shot himself in the head — but I don't believe it. I'm not God; I wish I *was*. But I don't believe it."

"Because?"

"We heard two shots that day, my wife and I."

"Maybe it was an..."

"Echo? Bullshit, man. Two distinct shots. You don't kill yourself with two shots. If you miss on the first one, you don't keep tryin' now do ya? "

I don't have a comeback.

"I know this is a lot to swallow," admits Richard.

"No, no. Go ahead." What the hell, I might as well encourage him.

"Well, the main thing is I don't want to tell you too much, but I want something to become of this because it is true. The kid just couldn't go through with it, so they killed him."

I figured it was time for me to give Richard a sense of perspective, at least the best I could.

"We have a situation where you've been hassled by quite a few different people, things are going on which seem off-kilter, and it's like your finding yourself in some sort of a vortex — an emotional storm or something — and you don't know where it's coming from..."

"Oh, I had my suspicions," Tibbit jumps right in as if two steps ahead of me. Perhaps he is. "I really did. And I think it all came right back to her. – my Dad's wife – *but I'm not done.*"

So emphatic is the last phrase, I drop any intention of speaking.

"I kept takin' my walks. Before they found the kid's body, I even smelled it, smelled the death. I mean, we had no way of knowin' those shots we heard had anything to do with him, you understand. You ever smelled death, you know it. This is weird man – I know what a falcon looks like..."

"You mean a Ford Falcon or a bird falcon?"

"Bird falcon. I can tell when I see a falcon. Well, there was a falcon sitting on that bridge up on Mill Creek I got off the bridge, and you look out and there's bushes, and I swear to God there was some kind of creature moving through there – like a *jackal*!"

Oh boy. I'm thinking of returning the thousand bucks

"You don't see very many jackals in the city parks now days," I offer, trying to sound like I'm following this story with a major degree of interest, "maybe it was a bobcat down from the mountains."

"Maybe, maybe*not,*" Richard snaps. He's talking faster now, as if someone has thumbed a variable speed control.

"We started to cross the bridge. I don't know what made me turn. There was a *man,* he had *a surgical mask*, and if you wanna call it a walking stick, it was about *twelve foot long.* He raised it up as if he were gonna whack me over the head with it. When I whirled to face him, he turned as if he was looking down into the creek. We made it back to the car and took off."

The little cassette tape in the answering machine is about to run out, and so am I.

"Let me guess. There was only one thing to do — you changed parks."

He either ignores it or doesn't get it. He's on a roll.

"I'm almost to the point, now, Jeff. Hold on. I don't want to bug ya, but I've paid ya and you need to know this shit."

Right. He paid me, okay?

"So, I waited 'till the next day and then I went back up there. Several people are back in the brush, cleaning it out, and they're putting up a sign, I swear to God, and it says `No Guns Allowed.'"

He pauses as if that cinches it, as if now it will all come together for me in a blinding epiphany. He says it again, slowly, rolling the words around in his mouth as if they were the chewy center of a Tootsie-Roll Pop.

"No Guns Allowed. I didn't pull my piece, but I put my hand on it. So...." Here comes the inductive reasoning climax, and he orates with near missionary zeal. "I think it was either (a) real, to do me, or, (B) they had a camera."

Jackals. A man in a surgical mask.

There are no jackals in heaven, not even pretend ones, or in Walla Walla, either.

I know what I'm going to do – the one thing I pretended I would never do again and always knew I would. I'm like an addict mouthing "I'll never use again" while driving to the dope house.

"How old are you, Richard?"

He tells me.

"I'm gonna set down the phone for a minute, but you hold on because I'll be right back."

I rest the black hand-held on the counter. I close my eyes. Why the hell am I doing this? I know it's not for the thousand bucks, but I have no other reason. I clear my mind, bring the tips of my thumb and first two fingers of my right hand together, and recite to myself his name, age and location.

It still works, but I'm not going all the way in – I'm just skirting the edges of ESP Boulevard, cruising the redlined residential district just past Inspiration Point. I promised myself a hundred times I wasn't going back. My days as "the new Peter Hurkos" are long over.

Hurkos.

He fell of a roof and woke up psychic. He could hold a victim's earring and describe the murderer. I wanted to be him when I grew up. I also wanted to be Hopalong Cassidy. I've been Hurkos, now I'll settle for Hoppy.

Thirty seconds later, at most, I pick up the receiver.

"You still there, Richard?"

"Yeah."

"You ever been tested for allergies? Coffee, especially?"

"No. Why? You think some allergy is making me crazy?"

The answer is yes, but I don't tell him that.

My sixth sense tells me he is one of those seven million Americans with a coffee allergy. Two cups and they think they're being followed, or that their co-workers are plotting against them. Tell them it's the coffee, and they would rather spend a fortune on group therapy than give up the java.

Who can blame them? There is nothing like a good cup of coffee, especially with a chunk of chocolate and a good smoke.

Over the phone, I hear the metallic click of Tibbit's Zippo.

BURL BARER

Another Bel-Air goes up in flames.

"I was just curious, Richard, that image sort of came to mind."

He doesn't buy it. He knows I think he's a nut.

"You think I'm nuts, right?"

"Possibly, but I don't think you're wrong."

"What does that mean?"

"Exactly what I said – you can be nuttier than Auntie Esther's fruitcake and still be absolutely correct about hard facts."

He makes a quizzical noise; I explain.

"Let's say that all this about the body in the park, the falcon, the bobcat…"

"Jackal."

"It could be the fuckin' Trix rabbit, Richard, it doesn't matter. That could all be supposition, superstition, or an undigested bit of brisket, but none of that negates the absolute fact that your father was murdered, the murderer got away with it…"

"His brains exploded…"

"Yeah, I remember. Probably just like in *Scanners*."

"*Scanners*?"

"A movie."

"I don't see much movies."

"Here's the problem, Richard: I believe you."

"That's a problem?"

"Only for me. I was thinking of giving you back the grand, now I can't."

Pooter, the wheezing cat, drags his arthritic body into the kitchen and flops face first in the water dish. He's fine. He does this every day. He stretches full length, with his face in the dish, and slurps. He's not crazy; he's just thirsty.

"This isn't a whodunit, Jeff. This isn't even a whydunit. She killed him for the insurance money, my dad's wife, right? I just wanna know…"

"Is it safe?"

"What?"

"Is it safe."

"Yeah. Is it safe?'

There's not too much more to say.

"Richard, you didn't see any mimes in the park playing tennis did you?"

"Hell, no. Mimes? Tennis?"

He laughs, and it turns into a hacking cough.

22

HEADLOCK

"*Blow-up*. It's another movie."

"Like I said…"

"Yeah, you don't see much movies."

"Well, sorry for using up more of your time, Jeff. I mean, I got more to tell you. Lots more. But I don't want to bug ya, right? I bet I'm a real pain in the ass."

"Not yet. I'll tell you when. Anyone who gives me a thousand dollars cash gets plenty of latitude."

He chuckles, and it's not fake – a real, honest to God chuckle.

"What now?" He asks.

Hell, it's not even noon. The day is young.

"First things first, Richard. I'm heading to Seattle. It's a mystery thing – Mystery Writers of America Fan Night. I gotta go be famous."

"That must be rough."

"You don't know the half of it."

Fame.

It's acceptable for Hollywood celebrities, but when you're a mid-list mystery writer from Walla Walla, it's called being uppity. Besides, once you're famous enough to have your work reviewed by the Times of London, people assume you're rich.

You can't eat fame. Mom always told me to have something to fall back on, something stable. Right. An ex-psychic private eye novelist who once worked the wrestling circuit and played rock' n' roll on the radio doesn't have a sizable stability quotient on his resume.

A Rabbi is stable.

According to Talmudic commentary, the three criteria for defining mental instability are (1) going out alone at night in an area where people do not usually walk alone, (2) sleeping in a cemetery, and (3) tearing one's garments.

"You ever sleep in a cemetery, Richard?'

"Hell, no."

"Ever rip your clothes up?"

"What? Not on purpose."

I'm a bit worried about his answer to the next one.

"You ever go walking at night where people don't usually go alone?"

He thinks it over.

"Only if they have punchboards."

That settles it. He's no crazier than Pooter.

The conversation concluded, I kick the cats out of the house, scoop up the cash, throw some clothes in a garment bag, and take off. I'm halfway down snob hill before I remember that I didn't leave out any cat food or water.

Heading back up the hill, I see a car in front of my house. It's not parked, but it's not exactly moving either. Big, maroon, and I swear I see a "D" on the license plate. If so, it's an unmarked cop car. As I pull up, the sunglassed driver smiles, points his index finger at me, cocks back his thumb as if it were the hammer of his service revolver, and then he drives on down the hill.

I go in the side garage door, and kick open the little cat hatch. I'm still thinking about that finger gesture as I prepare the cats' cafeteria. This is the first time I ever looked over my shoulder while pouring Meow Mix into a Tupperware bowl. Whatever Richard has going on between his ears, I hope it's not catching.

Back on the road, my first stop is Washington Mutual Savings Bank to deposit the loot. My temptation to give it back was overruled by more than monetary need. While Richard detailed his Rooks Park adventure, I thumbed through his copies and clippings. One news item concerned a young drifter's Rooks Park suicide; another noted the arrest of a long-sought peeping Tom. His interpretations may be skewed, but his facts are one hundred percent accurate.

There's more.

When I gave myself his name, age, and location, I saw more than a coffee allergy.

Check this out:

Richard on his knees clutching the windowsill, staring outside, scanning the horizon for signs of folks coming for him. Outside the window there is absolutely nothing. Nothing at all.

Now, rotate the scene as if it was a revolving stage, and behind Richard are two more windows, each smaller, and in each one stands a man with a high-powered rifle. One of the men looks…well, "electric."

Go figure.

Keep in mind, this is coming from just the suburbs, the brink, because I'm not going in. But if the images are that strong from the outskirts, the poor son of a bitch – never call him that – really is, or was, onto something decidedly dangerous, deadly, and/or unsavory.

Is it safe? Is it over?

HEADLOCK

When I was a kid, I watched William Boyd as *Hopalong Cassidy,* and Chester Morris as *Boston Blackie.* Blackie was "friend of those who have no friends." So was Hoppy.

Me too.

It's a matter of ethics.

I'm on the case.

Less than a half block from the bank is the McFeely tavern. Over fifty years old, it has never been remodeled, not even once. The owner, same one since 1947, has put new bulbs in the signs, but that's about it.

Smart. Real smart. Time waits for you at McFeely's. In it's own way, McFeely's is an American cultural museum. And I love museums.

The joint's original motto was "Drink Freely at McFeely," and back in the late '40's they emblazoned the slogan on an old Model T Ford and entered it in the local parade. The next day the liquor inspector told them it was illegal to advertise the word "drink."

"Is that a true story?" That's me asking.

The bar is handled by a slender blond in her late thirties who's seen just about everything and pretends she didn't. She's told the story before, but it's one she enjoys retelling. The next slogan was "Feel Freely at McFeely." Consider the possibilities.

"That didn't sound too good either," she admits, wiping an invisible stain from the bar, "then someone came up with `Relax Freely at McFeely,' and everyone decided that would be best."

Better than best. Perfect.

McFeely's atmosphere is 100% pure rural Americana. There's a stuffed elk head hanging over the pool table, it's antlers draped with Christmas lights. Sometimes there's a cigarette hanging out of its mouth. Not today. Somebody swiped it.

You won't find pretensions at McFeely's; you'll find convivial cowboys, beer-breathed babes, working class heroes, professional drunks, octogenarian geezers, pool hustlers, and good ol' boys who've aged like cheap wine.

This is a real Walla Walla kind of place. No hanging ferns or raspberry wheaton, this is where a guy in dirty work boots can lay down a buck for a ten-ounce glass of Heidelberg and still get back change

I don't drink alcohol. I order a can of Squirt.

McFeely's is not only "The Biggest Little Tavern in Town,"

it's the only tavern in town where you can play the punchboards. Big Indians go there.

The saloon retains its original paint scheme – tan and orange – and the joint is decorated with an astonishing display of kitsch both priceless and worthless. 140 collector's edition Jim Beam bottles are displayed above the bar, and a pack of Lucky Tens – low tar Lucky Strike filter cigarettes made back in the 1970's — is taped to the cash register.

Nine prints of dogs playing poker adorn the walls. I almost expect to see dogs playing poker at the Last Supper. None of these are on black velvet. Another set shows animals with guns setting out to hunt people.

Welcome to McFeely's.

The empty seat to my right waits for the next customer while the occupied seat on my left supports the sagging posterior of an elderly gent who proudly asserts he's lived on that perch for the past ten years. A GPC ultra-light clings tenaciously to his lower lip while he extols the virtues of McFeely's.

"I could tell ya a million stories about this place," he insists happily, "this is a wonderful neighborhood tavern."

I've got my eye on the door. I bet Mr. Maroon Car has cruised around the block twice since I've been here.

"Tell me your best memory," I encourage, "an example of McFeely's at its finest."

He guffaws. Really.

"One time this Mexican comes in and orders a bowl of chili," says the old guy, "and the bartender gave him a little package of crackers to go with it. Well, then this other Mexican comes in and sits down next to him. The new fella says to the bartender, `Hey, where's my crackers?' and the bartender just says, `Fuck you, you son-of-a-bitch, you ain't even ordered nothin' yet!'"

The old guy starts shaking as if some sort of seizure is setting in. This is apparently an expression of intense humor.

"That's it?"

He regains his composure by allowing ash to fall in his beer.

"Oh, I could tell you a million more just like that!"

The door opens. He's here. Mr. Sunglasses from the maroon car. I look right through him. He walks over and sits down on my right. I swivel, face straight ahead, flip back the top of my boxed Old Golds, fish out a fresh smoke, and light up.

I nod at him the way you nod at anybody you don't know

who sits that close to you.

He orders a beer. I check him out. Dumb shmuck is wearing a tie. No one in McFeely's wears a tie.

I sip my Squirt; he sips his Heidleberg. He speaks as if I'm expecting him to. I am.

"You know what makes this such a nice place," he asks without looking at me, methodically lighting matches, blowing them out, and arranging them in a little pile, "I'll tell ya. It's that it's been left alone. No one's tried to fix it up, make it right, do anything at all except let it be."

I nod and make one of those noises that doesn't say anything.

"Yeah," he wraps it up fast, "some things are best…"

I finish it for him.

"…left just as they are…"

"Right."

"Dead and buried."

Silence. He blows out the last match.

He turns facing me. I'm still giving him my best profile. I let my eyes slide over and take him in.

Mid-sixties maybe, or late fifties with hard living. Thin blond hair is slicked back as if he's impersonating his high-school graduation photo. He takes off the sunglasses and sets them next to his keys on the bar.

Cop's eyes.

"I was reading in a magazine," he begins softly, leaning a bit towards me, "about this new thing the CIA or somebody invented. It looks like this…"

He pulls a ballpoint pen – the kind you click — from his breast pocket.

"Inside the barrel is a small charge. It's loaded with a tiny projectile. If you wanna kill somebody and make it look like nothin' but a heart attack, you just…"

I turn towards him and he clicks the pen at my chest.

His laugh is steel on chilled steel; his eyes are iced lapis.

Fuck him. I'm six foot two, one hundred eighty five pounds, and can move with the speed of a compressed steel spring suddenly released. In my mind's eye, he's already down.

I can see past him where two heavyset women are up to their eyebrows in smoke and inconsequential conversation. The bartender is occupied elsewhere. The man puffin' the GPC can't see past the end of his ash.

27

My left hand sweeps Maroon's keys from the bar as I grab his tie and jerk it hard as hell. His head goes down like a fishing bobber, whacking against the hard wood bar. My right hand has already jabbed him in the solar plexus and moved up to press the carotid artery in his neck as he plunges from the stool.

It's all that fast.

"What the hell?" That's me yelling as if his sudden mishap has caught me off guard. I follow him down, my thumb pressing him dangerously close to the next world.

I release my pressure quickly, he gasps, and we're eyeball to eyeball.

"You're okay, man," I intone, "you just fell off your bar stool goin' for your keys."

He may be woozy, but he understands me perfectly.

His wallet is already in my hand. Prudent, just in case he's injured or unconscious. This way we know who he is. The drivers' license says he's Jake Livesay. He doesn't look like a Jake anything.

A goose egg forms on his forehead, and he moans as if very unhappy. The two women help me get him to his feet.

"Hey, it's ol' Jake the dickhead," exclaims one cheerily.

He glowers.

"Dickhead?"

I slip his wallet back into his jacket.

"Yeah. Jake here used to be a cop, didn't ya, dickhead?"

Swell. I had that one nailed.

"You okay, pal?"

"Yeah, fine," he wheezes like Pooter the cat, " I just fell off my stool. Lost my balance when I dropped my keys."

Dickhead is no fool. No need to cause a fuss. He wanted a quiet threat; he got himself a headache.

He sits back up and rests his head in his hands.

I shrug at the women, give a cavalier wave, pick up my smokes, and ease my way towards the door. One of the women follows me out.

"I'm Verna," she says, tugging at my sleeve.

So, this is Verna, local hooker. Low rent retail sex. She's not batting her eyelids nor giving me the come hither look.

"I've never known Dickhead to fall off a stool before." She's wise to what happened, even if she didn't see it. "You did something, to him I mean, didn't you?"

HEADLOCK

"I simply utilized the basic concept of *pikuach nefesh*," I say offhandedly, "Even potential endangerment to life demands violation of all the commandments."

She scowls. Maybe she agrees with famed Judaic scholar Moses Maimonides that "a warning, whenever possible, must be given."

"He's not a safe guy. No way," insists Verna, "I mean, if you're into that stuff. They say he took early retirement, but people talk."

She must be an ambiguity expert. I don't know what she means, but my time frame doesn't allow for anymore time relaxing freely. Seattle and fame are calling from the sidelines.

"My name is Reynolds, Jeff Reynolds. I'm headin' East. Want a ride?"

Poor choice of words.

"Ummmm," she purrs like a faulty Kirby.

"Information, Verna, information." I keep walking towards my car. It's not far, just in front of 1-2-3 Pawn where fast cash is a fact of life.

"Well, a girl can hope," coos Verna aviarily, "the price could be the same either way. You got a cute accent. You sort of sound like a guy I met once who said he was from Argentina. You from Argentina?"

"No, Señora."

"It's Verna."

"Sorry. Verna."

"Goin' to the Green?"

She means the Green Lantern, another neighborhood tavern on Isaacs Avenue in Eastgate catering to the tattoo and Harley crowd.

"No, airport, but I'll drop ya off."

"You can usually find me at McFeelys, the Pastime, or sometimes the Green," she says with a mascara laden wink as she slides across the red leather seats, "everyone knows Verna."

"Including big Indians?"

The color drains from her face and her eyes freeze.

"That's not fuckin' funny, mister. Not fuckin' funny at all."

She obviously has an issue with big Indians.

We head East on Alder Street, my massive Buick dominating the boulevard.

"What's the story on Dickhead?"

"What's it worth to you? I mean, after all, you know him well enough to knock him on his ass."

"I don't know him at all. He showed up and threatened me. You said he used to be a cop?"

She dug a used Kleenex out of her purse, laboriously uncrimped it, and blew her nose into its hardened folds. Endearing gesture.

"Yeah, but that was years ago," she explained with a wet sniff. "He wasn't a good cop, if you know what I mean. I think they booted him out. Cops may protect their own, but only up to a point. He crossed the line. Some of them do, ya know."

I know.

The local "boys in blue" range from one end of the morality scale to the other. Always have. There's been a few on the force I'd nominate for Sainthood – honest, dedicated professionals who'd lay down their lives to protect you. Then again, I've seen the rogues who belonged behind bars for community safety. The latter don't last long. Criminality raises hell with socially acceptable corruption.

If Internal Affairs ever wanted my advice on how to spot a crooked cop, I could give them the world's simplest clue – if a cop will lie, a cop will steal. A cop who's a thief will take payoffs and deceive anyone. Simple. Corruption starts with the first lie.

Go to traffic court and watch their faces. If you see Officer Friendly put on that fake set-jaw look of public service seriousness while spinning a palpable yarn of imagined infractions, I say kick the cop off the force now and save yourself a scandal ten years down the road. Ok, maybe fifteen years. But you know that sooner or later you're gonna find that guy up to his gun belt in meth, fabricated evidence, and false testimonies in major convictions.

Internal Affairs never asks my sage advice. Every profession has its temptations, even Verna's. What's the old adage? "When you start coming with the customers, it's time to quit." Judging from the mileage racked up on her facial odometer, Verna's never had twenty bucks worth of honest pleasure.

"What did Dickhead do to earn him early retirement?"

Silence. She looks out the window as if there's something really interesting happening at the Walla Walla Public Library. Not likely, not unless they suddenly decided to carry my books in a last ditch effort to make sure I don't sell another retail copy in my own hometown. I love it when folks tell me they'll wait and get my latest masterpiece at the library.

She exhales a long sigh.

"Oh, rumors. He's married, got kids. A little affair on the side is nothin', or even a mistress around here...even the other kind, if you catch my drift, but..." She shook her head in disapproval.

"The other kind?"

Her artificially arched eyebrows arch.

"Guys. He liked a guy on the side, or on top or whatever. I mean I can understand wantin' guys 'cause I want guys too, so that's not the problem. Consenting adults are one thing, kids are another."

Swell. An ex-cop who's also a bisexual pedophile. If I put this in a work of fiction, I'll have more activists on my ass than Dickhead could dream of.

"Is this true? Do you know that's why he was kicked off the force?"

Verna gives me a look, the kind that says, "You're stupid."

"I said he took early retirement. It was just a *rumor* that he was canned." And then, under her breath, "But I believe it, the little dickhead."

I could make better time driving on Isaacs, but I'm taking the scenic route down Boyer, past Whitman College. Not a long route – all of three blocks – but remarkably lovely.

An educational and cultural resource to the community, Whitman College derives its name from Christian missionaries Marcus and Narcissa Whitman. This adventurous couple attempted bringing Jesus and farming to the nomadic Cayuse Indians in 1836.

For their part, the Cayuse were remarkably unenthusiastic about either.

After eleven years of relentless work, painfully punctuated by the accidental death of the Whitman's little girl, a measles epidemic killed half the Cayuse tribe. Believing they were being poisoned to make way for white emigrants, a band of Cayuse attacked the mission on November 29, 1847 — the famed "Whitman Massacre."

Marcus died from a hatchet to the skull; Narcissa, wounded in the breast, was carried out of the house on a makeshift stretcher, dumped in the mud, and riddled with bullets.

Whitman College, blessed with a superb sense of irony, named their championship basketball team, "The Fighting Missionaries."

Fighting Missionaries.

Think about it.

I'm still thinking about it as I ask Verna, "What's the relationship between Dickhead and Richard Tibbit?"

Had Verna been walking a tightrope, she would have fallen to her doom. She shook so hard I feared she was going to soil the red leather seats of my '83 Park Avenue. She was laughing. Perhaps she's related to Mr. GPC in McFeely's.

"Richard Tibbit?" She honks out a loud snork.

"I haven't seen him in years!"

"Not since the days of the big Indians?"

She stops laughing.

"I told you not to mention that, Mister. That ain't funny, and it ain't polite."

"Forgive me, but I don't know what I'm saying that's so offensive." I mean it.

She pulls back a bundle of permed curls clustered around her thick shoulders. A long scar runs from underneath her left ear to just above the lump of muscle by her neck.

"Big Indians, OK? Big fucking Indians about five years ago in Umatilla, Oregon. Not on the reservation, but just in Umatilla."

"I'm sorry, Verna, really. I didn't know."

"Well, what big Indians are you talking about then?"

"The ones who hassled Richard Tibbit."

"Oh, shit. Those Indians? Hell, that was about a hundred years ago. They backed off once Supertongue said Tibbit used to be a wrestler."

"Supertongue?"

"Her name is Riki, but I call her Supertongue because she's got the biggest, fattest, longest tongue you ever saw in your life. You could charge money for people to watch that girl at Baskin and Robbins slurpin' up a double-decker ice-cream cone. I swear it's like something from Mutual of Omaha. You know, Marlon Perkins' Wild Kingdom. She's like one of them `Hall-Monitor Lizards' or whatever you call 'em. Or a giant Gila Monster like in that old movie where it comes over the top of this little hill and eats a couple of cops."

We're turning left onto Clinton Street, and about to turn right on Isaacs.

"This Supertongue Riki? Did Tibbit know her?"

"No. Riki was down from Seattle. She had an aunt or something living over on Bonsella or Valencia or one of those `uh' sounding streets. I talked to her some later. She was tryin' to decide if she should move here or not, being as the property was in the family and I guess the aunt or something was gonna kick off. Anyway, she just recognized him from some grunt 'n' groaner match she saw in Seattle, I guess."

"Was there any relationship at all between Tibbit and Dickhead the ex-cop?"

She scowls and shakes her head.

"Nah. Different circles as far as I know. But I didn't know either one of them intimately, and I wouldn't say if I did, but I know that I didn't. Tibbit was never interested in me, just in punchboards of the other kind," she says that like she thinks it is really clever, "and Jake would just shake down a few drunks or cooperate when those crooked drug cops — you know, like the one that gets in trouble but nothing ever happens to 'im– would put the hammer on some local snitch."

I know those drug cops, thank you. One is Thomas H. Carter, a beefy fellow known to friends and enemies as THC. One of many who wishes they'd never heard of THC is the Walla Walla city attorney, currently negotiating settlement of a ten million dollar judgement for civil rights violations. Hell of a story, and one that would make you think twice about ever walking into a 12-Step meeting. It's one cold story. Almost as cold as the way Verna snaps out the word "snitch."

'Which snitch?"

We're here. The Green Lantern

"I don't even snitch on a snitch...unless..."

She doesn't finish, but she waits for me to do something, say something. I figure it out. I pay something.

I stuff two twenties into her palm, twice as much as she expected and perhaps less than she deserved.

I have another thought, and I express it.

"Richard knew how to play those punchboards, right?'

She gives me that look again.

"What did you say you did for a livin'?"

"I didn't, but I'm a private eye."

"Yeah, well that's why you're working in Walla Walla. You're not exactly Perry Fucking Mason."

"Perry was a TV lawyer," I am quick to correct her, "not a

private eye."

"Yeah? Well, fucking Richard Diamond then."

Wow. Richard Diamond. She's older than she looks.

"Richard, Richard Tibbit I mean, not Richard Diamond for God's sake, *always* won at punchboards. It wasn't luck, but I don't think he was cheatin' either."

"Listen Verna. I appreciate your help. If Dickhead asks you anything about me, you don't know...."

"Well, I don't know so I can't tell 'em shit."

She's right.

I dig a scrap of paper out of my pocket.

"I'm going to Seattle today, but I'll be back in a day or two. I'll write down my phone number. If for any reason you need to get hold of me, you'll have it, okay? Just leave a message."

I take out a pen.

What the hell?

I've got Jake the Dickhead's ballpoint pen. Damned if I'm going to drive to McFeely's and give it back. Not trusting it, however, I dig another one out of the glovebox.

"Don't bother givin' me your number," says Verna. " I ain't gonna interrupt your business – like you got a real business, which I doubt 'cause if you did you'd have business cards."

Right. And she has a business card?

"Besides," she continues with relentless nasality " if it was urgent, calling somebody two hundred miles away ain't gonna help much."

I briefly contemplate giving her my cell-phone number, but decide against it. I write the local number, the one with the answering machine, insist she take it, and wish her well. She swings the Buick door wide open, then stops for parting philosophy.

"We used to own this town, women like me. We were sumpthin' then, I guess. Not like now, not like this."

I'll be damned. The lady knows history. Christian missionaries may have founded Walla Walla, but prostitutes developed it. Bordellos were rich and plentiful in downtown Walla Walla up 'till the mid 1950's.

The big-name wheat ranches handed down by agricultural dynasties to their well-bred offspring owe their origins to dust bowl refugees' unions with entrepreneurial outlaw women. Within a few gentrified generations, everything was old money and respectable families. Verna didn't come from such historic stock — a fact plainer than her face — but I guess you take comfort and pride in whatever most resembles an admirable heritage. It's the "dogs in heaven" syndrome.

A solid door slam later, she's entering the Green.

I'm off to the airport, keeping an eye on the rearview mirror for signs of Dickhead. You can get anywhere in Walla Walla in seven minutes, and if he wanted to find me, it wouldn't be difficult.

Sure enough, I'm piloting the Park Avenue into the Walla Walla City-County Airport and here he comes up the road. I pull into a two-hour parking spot. I'm going away for two days, but the two-hour slots are right in front of the Airport door. Prudent.

He knows I see him, and I know he knows. He's not exactly sneaking up on me.

Sometimes you just gotta meet a situation head-on. I reach under the seat, grab my high-tech "protection," exit the car, aim it right at him, and start walking in his direction.

The maroon Dodge lurches to an immediate halt, he gets out quickly, his hands open and palms out.

"What the hell are you doing?" He's pleading. I like that.

"Hey, this made Rodney King famous," I call back cheerily, focusing him in my viewfinder, "except this one is Hi-8, well lit, and full color."

There's nothing like a video camera for intimidation and documentation. Private Eye tip #102.

"Put that thing down and let's talk. C'mon Reynolds, really. I know my initial approach was out of line..."

He knows my name.

"You got approach problems, talk to your golf pro," I snap, feeling witty, "I don't appreciate being threatened, especially when relaxing freely."

He looks worried. This video gambit is pure genius. I'm closer now, keeping the lens trained on him but lowering the camera.

"We're talking today to Jake Livesey, former police officer," I intone in my best announcer voice, "tell us, what inspires you to threaten private investigators at the McFeely Tavern?"

His eyes are darting around the parking lot like epileptic pidgins.

"I didn't mean to threaten you, honest. It was a misunderstanding."

"And you fell off the barstool..."

"Yes," he lies, " I dropped my keys. I just wanted to talk to you. Honest."

"So, talk."

"Can you put that damn thing away?"

"Of course, but I won't, not yet. What do you want?"

Something resembling a cheap grin distorts his lips.

"My pen. I believe you walked off with my pen."

Damn, that was good. I find it with my left hand and toss it over. He actually catches it.

"Sorry 'bout that, Jake, I'm not a thief or a thug or ...why was it you left the force?"

Never lose an opportunity to needle the bad guys. It may irritate them, but it establishes your ascendancy. I just hope Dickhead's a bad guy.

He spits out the answer, momentarily forgetting the lazily carried video camera.

"Early retirement, no matter what bullshit you've heard from that bitch, her sleazy friends, or that psycho Tibbit."

Well, there's a memorable litany.

"I gave you back your pen, I've got a plane to catch, and I've got your outburst preserved for posterity — so tell me, Dickhead, are you the shmuck making Tibbit paranoid?"

His head drops in exasperation. He looks beat.

"You don't understand. I came to warn you, not threaten you. You don't know what you're getting into. Whatever Tibbit told you..."

"Is confidential between him and me. He's a client."

He takes two steps towards me. I don't know if he wants to hit me or hold me.

"I'll be your client. I'll write you a check right now. How much do you need?"

"The minute you write me a check for a thousand bucks, whatever you tell me is confidential — assuming the damn thing clears the bank."

He's scrambling to get out the checkbook.

Amazing.

He trots hurriedly back to his Dodge, using the hood for support as he scrawls out his signature. The guy's serious, desperate, or full of shit. Maybe all of the above.

"Here. It's a grand. Take it. You're hired. Let's talk, okay?"

I make show of turning off the camera, step forward and extend my hand. He reaches out to shake it.

"The check, Jake."

"Oh."

He hands over the check. Even if it's no good, I want it.

"Jake and Dorothy Livesay. Tempe, Arizona" It even has their address and phone number. "You're a little far from home, aren't you Mr. Livesey, Sir?"

I call him "Sir" because you should never call a paying client "Dickhead."

A West Coast Airlines propjet just landed on the runway. That's my plane.

"You gotta watch your step, Reynolds. Listen, we can help each other. I've hired you, Okay? Don't tell Tibbit, don't talk to the cops, don't do a damn thing until we have a chance to sit down and talk."

I'm walking back towards the Buick with him scurrying after me.

"One quick question, Mr. Livesey," I call out over my shoulder, "I didn't meet Richard until this morning, how did you get here so fast from Tempe?"

"He may not leave the house often, but Tibbit has telephone-itis. A few days ago he called the wrong person looking for verification of one of his little `delusions' before he contacted you. I don't know if he's trying to sell you a story for one of your books, or hiring you to investigate one of his conspiracy theories, but either way...."

My cellular phone is ringing. It could be anyone of a dozen people, but I bet it's Richard. What a sense of timing.

I snap it open.

"Yes, hello."

"Sorry to bother you, Jeff. I know I'm a real pain in the ass."

I look Jake right in the eye.

"This isn't a good time, Richard, I'm with a client."

"Well, I had a phone call. This guy said I better be careful. I just wanna warn ya. I think you're in trouble."

No shit.

"No shit?"

"Yeah, if some guy named Jake Livesay gets hold of you, well, watch your back. He was in on it, buddy. He's one of them."

The guy who is "one of them" can't hear the other end of the conversation, but he's no fool. He mouths Richard's name. I nod;

he grimaces.

"Thanks for the tip, Richard, but I gotta go. Just stay in the house. Play *Uno* with the wife or something. I'll be back in a day or two. You hired me to find out if it was over, if it was safe, and who all was involved in your father's death. I can tell you right now it's not over, but you are safe," I say this staring at Dickhead as if looks could kill, "at least for now. Just be cool, sit tight and wait 'till you hear from me."

"Okay. I won't bug ya. I'll be cool, okay?"

That's it, and I click the phone shut. I'm pulling my bag out of the car. I didn't intend to bring the video camera, but now that he's seen it, I have no choice — if I leave it behind there's no doubt Livesey will steal it. Hell, I can't let him find out the damn thing doesn't have a tape in it.

"I've told you too much, Dickhead...I mean Mr. Livesey, but I don't want a conflict of interest situation. Right now I've got things to deal with other than you and wacky Richard. You want your grand back?"

Before he can answer, I grab my bag and head for the airport door.

"I didn't think so. Trundle back home and get hold of me Tuesday or Wednesday. I'm sure we can work something out that will make you very happy. Meantime, stay away from Tibbit; stay away from Verna. Deal?"

"Deal." He answers while haltingly scurrying after me.

Opening the vestibule door, I make a sudden stop, turn, and pose one last question.

"Jake, what's your exact age?"

"What?"

"Your age, Mr. Livesay."

He says fifty-nine. I know he's lying; he's sixty-two. I read his drivers' license in McFeely's. Maybe I'll do a mini-reading on him once we're airborne, then put him and Tibbit out of my mind for a while. I have Richard's photocopies in my pocket, and I figure I'll look them over in complete detail during a dull moment in Seattle.

I board the propjet in the nick of time. In a few hours I'll be enjoying laughs with fellow literary luminaries at the Mystery Writers of America Fan Night. This year, due to a twist of scheduling fate, it occurs only a week prior to Left Coast Crime —a larger convention of four to five hundred fans and authors invading the sunny climes of Palm Springs, California. It's a fun weekend of panel discussions, mutual back slapping, and endless opportunities to glean advice from the genre's more prominent authors while buying more and more of each others' books.

As for Fan Night, we'll gather for cocktails and Cajun peanuts about six o'clock at the Madison Hotel. I can already guess the number one topic of conversation: Ms Tony Fennelly's breasts.

II

"The proper term is `bosom,'" clarifies G.M Ford, author of the Leo Waterman mysteries, "'twas her bosom the woman exposed."

Indeed, I was right. Fennelly's mammary glands are the hottest MWA topic since the fracas over whether or not to disband the regional chapters. Tony's anatomical exposé overshadows such puerile concerns as the need for a full audit, or the budget of our annual Edgar Awards banquet.

In case you don't know, the Edgar is the Mystery Writers of America's highest honor. Winning the Edgar is like winning the Oscar. Unlike the Academy Awards, however, the Edgars aren't televised world wide, and People Magazine doesn't usually comment on who wore what. Usually. This year is the exception, thanks to the "accidental" exposure of Ms Fennelly's ample bosom before a drop-jawed crowd in the Sheraton Towers.

"She got right up there in front of God and Mary Higgens Clark — not necessarily in that order," Ford elaborates, "and when she raised the award above her head, her dress strap broke, and out tumbled her well formed, shall we say, `hooters.' Whatcha think about that?"

"I refrain from commenting on the behavior of others," remarks Meg Chittenden gracefully. "Can't we have a more uplifting topic of conversation?"

Meg, who has written more novels in more genres than everyone in the room combined, is delightfully refined. As for uplifting, Fennelly gave the Edgar Awards much needed exposure and boosted her career's profile by several cup sizes. Within a week she was booked on Leno and Letterman, and Oprah selected Fennelly's literary effort for relentless television discussion and unprecedented sales.

"This type of behavior cheapens the genre," grouses one disapproving pre-published author, "readers will think all mystery writers are flashers and perverts."

"What's wrong with realism?" offers Ford pleasantly, "besides, she won the Edgar for her novel, not her nipples."

True. Fennelly's brain-twisting mystery of culinary creativity and murderous mayhem in Missouri, "Eat Me in St. Louis," was an unrelenting page-turner.

"And remember, this was her third Edgar nomination. She was nominated previously for `The Glory Hole Murders' and `Worse than Dead.'"

I'm overhearing this conversation in progress while hovering around the book display, and watching authors buy each other's tomes. Sometimes I think all mysteries are sold to writers supporting their friends. I purchase Lawrence Block's newest Bernie Rhodenbarr novel of breaking and entering, *The Burglar who admired Mercedes McCambridge*. The book table is well arranged and fully stocked by Bill Farley of the Seattle Mystery Bookshop. Of course, he carries my true-crime Edgar Award winner from a few years ago, *Finding Sarah*. Its success, and the subsequent disappointing made-for-TV movie, paid for the snob hill house and high-tech audio/video gear. When I say "high-tech," I'm not referring to consumer gear. My top-end equipment is all professional broadcast quality, perfect for surveillance: catch crooks; capture character. I've never caught a crook. If I didn't live alone, I could make marvelous home videos. In truth, the gear was a tax write-off. Next time, I'll buy a new car. I've had my eye on the Volvo C-70 coupe.

My post-*Sarah* crime fiction sells well enough to keep Pooter and Angel in Friskies, and earned me a couple Anthony Award nominations from the World Mystery Convention. My fiction isn't in the same literary universe as *Finding Sarah*, but that book is something you only write once. I endured months of dredging up everything from as far in as the "gift" would take me — including the human bone yard outside Issaquah, Washington where the remains of twenty-three year-old co-ed Sarah Nussbaum were eventually unearthed. Never again. No more Mr. Hurkos.

"Hey, Reynolds," calls out Ford, "you still hiding out in Walla Walla?"

Hiding?

"I'm not hiding, Jerry," I answer happily, "I'm right here in plain sight."

"I see that. Got another mystery in the works?"

"What I'm really working on is a P.I. case that could be a book," I say, joining him at a corner table, "in fact, I've got the pitch ready."

"Let's hear it."

I clear my throat and give him my best impersonation of that announcer on NBC, the one who does the dramatic voice-overs for upcoming shows.

"A paranoid recluse lures P.I./ author Jeff Reynolds into a complex web of intrigue, murder, and conspiracy where delusions are deadly, and life-after-death can be hell."

"Not bad," says Ford, "is this is a true story?"

Jerry, a former high-school teacher who crafts clever private eye capers transpiring in Seattle's darker downtown environs, has a quick mind and a good heart. I tell him about Richard, the exploding brains, and my pre-flight encounter with Dickhead. This cracks him up.

"Who's writing your life, Elmore Leonard? Sounds like you need Leo and the boys."

By "the boys," Jerry means the rag-tag gang of homeless men who help the fictional Leo Waterman crack heads and solve cases.

"Any of Leo's boys ex-wrestlers?" I ask.

"Wrestlers? You mean collegiate, or like Jimmy "Superfly" Snuka?"

"Like Snuka, except more local/regional. You know, guys like the Irish Rogue, the Mongolian Mangler, Greg Lake, Shag Thomas, Hell's Demons..."

Ford's eyes focus on a distant point somewhere above Steve Martini's head, just to the left of. J. A. Jance.

"There's a guy I see at the J&M Cafe in Pioneer Square. He walks with two metal bracing canes, you know what I mean? We were shootin' the breeze one night over numerous bottles of pale ale. Seems steroids turned his bones to peanut brittle. Anyway, he used to wrestle years ago. If you don't ask me, I'll remember his name."

"What's his name?"

"Jesus, you're a smart ass. You must be a writer. No wonder were on the same panel at Left Coast Crime this year – "the Smart-Ass Author Panel" He scoops up another handful of Cajun peanuts. "The guy with the braces — Sullivan, something Sullivan — practically lives at the J&M."

"Lightning."

"What?"

"Lightning Rod Sullivan, that's who I bet he is...or was."

"Lightening Rod?" Ford extends one arm in the air and shakes as if being struck by a thunderbolt.

Writers.

Steak Terryiaki and vegetable medley followed by blackberry pie and coffee, signals the much anticipated and often-dreaded moment when we swing wide the doors, allowing our legion of fans unlimited access.

Well, not exactly a legion. Among the dozen or so eager attendees is a knockout blond wearing an unbuttoned light green suit, masculine style. Under the open jacket is a white blouse barely skimming the top of her navel.

She heads for the book display, snaps up *Finding Sarah*, and asks Farley where she can find Jeff Reynolds. He points. I smile. She walks over. What a dream. She reminds me of a super-stacked Ellen Barkin. Maybe she'll star in the "Tony Fennelly Story."

Jerry, more popular than I, already has three or four admirers shoving "The Bums Rush," "Slow Burn," or "The Deader the Better" under his nose. Judy Jance has almost everyone else. At least I've got *one*.

"I must have you sign this," she insists, "my name is Randy."

I take out my pen.

What the hell?

It's Dickhead's. Obviously, I tossed him one of mine and kept his. His says "Classic Wax Musical Memories 45th & U. Way." This is what we call an opportune clue.

"Thanks for supporting your regional author," I murmur sincerely.

She laughs as if having vastly amusing sex.

"I've already read it at the library."

More advice: never tell an author you got their book from the library. She almost didn't look as good now as she did two minutes ago, but buying a copy redeemed her.

She opens her little purse, and out tumbles a half-empty bottle. Not booze, Pepto-Bismal.

She giggles self-consciously, picks it up, and pats her undeniably attractive tummy.

"Stomach trouble," she admits as she replaces the plastic flask, "chug-a-lug a half bottle of the pink stuff and you can go anywhere, do anything."

"I'll remember that if I'm ever invited to go sky diving with the Queen of England," I respond warmly, even compassionately. Her eyes are already skimming the crowd.

"Is that guy over there Earl Emerson?"

She points at table number five.

"No, that's Jack Mullen. Emerson is the chap surrounded by arsonists at table number three."

Randy and her tummy take off. She gets halfway to Earl's table when she lurches to a stop, swivels on her heels, and races towards the door. Next time she'll chug-a-lug an entire bottle.

Time goes by, the crowd thins out, we've all bought as many of each other's books as we can afford, and the event is ready to be immortalized on a web-site somewhere. I still cringe at my photo from last year. I looked like Hitler getting an enema.

The few conversations still continuing are between Ford, Jance, Martini, and a handful of hangers-on. Randy and her attractive, if troubled, tummy are no where in sight. It's only nine o'clock. I'm thinking about wrestlers, take out the cellular and dial Tibbit in Walla Walla.

"Richard, this is Jeff. Yes, I'm still in Seattle. Got a question for you. A name, actually. Lightning Rod Sullivan. Ring a bell?"

"Jeeesus," replies Richard, "I didn't know that old bastard was still alive. He tried to take me out once, ya know."

"A date?" I'm incredulous.

"No, no. I mean take me out as in take me out like garbage. He didn't trust me. None of them did. Sullivan was one of the best heels, though."

Heels. I hadn't heard that term in years. Wrestlers come in two categories, "Babyface" and "Heel." The babyface is young, handsome, and squeaky clean, and wrestles by the rules. In reality, he's usually new to the business and can't wrestle all that well. The heel is an old-timer who knows how to work the crowd. An expert heel can make a novice babyface seem an Olympic champion.

Heels are great fun to watch. They have the most colorful gimmicks, and spend most of their time stalling, jumping out of the ring, and doing cowardly acts.

Lightning Rod Sullivan was a first-class heel. The fans hated his guts, which means they paid good money to see him pull dirty tricks on a babyface.

"I think I might bump into this Sullivan guy while I'm here."

"If he talks about the bank robbery, I can explain that, okay?"

Bank robbery. I let it pass.

The conversation concluded, I re-pocket the cellular and Dickhead's pen, scoop up my new Larry Block book, and bid my good-byes. The night is younger than I, but I have no intention of going up to my room. I take the elevator to the lobby and stroll towards the revolving door. I'll go outside for a smoke.

Sitting in the lobby reading *Finding Sarah* is Randy the tummy lady. She sees me, smiles, and rises as if meeting an overdue bus. This is no accidental meeting. She's been waiting.

"Hi!" She calls out as if I was the last person on earth she ever expected to see again. I feign appropriate surprise, and succumb to a few irreverent fantasies regarding her physical charms.

"Got a minute to talk?" That's her asking, cranking up her smile's temperature.

"I have many minutes," I confirm pleasantly.

She cocks her head to one side, opens her jaw slightly, and raises her eyebrows. Her body language has just been rated "R" by the Jeff Reynolds board of review, my mind calculating our age difference and hoping it's not so vast that my fantasies humiliate me.

Maybe she's the babyface and I'm the heel, but the grappling so far is entirely interior. First of all, she's knows she's pretty. Second, she knows I know she knows. On the subject of her physical beauty, we are, without discussing it, in agreement. How my personal attractive quotient figures into this equation, I'm not quite sure. I don't have to be handsome; I'm the guy who wrote *Finding Sarah*.

"I haven't had a smoke for a few hours, Randy, so how about if we step outside for a minute," I gently touch her shoulder and apply directional pressure, "anything special you want to talk about?" This is a good discovery line. If she only wants sex, she'll make a thoughtful noise and refrain from specifics while giving seductive hints.

No such luck.

"Yes. For you, is it over?"

"Over?" I know what she means, I'm just surprised she asked it.

We're outside now, facing 6th Avenue and looking up Madison Street. I light up an Old Gold.

"Yes," she continues seriously "Is it over? I mean, you actually found Sarah, found the bone yard..."

"It was more like a lair, actually," I clarify, "more like some wild animal's lair." I see it again in my mind's eye, and I shudder against the night air. "I haven't talked about this before, ever, not even when the book was first being hyped."

"I'm sorry, if you'd rather not..."

"I'd rather. It's about time, and this time is as good as any," I say, surprising myself, "for a long time I wouldn't...I couldn't bring myself to verbalize it. I've kept my mouth shut, okay? I mean, after the book came out there were the accusations. After all, I found the lair by virtue of the `amazing gift,'" my tone is somewhere between ironic and sardonic, "but according to the tabloids `the new Peter Hurkos' was suspiciously unable to identify the heinous killer. Guess who was public suspect number one? There were other negative consequences, but my career flourished."

"And you're not married anymore."

Ouch. Direct hit.

"You know your authors," I remark evenly.

She shifts her weight, although there isn't much to shift, and shoves her hands deep in her tailored pockets.

"Well, I read your book when it first came out. I already mentioned that, didn't I? Anyway, it, and you, fascinated me."

"And now?"

She gets one of those coy looks that delicious women master during adolescence.

"Even more so, if I can be perfectly honest," she says, bathing her answer with just the right hint of illicit promise.

I'd better answer her question.

"I was married thirteen years to a long-suffering woman of stoic practicality. Worlds beyond these worlds and dimensions beyond these dimensions were unsettling topics. She liked things simple, physical, and easily categorized. When the man of her dreams became the man who manifested nightmares; the man who, by simply holding a dead girl's earring, knows every horrid detail of her violent and degrading murder..."

She looks at the pavement. I flick the last of the Old Gold into the gutter.

"Her biggest fear was that I could be the killer."

Randy's eyes are scanning me as if I'm a universal pricing code.

HEADLOCK

"She didn't worry that I *was* the killer, but that I was someone who could be. The cops never thought so. It was never an issue. In her mind however, the logic was simple: only one person could know what happened to Sarah Nussbaum: the killer. I knew what happened to Sarah Nussbaum, ergo even if I wasn't the murderer, I was too close, too similar, or how could I know so much?"

"Kids?" She's changing the subject, or maybe not.

"I have a six year old daughter I never see. I get postcards from China where her mother teaches ESL."

We move back inside, not heading anywhere in particular.

"Perhaps if my gift had aided in the killer's capture, I'd be the family's literary and intuitive hero. Instead, I'm the guy who's so sick he can find dead coeds without leaving the comfort of his living room." We stop halfway between the cluster of chairs in the lobby and the elevators "Yep, just give Jeff Reynolds a blood soaked trinket, or stained panties found by a roadside, and he'll lead you to the most stomach turning sight ever to shake your faith in God."

She looks me right in the eye. Her's are deep blue and increasingly alluring. Maybe she took the stomach reference personally and positively.

"Did it shake your faith, or did you have any to shake?"

My faith was stirred, not shaken.

I shrug. Let's not make a big deal out of this.

"Someone had to find that corpse; I guess it was up to me."

She winces. I could have been more delicate.

"I have another question, but it may be silly."

"Go ahead."

"What British protectorate are you from? I mean, you don't sound exactly American, or Canadian. And you don't have an English or Australian accent, but..."

I've had this question before.

"Never underestimate a mother's influence," I answer pleasantly, "mine was born in England; raised in Canada, moved to America in the 1930's."

"Oh," she accepts my explanation easily, "that makes sense. It sounds nice. I like it. Always did like English accents, Anglo/ British or whatever it's called."

Anglo/British?

"You know," she elaborates, "like the Moodie Blues or whatshisname, Gary Grant."

"*Cary* Grant."

She giggles

"Yes, I mean him."

And then there's the silence when two people who want each other are halfway between fearing personal affront and throwing themselves into a vortex of impersonal passion.

If this is a dance, I'm taking the lead.

"So, Randy, are you mature?"

A question from left field, to be sure. She wasn't expecting it, but she remains unfazed.

"Mature? Do you mean as in `mature, consenting adult'?"

"It is the immature person who can't delay gratification."

She smiles wickedly

"Anticipation is the most powerful of erotic intoxicants," she states, obviously speaking from experience.

"Really?"

She hums in affirmation.

"I thought it was Pepto-Bismal."

Her cheeks flush with embarrassment. Trust me, embarrassment is more powerful than anticipation.

"Oh, Jesus," she laughs, her hand over her mouth, "I forgot about that. Not too inviting, is it. Really, I don't have..." She can't go on. I stand back with my arms crossed and eyebrows raised — the gentle mocking stance.

She composes herself and continues.

"I don't have stomach flue, if you're afraid of catching something. My stomach gets that way from nerves."

"Let's all hope you don't find romance nerve-racking."

I move closer, bringing down my arms. Less defensive; more accepting.

"Were you nervous about MWA Fan Night?"

"No," she giggles, "nervous about meeting you."

Ooops. I didn't expect that.

"Me?"

Her features soften, and she moves closer yet.

"I didn't know what you'd be like. I've wanted to meet you ever since I read *Finding Sarah*.'..."

She's so close now that I can inhale the fragrance of her lipstick.

"Because?"

"A man who can...I mean...someone who can know so much

48

just by touch...would, well...know..."

Her blush becomes more heated. I gently smooth a strand of hair from the side of her cheek.

"Attraction and desire are tricky topics, Randy. Desire is, in itself, subject to amelioration. According to the Talmud, " I relate evenly, "if a person has a burning desire to amass great sums of money, then they should become a fund raiser for a charity organization."

She knits her eyebrows together with mock impatience. Or maybe it's real impatience. It's her turn.

"And if my desire is for you and me to take a tumble on a firm mattress," she asks good-naturedly, "what should I do instead that would serve humanity? Be a sex therapist?"

"No, a professional wrestler."

She likes that. She scrunches her nose in an unconvincing scowl and growls.

"Ya wanna go two out of three falls?"

"One fall, no time limit. At my age I'm not as good as I once was, but I'm as good once as I ever was."

"What if once isn't enough?" She's enjoying this as if she's Lauren Bacall in *The Big Sleep*.

"We'll make it a double-header, or I'll call room service for reinforcements."

She laughs, more from trying to keep a straight face than the hilarity of the dialog.

"No way," she objects, "no extra men in the ring."

"Well, " I conclude with feigned reluctance, "there goes our tag team belt."

The elevator doors open and out steps Jerry Ford and Steve Martini. Jerry eyes Randy and gives me the thumbs up.

"And so," I remark officiously to the young woman, "that's why you should never sign with an agent who demands a reading fee or refers you to an editing service."

"Thank you Mr. Reynolds," she says as if auditioning for the Little Theater, "I'll certainly keep that in mind."

Ford rolls his eyes. We don't fool him for a minute. I'll be hearing about "the blond in the lobby" for years. This isn't quite as scandalous as Tony Fennelly's "unveiling," but any author activity more adventurous than Leslie O'Kane getting a new fax machine is grist for the gossip mill.

With our verbal *coitus interruptus* concluded, she hooks a

well-lacquered index finger into my waistband and pulls me close.

"So, Mr. Reynolds, ready to hit the canvas?"

"If you're going to jump on me from the top rope, I have to trust you."

Her lips brush mine. I can't tell if she's teasing.

"If you can't trust a total stranger who propositions you, who can you trust?"

"My agent," I answer honestly. "He told me `never use female characters as sex objects'."

"If you don't use females, what do you use?" She looks mildly disappointed.

"Farm machinery," comes the happy reply, "in Walla Walla it expands my agricultural market."

Silence. She's giving me the ultimate pseudo-pout.

In truth, I want her. That's the problem.

I know nothing about her beyond the alluring looks and adequate repartee. Sexual union is powerful stuff. I remember every woman I've ever slept with, even if they don't remember me. Do I want to be linked with her, in one dimension or another, forever?

"I'll still respect you in the morning," she murmurs convincingly.

There's only one thing to do. I pull her into the elevator and push the top button.

"Put your mouth where your mouth is, Randy. Kiss me like you really mean it."

She does.

Whammo!

Wow.

Now, this kiss is hot enough to melt the paint off the walls and make the light bulbs explode. She's wrapped around me like an enraged anaconda, her mouth about to swallow me whole. This woman is one hell of a kisser, and I'm doing my best to maintain passion parity and ardor intensity. My mind, however, is otherwise occupied. Believe it or not, this kissing episode is neither gratuitous nor superfluous — it is an aspect of professional inquiry, personal investigation of integrity, and responsible discernment of truth.

We reach the top floor while still escalating our osculation, the little bell rings and the door opens. We part lips and strike a responsible pose. Nobody enters. We kiss again all the way back to the lobby.

She's good, no doubt about it. I don't know what she sees in me, but her heart is pounding against mine with astonishing rhythmic intensity.

"What floor is your room on?" She whispers, her breath hot on my face, "I want to get busy."

"You might have to start without me," I say hoarsely, "I have to meet a guy in Pioneer Square."

"Talk to him tomorrow, I come first." She is, I believe, feeling my pockets to locate my room key. In the process, she becomes distracted by other items.

We reach the lobby, the door opens, and I pull her gently back out into the foyer.

"Listen, Randy, how about if I start you a tab in the lounge. Amuse yourself with drinks and whatever passes for entertainment. You can wait for me to get back, or, if you cool off and have second thoughts, you can leave if you so decide. Either way, I'll respect you in the morning."

"How about a quick preliminary match before the main event," she asks with hopeful insistence, "Maybe no knock-out, but a good split decision?"

Her life, I believe, is based on split decisions.

I smile in friendly negation, and we ride the lobby's escalator to the mezzanine's cocktail lounge. A Sonics' game is in full swing on the color TV, and everyone is relaxing freely just like McFeely's. Beer here, however, is more than ninety cents, and I don't see any Native Americans, big or otherwise.

I lean across the bar, handing my room charge authorization card to a uniformed lovely.

"Give this young woman whatever she wants, I'll be back later if you need my signature."

Randy slides her well-formed derriere onto a barstool and orders a straight shot of whiskey. I know what I'm doing.

She swivels towards me for an affectionate good-by.

"I will await your return, " insists Randy, "besides, delayed gratification is the best kind."

"For the time being, I'll take your word for it," I say, reaching out and shaking her hand. Her grip is warm, firm and slightly moist. I hold it for a few beats before letting go.

"It's a pleasure, Mr. Reynolds," she says with charm.

"Indeed it is," I hold a slight pause for dramatic effect, "Ms Nussbaum."

Bombshell.

Her jaw drops.

"How did you ...?"

"I'm psychic, remember?"

She's temporarily speechless.

I hear her next words as I head down the escalator. She addresses them to the bartender.

"Make that a double."

III

Randy Nussbaum.

When I told you that kiss was personal investigation, I meant it. I wasn't merely taking a guided tour of her taste buds.

I used the intensity of personal contact and open vulnerability to capture as many images as possible.

I'd heard of Randy Nussbaum, but that's all, and that was several years ago. When I wrote *Finding Sarah*, I didn't interview the deceased's extended family. They had enough pain. My contacts were law enforcement agents, federal investigators, and sincere sympathizers. Besides, Randy was Sarah's older half-sister. Separated by familial splits and widely divergent life-styles, her proclivities and activities stood — or should I say reclined — entirely dissimilar to her semi-sibling's studious example.

In short, Randy was a party-girl, the top of her head a familiar sight to local musicians. If Sarah was a babyface, Randy was a heel. What she wants with me isn't clear, unless there is some sort of perverse pleasure in having sex with the psychic who found her dead half-sister. Then again, maybe that's important to her as metaphor. Union with me could be her version of closure.

Maybe women such as she listen to Dr. Laura

Funny. She asked if it were over *for me*.

No. Not now. But first things first.

Randy isn't my client and the J&M Cafe in Pioneer Square isn't McFeely's Tavern. That's where I am, the J&M.

Spotting Lightning Rod Sullivan is easier than picking out hooker Verna from a big-hair line-up under the moose head.

There are no punchboards at the J&M, but a crowd of hipified yuppies, yupified hippies, well-known has-beens, and up and coming losers. Sullivan is here all right, slurping up pale ale through his silver streaked beard.

At this particular moment, he's drinking alone. Maybe he just arrived. He won't be alone long, not if he's a regular. Predictable patrons gravitate towards each other for the simple safety of hearing the same old stories over recently poured beverages.

"Excuse me, Mr. Sullivan, may I join you for a moment?"

Before he can answer, I'm already sitting next to him.

"You probably don't remember me, but we crossed paths years ago and we have a mutual friend."

"Oh?" He looks gruff and soft, mean and mild. He could scare the hell out of you if he wanted to, or he could be the nicest man ever to put you in a submission hold.

Of course, I'm not going to mention Larry Large — Richard Tibbit— right off the bat. No way.

"Yeah, you know Billie Lee Kafabe from Texas?"

Billie Lee Kafabe.

This is wrestler talk. Wrestlers and carnival workers have their own jargon — Tezar Kezar. Professional wrestlers determine if you're one of them by asking if you know Billie Lee Kafabe from Texas. If you know the answer, they know you're not a "feazan" and are "smart" to the business.

He knows the answer, and soon we're swappin' remembrances of the days before the WWF more or less put the regionals out of business.

Back in the 1970's three main wrestling alliances literally carved up the American continent. The West Coast was the NWA, the Mid-West and South were the AWA, and the WWF covered the North-East.

"You get your start back in the ol' AWA?"

Sullivan slams his mug on the table and lets loose a hearty, if somewhat resentful laugh.

"Oh, fuck the AWA, God love 'em. In the AWA my week would start in Shreveport, Louisiana, there they had matches on Tuesday nights, then we'd tape a double wrestling show — four goddam hours — on Wednesday *morning.*" He shakes his head as if even he can't believe it.

"Well, God on a pogo stick," He punctuates his sentences with these unique images of the Divine. " During the taping, we'd get our `booking sheets' tellin' us where were gonna work that night and the rest of the week. Now, that doesn't sound bad, 'cept that the Monday night show was in Tulsa, Oklahoma and we'd spent all night driving to damn Shreveport. Hell, I was puttin' seven thousand miles a week on my car, spent most of my waking hours driving."

He's downed one ale and is ordering another. I settle for a Sharp's. I have the distinct impression that old Lightning Rod had a few pops before he arrived, and he's fairly well lubricated.

"You know what being a jobroni's all about, right?"

"Right. Ten pounds of shit in a five pound sack."

A jobroni is a kid learning the business. He helps drive the truck, set's up chairs, the ring, ushers, works the snack bar, and does crowd control. For all this work, he's paid minimum wage and has to cover all his own expenses on the road.

If he's lucky, he'll be allowed to pay one of the "workers' to teach him how to wrestle. He'll still do all the jobs, but now he'll be a rookie jobroni. The only exceptions are midgets, women, athletes from other sports, and family.

"Here's the way it worked, if you were ever gonna make it even into the AWA, let alone the WWF," elaborates Sullivan, "a jobroni would show a little promise, so the promoter would send him to the NWA which was a combination retirement/nursery. The territories were small, the trips between towns were short, and the jobroni got the benefit. He worked his way from Washington Territory to Oregon Territory, to Vancouver B.C. Territory. Then, if he survived the rigors of the business and getting slammed on his head allot, he's be ready to hit California. The poor bastard spends six to eight months in each territory. If he's a decent flyer or fatboy and doesn't fuck up, the last promoter will recommend him to the AWA. Then if he really stands out, he'll be approached by the WWF."

I'm still chuckling over "flyer" and "fatboy." Sullivan likes my laugh and the fact that I've now started buying the drinks.

"Flying" — aerial stunts — are usually done by the babyface. He may be working with a "fatboy" who has to use an "Illegal Object" to beat the flyer. Of course, this dreaded illegal object may not exists except in the crowd's imagination

"Jesus in a side-car! Those were the days when we could still `juice,' `pull a work,' and the Arena Rats were pure `peanut butter'."

Juice. That means cutting your forehead with a razor blade. Take a good look at any pro wrestler and you'll see cuts all along the hairline. As the saying goes, "Red makes Green." The sight of some poor babyface covered in blood brings in bigger crowds for the "grudge" match in the following weeks.

It was the referee's job to slip a corner of razor blade to the babyface or heel. When the babyface juiced, he'd do an "easy" cut in his eyebrow or scalp. In the follow-up grudge match, the heel did a "rough" cut parallel on his forehead. The promoter used to pay extra for a rough-cut.

"Moses in mothballs! I haven't seen anyone juice since AIDS," comments Sullivan wistfully, "besides most states made it illegal to juice — heavy fines if they caught ya."

As for "pulling a work," that was a trick promoters used to goose up the gate during an economic slump. They would advertise a big draw such as the midgets, but on the night of the show, the announcer would break the news that they couldn't make it due to car trouble. Most people didn't ask for their money back. If a promoter tried that stunt today, it would cost them more than the night's receipts in fines.

Arena Rats are groupies. The boys called them 'Peanut Butter' because their legs are smooth and easy to spread. This has me thinking of Randy back at the hotel swallowing doubles.

"Hey," I say if the idea just entered my head, "what was the story on whatshisname, the bank robber?"

"Bank robber?"

Maybe I've screwed up.

"Yeah, back in '74 he worked as Larry Large. A rookie jobroni."

"Jesus on a stick! That son of a bitch. Tibbit. Yeah, Richard fucking Tibbit. He tried to sue our ass!"

"I thought that was it," I lean back like I can't believe it. "What was that all about, anyway."

Sullivan signals for a refill and waves at some drinking buddy. I'm praying he doesn't get really drunk or distracted. I've nursed this conversation too damn long already. Randy may have passed out by now.

"God on a donkey! What a sack of shit," growls Lightning Rod, "he asked to learn the business, him and Tommy Pain about the same time. Don't know what happened to either of them in the long run. But I remember that Tibbit bastard was trained by Joe Ferguson, The Irish Rogue he called himself. Tibbit would meet Joe in the Tri-Cities and they'd go to a gym and practice, you know, Joe teaching him all the moves...well, not all the moves. We'd never teach a rookie jobroni a real submission hold just in case he was a smart ass and got carried away."

I nod like I'm with him all the way.

"But there was something wrong with Tibbit, see. He said he'd never worked before but he already knew the moves. Not the lingo, but the moves. Oh, he worked the NWA circuit — Seattle, Yakima, Wenatchee, Walla Walla — but because he knew more than he was supposed to, none of us trusted him. Well, it turns out we were right. He was up to something."

"Like what?"

"Shit, I dunno, somethin'. Anyway, a bunch of us decided to really put him through it."

Wrestlers can hurt you if they want. It happens usually when a rookie connects hard, or is stupid enough to throw a real punch. To be on the receiving end of this misbehavior is called getting potatoed. If an experienced worker gets potatoed by a rookie jobroni, he'll retaliate by "pulling a shoot." The rookie winds up bleeding if he's lucky. If not, he'll be seriously injured.

"Tibbit got stretched but good. Not like the fans think, of course," Sullivan elaborates, "a figure four leg lock is just a good way to look busy while taking a rest, but the `surfboard" can put a jobroni out for a long time if a foot `accidentally slips' and too much downward pressure is applied. Well, one night ol' Tibbit got stretched. In fact, it was me that stretched him. He knew it was on purpose and tried to sue me and the whole damn federation. He gave it up though – we put a little pressure on him, if you understand. Besides, I think the guy had a rap sheet as long as a damn heeb's nose."

I rankle at that last remark, but suppress my distaste.

"Rap sheet?"

He belches.

"Yeah, and I don't mean `rap' like those jungle bunny-boombox bastards – I mean an arrest record. That Tibbit shit was a car thief and I understand he even broke a murderer out of jail once."

"Do you know about some bank robbery deal?"

Sullivan points his increasingly glazed eyes as the ceiling.

"Well, my drug-addict asshole son has a buddy from Walla Walla who told him that Tibbit robbed a goddam bank, for Christ's sake, and got away with that too. Never busted, not even questioned. Can you believe that? A bank robbing car thief ex-wrestler. Jesus. That kind of crap gives us all a bad name."

As if nothing else would.

"No shit. Hey, did you know I once had five wives?"

Guess I missed that.

He laughs so hard that he hacks up some horrid thing from his lungs and spits it into the ashtray. Disgusting.

"What happened with your drug-addict son? That must have been rough."

"Nah, the little prick. I love him, understand, he's my son, but he's a drug-addict asshole. But look at me for Christ's sake."

I'm not sure if he means his alcoholism or his crippled condition. He rattles the metal crutches for clarification. The booze problem is invisible.

"My kid got into a drug deal – a trunkload of grass — with some other little prick from Walla Walla. Seems that kid — hell, he was twenty — was the son of some shithead snitch. This snitch was talking about this ex-wrestler down there who robbed a bank."

Snitch. Richard used that word, so did Verna.

"Which snitch?"

"Yeah, *which* snitch." Sullivan laughs. He doesn't realize I'm asking a real question.

I re-phrase it.

"His name. Do you remember the snitch's name?"

Sullivan sucks some foam from his beard. He is increasingly repellent.

"Oh, God on a boat..."

That's a new one. I should be keeping a list.

"Bane the snitch. The prick's dad's name was really Derek, but everyone called him Bane. Met him when we were both visiting our boys in the slammer. Sort of a weird character, ya know, had a funny look in his eye. Loved wrestlers in more ways than one," says Sullivan with a droopy wink.

Okay. Now we're getting somewhere.

"Bi-sexual?"

"Tri-sexual, quadra-sexual, fucking pentasexual!" Sullivan roars with fermented mirth. "Ol' Bane was a mark on the NWA circuit. He wanted to be pals with the boys. Pumped iron, got muscles, but he could never be a worker, not in a million years. Guys like that are good for money, cars, or, if they got a secret side, sexual favors. Jesus in an evening gown! I was never into the boys, just the wives and the arena rats. Oh, there were some little cuties that could tumble in the sheets better than any worker could in the squared circle."

I'm sure he's right, but I'd rather not visualize it.

He rattles his braces again.

HEADLOCK

"Now, if you want the whole sordid story about how I got talked into downing all those damn steroids and wound up like this..."

"No, man. I know. You was robbed."

He wasn't robbed. Neither were the other fools who destroyed their bodies with perfectly legal steroids and then tried to sue the promoters who either made steroids available, or gave booking preference to the spectacularly large. Even wrestlers have to take responsibility for their deeds.

"Moses up a tree, pal," insists Sullivan, "I like you, you're all right."

That's because I'm such a sponge. I'll listen to all manner of nonsense.

"Write down your name and number for me," he says shoving a J&M coaster in front of me. "Don't give me no business card, I'll just lose it, but I got a stack of these sons of bitches." He means coasters.

Cool.

I take out Dickhead's pen.

"I gotta pee," says Sullivan, and he pushes back his chair, struggling to his feet. He pauses and looks down at what I'm writing.

I'm just about done when I see it in my mind's eye — a sudden flash, an adrenaline rush, and the man with the surgical mask raising that walking stick in Rook's Park.

Instinct.

I throw myself out of the way as Sullivan's metal crutch crashes down. The beer mug shatters, and glass shards are flying as I scramble for footing. He swings the other brace in a wild, angry arc. I put up my arm. The crutch smacks me hard across the shoulder. Painful, but not damaging.

"Jesus on a rat's ass!" screams Sullivan. The tavern crowd is noticing now, they don't know what the hell is going on. Neither do I.

"What's wrong?" I yell at him, open palmed, pleading. He's advancing, wobbling, and swinging one brace after another.

"You son of a bitch!" He's wielding those braces like some crazed sci-fi transformer. I half expect smoke and flames to shoot out his nose.

At this moment, I can't recall if the Talmud says anything about decking a crippled grappler. I'm sure it does somewhere.

He may be brittle-boned, but his upper torso is massive muscle. The force behind each thrust is potentially bone crushing.

He lunges again. I grab the brace, twisting hard to my right and then jerking back. I'm desperately trying to throw him off balance.

"Sullivan, wait, please," I'm reasoning with him through his alcohol fog, "whatever I did, I'm sorry. I was just writing my name and number like you said..."

Well, that just pisses him off more.

The other brace whooshes towards me, I duck, and pull on the other crutch as hard as I can. He's got his momentum moving towards me, and I'm helping him along. He falls forward, braying like a wounded donkey.

We crash over another tabletop, patrons screaming. He's swearing, shouting, cursing, and I'm trying to get away. And then Lightning Rod Sullivan says the magic words that turn your basic mild-mannered P.I./author into the Ultimate Fighting Champion.

"That goddam JEW sent you! You're probably a goddam KIKE yourself!"

Somehow, I don't think Sullivan plants trees in Israel.

The next thing I know, several guys are pulling me off of the old fart because I'm pummeling his face.

Advice: never call Tibbit a son of a bitch; never call me a sheenie, kike, nigger, or any other racial/ethnic slur. I don't look black or asian, but I have blacks in the family history. A simple twist of Mendel's Law and I'd look a lot more like George Washington Carver and a lot less like George Clooney.

Perturbed customers, outraged that I would beat up an old cripple, are dragging me towards the door; Sullivan's ranting like Mussolini and waving one metal crutch in the air. The entire place is pandemonium.

"And take that goddam pen with you," shouts a bloody-nosed Lightning Rod, "you motherfucking queer-ass Jew!"

Fine way for a wrestler to talk. He probably has a swastika on his disabled parking permit.

Nazis

I hate those guys.

Well, here I am out on the pavement damn lucky they didn't call the cops. The door opens and someone throws Dickhead's pen into the street. I know a Falcon when I see one, and it's a Falcon Futura that runs over it.

So much for opportune clues.

You don't have to be a Shamus Award winner to figure out that Dickhead's pen from "Classic Wax" triggered an anti-Semitic explosion from Lightning Rod Sullivan.

Anti-Semitism.

I've never understood it.

There's a theory, one among many, that Jews are hated because they gave the world ethics — accept the message and kill the messenger. This concept finds verification in the Talmud in a play on words when it says that Sinai caused *Sinah. Sinah* means hate. Perhaps in Sullivan's case the explanation is simpler. Maybe his mother was bitten by Jackie Mason.

I cab it back to the hotel. My body aches and my head hurts. Obviously, this is God's way of keeping me from having too much fun with Randy

"Jesus, you look like you've been in fight," she slurs sympathetically, "that man you were in such a hurry to see must not have been too thrilled to see you."

"Brilliant observation," I mutter, and take the seat next to her at the bar. "Sonics win or lose?"

"Hard to tell," admits Randy, "every time the Sonics made a basket, I took a drink."

The bartender interjects.

"We lost."

Figures.

I order coffee. She looks at the cup with undisguised derision.

"Why don't you put something in it?"

"Because I don't drink alcohol."

She's not as drunk as she pretends. Maybe a bit tipsy, but that's it.

"Listen Randy, if you want to get close to me, you don't have to sleep with me. You can ask me anything, keep your clothes on, and still have whatever pillow talk your little heart desires."

"I don't want to keep my clothes on,"

It's hard to argue with a woman of such consummate debating skill.

I'm already working out my rationalizations. She's in no condition to drive, I'm not up to driving her home, what with just having battled the Fourth Reich...I'll think of more reasons in the elevator.

A few minutes later, I'm watching her flop face first on the bed. She rolls over, sits up, peels off the suit jacket, tosses it towards the chair, and pulls her little blouse off over her head.

"How do I look so far? Wanna see more?"

She expects a compliment.

"If I haven't seen it before I won't know what it is, if I have, it won't bother me."

She falls back and laughs. Then, she suddenly stops and sits back up.

"You gay or something? I mean I don't have anything against gays or anything, but most guys would have jumped me by now."

"No, I'm not gay," I answer sitting on the edge of the bed, "it's just that I don't think casual sex is..."

"I don't have AIDS or anything, I'm not some whore."

She's half-naked and half-irked. I take her hand in mine.

She's kind. For her, kindness is best expressed by sex. Maybe it's all she knows.

I pull her gently from the bed, fold back the covers, fetch her an extra large T-shirt from the dresser, and turn off the lights. Together in bed, enveloped in darkness, side by side, we talk.

She speaks of her response to my book. Between the lines she found a man who manifested the virtue of selflessness. For her, Jeff Reynolds was a hollow reed from which the pith of self had been removed — a clear channel through which spiritual insight and justice flowed. He was the one man who, with no thought of his own emotional safety or the repercussions in his life, becomes a vehicle of truth. She believes I saw into Sarah's very soul, discerned her inner reality, and brought a least some closure to her fragmented family's pain.

How far, far indeed is the truth from what she attributes to me. She invests my fallible self with the robe of near-prophethood and crowns me with the diadem of undeserved admiration. Oh, I did all those good things, but it was half-unintentional and half-motivated by a lucrative book contract.

Somehow, some way, I knew I could tap that gift for a good purpose and reap a reward. The payoff was a nice house, no wife, and a daughter who'll be fluent in Cantonese before I see her again.

Silence. I listen to Randy's breath, and feel her warmth next to me.

I'm thinking of going ahead and doing it. I mean, after all, she's right here and more than willing.

HEADLOCK

She starts snoring. A blessing. Thank God she's not an insomniac.

Discomfort and pleasure. Morning. I blink at the hotel ceiling.

My shoulder aches were Sullivan's crutch connected; there's a silken leg wrapped around one of mine, and a lithe arm across my chest.

She stirs, awakening.

She opens those dark blue eyes, sees me, and smiles.

"You were wonderful last night," I remark affectionately.

"I was?"

I nod, smile.

"Damn," she mutters under her breath as she gets up, "I gotta stop drinking or get tested for Alzheimers."

"What does that mean?"

"It means I can't remember making love to you," she complains, "and I feel cheated. It's not your fault, it's the booze."

She plops down in the chair.

"That's it. I had a goddam blackout like some old alcoholic. Me! I can't believe it. Well, that ends that."

"We're through? Already? I was just becoming fond of you."

She puts her head in her hands.

"No, not you, the drinking. When a woman starts having blackouts, she better quit. It's like, you know, I mean, a girl can get, pregnant..." she says this as if the "p-word" is made of spun glass, "and never remember who she did it with."

Randy makes a sour face and stares at the carpet.

"Besides," she continues, "I love sex and don't like the idea of having it and not remembering it."

Time to come clean.

"We didn't have sex."

"Huh?"

"You started snoring before I could make my move," I explain, doing my best to phrase it warmly. "I'm obviously `Mr. Excitement.'"

This doesn't help her feel any better.

She blushes, and I mean she really, really blushes.

"I'm mortified, just shoot me, this is humiliating. I seduce you and then fall asleep before anything happens."

She gets out of the chair and crawls onto the bed.

"If you loan me a toothbrush first, I'll make it up to you."

"I don't think I'm up to it."

"You will be."

"But will you respect me at lunch time?"

She thinks it over.

"If you also lend me shampoo and buy me breakfast, I'll never say an unkind word about you as long as I live."

"Sounds highly conditional to me, but I do have shampoo and a toothbrush."

"Ummmm," she purrs from practice and habit, "are your bristles firm"

"Not as firm as my resolve."

I get off the bed.

"Randy, you're a knockout – attractive, the works – and I'm a normal...well, sort of normal man. But it's not about respect, it's about responsibility. If I'm a lousy lover you may never want to see me again, and likewise for me; if we are fantastic sexual partners that may keep us together as long as that initial fascination lasts, but no longer. If this were our honeymoon, no matter how disappointing the sex, we would stay together out of love and work on the sex part."

She's smiling, looking at me with an adorable cock-eyed expression.

"Our honeymoon? Is this a proposal?"

"Yes, I propose you shower and get dressed and we have breakfast and we have conversation. If, after the last cup of coffee, we still appreciate each other's company, we spend the day together before I fly home."

She gets up, puts hands on hips, and squints at me in an exaggerated posture of schoolmarm inquisition.

"You *sure* it wasn't shot off in the war?"

Bravo. She really likes me. Hell, she wanted to have sex with me. I figure that's good for something. Besides, she's Randy Nussbaum. I found her dead sister's bones.

IV

"I'm not trying to scare you, but you should be aware that you might get killed, and I don't mean by some old fart wrestler."

Randy's in the shower; I'm on the phone with Richard relating my one fall disqualification match with Lightning Rod Sullivan. He seems more amused than concerned.

"He always was too much to handle when he hit the sauce. Most wrestlers drink more than an athlete should."

I'm not going to ask how much an athlete should drink. I'm looking out the window. Seattle in the sunshine is the most beautiful city on Earth. Today, it 's cloudy. I must remember to ask Richard about the bank robbery.

"Of course, Dad was one hell of a drinker."

The bank robbery can wait.

"Tell me about your father."

A deep breath on his end of the line while I'm digging through my clothes looking for an Old Gold. Behind the sounds of her shower, Randy is singing "Relax" by Frankie Goes to Hollywood.

"My father, Russell Tibbit, was an alcoholic, okay, since World War II. Came home with the usual memorabilia and an unquenchable thirst. Beat the Germans but not the bottle. Anyway, he was chief engineer on a tug on the Columbia. That's where he met my stepmother. She was cookin'."

"The chief engineer falls in love with the cook."

"Right. "

"This a Foss tug?"

"No, Merril/Stroum – based in Portland. Anyway, he approached me and my older brother about it. Not the tug, the idea of marrying her. He said, `I love her and she loves me and she wants to marry me.' And so I met her, and he wanted to know our opinion. My brother was all for it."

"You had reservations?"

"I can' t explain – I can now, but I mean this is back then – at that time I couldn't explain this feeling that I got. I remember the exact words I said. I mean, this lady gives me a bad feeling. And so my father says, 'so, what do you think?' and I says....

The pause is worthy of a professional performer.

"'She's not who she says she is.' That was my words, I remember specifically. Dad looked at me kinda funny. `You don't like her.' 'No, I didn't say that, I said she's not who she says she is.' There's something wrong. Well, he went ahead and married her. And right off the bat, boy, I knew that she didn't like me and that was just fine. Well, I'd had trouble in school. I'd had a head injury. I didn't know it at the time, but I found out about fifteen years ago."

Peter Hurkos had a head injury.

"I didn't do well in school so I quit. She was gone most of the time and she didn't know if I was in school or not. I hitchhiked up to a construction site on the Snake River. Walked up there and the foreman hired me. Ya gotta realize I was a pimple-faced punky lookin' kid. He hired me anyway. I must have worked a couple weeks before a guy showed up and pointed me out. The jig was up and I was let go. He took his wallet out and paid me. I know this is boring to you."

"Keep talking"

"He paid me three-hundred fifty dollars right out of his pocket. That tickled the hell out of me. So there I was, hitchhiking through little Dayton, Washington.. There's this guy polishing his car with a `for sale' sign on it. It's an old 1939 Chrysler. I wanted transportation. Didn't have a license or anything. Went up to him and he was asking three hundred dollars. Paid him, got in, drove it home."

Cool. 1939 Chrysler. Randy is out of the shower. I can hear her in the bathroom.

"I pulled up next to the house. Dad was home. I parked and he come out. `How come you're not going to school, blah, blah,blah.' You know how parents are."

Yeah. They wonder how their kids are doing in China.

"He said I didn't have a license so I couldn't drive the car. I gave him the keys 'cause he was right. My dad went to work, and he was going to be gone for twenty days. Anyway, right out of the blue she says to me, `I hate you, I don't want nothin' to do with you, I've got my own family.' Ya gotta understand that it took me a while to figure out her motives, her ways. She wanted me out of there."

What did you do?

"I stole my dad's car and headed towards Idaho."

"You stole *his* car? What about…"

"The Chrysler? He hid the keys. I knew where there was a set of his keys, so I just took 'em, made a copy, and took off for Idaho – I had some family there. Actually, my aunt in Idaho raised me. Anyway, I was so damn tired drivin' all night that I drove the car off a goddam cliff. Okay, the cops come, lock me up, call Dad, bring me back, lock me up. Three days later he comes down with her."

Randy comes out towel dried and freshly scrubbed, her wet hair slicked back, no makeup, and she looks excellent. She smiles, sits down on the bed, and digs through her purse. I wiggle my fingers at her in a friendly wave. She gives me an exaggerated wink and a luminous smile.

"Dad asked me why I did it," continues Richard, "I said `If I told ya you won't believe me so there's no reason even conversing.' `Well, I'm your father and you shouldn't feel that way.' So I says, `Okay, that bitch said she didn't like me, didn't care for me, so I headed for Idaho.' He looks at her, then at me. She says, `That's a goddam lie!' He says, `I'm gonna believe her. You're just a trouble maker.' So, basically, from that point on, I knew where I was goin. I gave up. I didn't give a shit. I was sent to Chehalis prison. I figured how to escape. Me and this other kid escaped, stole a car, and took off. We made it to Seattle and stayed with some friends of his for two nights. We stole another car. In fact, we stole the same car he stole in the first place that got him sent to prison. We made it across the floating bridge, got as far as some little town and ran out of gas. Well, right in the middle of trying to siphon some gas we got busted by the cops. Blah, blah , blah, we're back in jail."

Randy is smoothing on her nylons.

"So, then they put me in top security there in Chehalis and to make the story short, I figured to hell with this. Now I've gained another year on my sentence. So, I straightened up, got out, came home, got a job washing dishes at that restaurant that used to be at 9th and Main, the Heidelburg Villa. I started drinking. Like I say man, what ya gonna do?"

"Yeah, what ya gonna do."

"Nothin' I could do about her, right? Ya can't change stepmothers the way you do bars. Besides she already got rid of my brother."

"Got rid?"

"Well, convinced him he should go in the service. You gotta understand that things were working out perfect for her. Hell, you know any other situation where a teenage kid takes his dad's car and gets sent to prison for a year?"

I thought that sounded peculiar.

'That was her idea. She told Dad I wouldn't mind her, that it would teach me a lesson, and so forth. Dad had a talk with the judge, and the next thing you know I'm in prison – the one I broke out of. But you see she was successful. That was always her plan – get rid of me. Remember I told you when we first met that she was smart - real smart. "

"Her name, Richard. You never told me her name."

"Didn't you read those papers I gave you?"

"No. I will."

"I'm rushing you, right?"

"Her name?"

"Violet. Her maiden name was Langness, Violet Langness."

Randy walks over and kisses me on the cheek before stepping in front of the mirror.

"And she was just a cook on a tug boat, right?"

"She said she was a nurse for five years and worked in psychiatrist's office, but she could have been lying."

"Where is she now?"

Silence. The clouds fall away and Seattle sun streams in through the window. Randy's hair shines as if she's in a TV commercial.

'They found her body in Nevada or Arizona – I can never tell those two states apart — the bitch was dead as a doornail. Natural causes – heart failure, as if she had a heart to begin with. We got a call when she was already in the ground. Dead or not, she got away with it, right? Everyone dies sooner or later, so it's not like she could get *away* with it and get it away *with* her, ya understand? "

"Gee, Richard, you mean you've never seen a Brink's truck following a hearse to the cemetery?"

He sort of laughs.

"It was almost half a million bucks. That's what killing my dad was worth – four hundred seventy five thousand dollars. She got it all, spent some, and God only knows what happened to the rest."

"Her death didn't end it?"

I hear his Zippo click and the crisp crackle of another ignited Bel-Air.

"Hell, no. She died almost right after she got the loot. I don't mean days after, but within two years. It was pretty intense for me, ya know. I mean it got even worse for a while after she died – the following, the threats, and all that shit. Then it sort of eased up a bit. That's when I came to see you, but it kicked back into high gear right away. Like I say, don't be surprised if you get killed."

I look at my watch.

"Happy anniversary, Richard."

"Happy anniversary?"

"Yeah, in thirty five seconds we'll have known each other exactly twenty-four hours."

"Speaking of anniversaries, did I tell you about the guy who shoved the shotgun in my mouth?"

He tells me, and it's one hell of a story. In fact, it's better than that, it's real Americana.

Richard, age eighteen and heavy into solo drinking, drove his Chrysler to the Sky-Vu Drive In for a double feature – booze and girl watching.

Halfway into the second movie, Richard stumbled out of the car and headed towards the rest room. On the way, he noticed a vehicle with one guy and girl in the front, and another attractive girl sitting alone in the back seat.

Richard knocked on the car door.

"Yeah? What do you want?"

"What the hell you got two women for?"

The explanation was simple: the front seat couple was on a date; the back seat girl was her younger sister's chaperone.

Richard, by either verbal artistry or intimidation, talked his way into the back seat. He was hardly in the car two minutes when he reached around and grabbed the girl's breast.

Big mistake.

The young woman went ballistic. Furious, offended, and kick-ass pissed, she beat the crap out of him. The front seat fellow rescued Richard by pulling him out of the car and throwing him on his face in the gravel.

Disgraced and disheveled, Richard slunk back to the comfort

of his bottle.

But it wasn't over, not over at all.

The next day he spotted the car heading down Main Street. He flagged down the driver – the same guy who'd thrown him out the night before – and asked, "Who was that gal, the one in the back seat?"

The driver revealed her name, but added a warning, "She told her daddy and he's looking for you. He's gonna shoot you, and that crazy son of a bitch will do it, too."

Richard found out where she lived, waited two weeks, then drove to her house, walked up the front steps, and rang the bell. When the door opened, there she was.

She was livid. "Get out of here!"

"Listen, I want to apologize. I was drunk and way out of line."

She was suddenly shoved out of the way by her father, brandishing a shotgun. He shoved the barrel directly against Richard's mouth, and his finger was on the trigger.

The father let up the pressure just enough so Richard could speak.

"Sir, I deserve it," said Richard flatly, "I deserve whatever you do to me. I apologize to her, and I apologize to you."

Shaking with rage, the father thrust the shotgun back into Richard's mouth. The girl, terrified, did nothing. And there the three of them stood – the father, Richard, and the girl.

"Understand this," hissed the dad, "I think you're vermin. I'll kill ya and I'll bury ya."

He eased the barrel slowly out of Richard's mouth.

"Sir, would it be OK I came back sometime and we all just sit on the porch and talk?"

That's nerve.

And that's how Richard met his wife.

"You kidding?" Randy asks as we drive towards the University District in her Subaru XT-4.

"Nope, true story."

"Weirder than weird," says Randy, "and I mean really weird...but sweet in a weird sway."

"Yes, very sweet. If he hadn't been drunk and rude, he never would have met her."

"Gives you something to think about, that's for sure."

"Such as?"

"How being drunk can screw things up, but doing the right

70

thing can make it better. I'm done with it. I decided this morning. That's it. Period."

"Good for you. Is it going to be a problem?"

"Nah. Piece of cake."

We'll see.

Classic Wax occupies a long, thin storefront at 45th and University way. Retro is all the rage with the college crowd and the university professors, so I imagine business is brisk. The store is a little too dark and musty to sell anything but oldies – it has the distinctive smell of those green paper sleeves for .45rpm records. The aged crone behind the counter is no college coed. She looks somewhere between seventy-five and one hundred thirty, has enough scrap metal in her ear lobes to set off an airport metal detector, and more chains around her neck than a busload of Isaac Hayes impersonators. Despite dual burdens of increased age and heavy metal, she appears impressively spry.

As an audio adjunct to the atmosphere, the prominent sound system is an antiquated 8-track. The song is familiar, but the artist's name eludes me.

I ask.

"*Los Indios Trabajaros*," she answers, "I think it means Big Indians."

It doesn't.

Randy is already flipping through the LPs, enraptured in vinyl memory world.

"Lovely place you have here, Ms...."

She thrust a long bony hand across the counter, each fingernail a different color.

"Yenta, Yenta Schnauser-Goldblatt. I know it's a mouthful, but I want to honor my maiden name. The Schnauser family had no sons. I, of course, have one – Dean."

It was a Goldblatt named Dean who was, for more than a decade, the owner of a chancy Seattle-based enterprise named Northwest Championship Wrestling.

A coffee mug full of Classic Wax pens sits on the counter.

"Mind?' I ask, gesturing.

"No, help yourself, that's what they're there for. My son, Dean, is always ordering pens. He uses them to write checks to the pen company."

I tell her I used to know her son back in the "old days," and give her the name he'd know me by. She's only passably impressed.

"Too bad he missed you," she says, "today's his day off. He doesn't care much for wrestling anymore. Won't watch WWF or WCW on TV, it just aggravates him. Wrestlers are trouble anyway. One of our guys even became a bank robber or something."

That story sure gets around.

She shrugs and her chains rattle. "That bastard Sullivan – he's nothing but a goddam Nazi, the putz, — sued my Dean because he got screwed up on steroids. Is that my son's problem?" She sighs, and the *greatest hits* 8-track pumps out *White Rabbit* by Jefferson Airplane. "Did anyone tell him to do that? Hell, no. Dean just told him to show up and wrestle. His case was thrown out anyway, but it cost us nothin' but *gelt*."

She lifts a thin wrist banded by heavy bracelets and waves her hand towards the record bins where Randy and a few tweed attired customers are browsing through album jackets.

"This is a lot less stress," she remarks with a smile, "and the music brings back happy times for these people. I like to think of this place as if it's a museum, except the customers can buy the artifacts."

I smile back.

"I like museums, but I don't listen much to oldies. Someone once said that nostalgia was just another name for depression."

The Jefferson Airplane tune does, however, sound spectacular.

"You want depression? Be a wrestling promoter, that's depression," insists Yenta, "I learned one thing from watching Dean go through that aggravation."

"What's that?"

"Good guys come and go, but heels go on forever."

Randy buys a Moody Blues LP, I tell Yenta to give Dean my best regards, and we step out onto University Way. The bass line from *White Rabbit* still plays in my head, and she's admiring the Moodies LP as if it's the crown jewels.

"I used to make love for hours to this album."

"Did it skip afterwards?"

Her laugh is wonderful.

"I mean the album would be playing while my boyfriend and I made love."

"Menage a'stereo. How romantic. We have the LP, but where's the boyfriend?"

"He dumped me years ago, or I dumped him. I don't really

recall. I remember the album better than I remember the boyfriend."

"And such is the secret of Classic Wax's success—memories of media replace memories of relationships."

"God, you're just too damn profound," says Randy, and she whacks me gently with the LP.

Jimmy Woo's Jade Pagoda on Capitol Hill serves a splendid Oyster Beef, and I prove this to Randy. Between bites she talks circumspectly about attempting to normalize her life after Sarah's murder.

"I could have really lost it," she admits. "I was already a wild party girl, and I can see that I could have really gone over the edge. Instead, it made me begin reevaluating my life. I went to North Seattle Community College, stopped dancing at Uncle Elmo's Good Time Arcade, got a real job in an office from nine to five. Lot's of filing and phone answering. I used to be jealous of Sarah because she was smart and pretty and got great grades. I thought she was the loser because her life was dull and mine was a big party. Yeah, right. Big party. When she got killed, I figured it could have been, maybe should have been me. So, anyway, I figured maybe I could be sort of halfway between what she was like and what I used to be like. Not that I don't still like to party, but you know, because, well…you never know."

I know.

"I talk too much, don't I? Guys don't like women who talk too much."

"No, guys don't mind the talking, it's the listening – most men are ill practiced at it. Toy stores sell "Talking Barbie," but you can't even special order "Listening Ken." As for me…"

"I know – you'll listen to anything."

"Fortune cookie?" I tilt the little black tray towards her as she dabs her attractive lips with a Jade Pagoda napkin.

"Why would I need a fortune cookie when I have a famous psychic friend sitting across from me with oyster sauce on his shirt?'

She's right. I have sauce on my shirt.

"I want to ask you a serious question, Jeff."

Jeff. That's me.

"Another serious question? You've asked me `if it's over,' about my failed marriage and my Macao resident daughter, my accent, and what it was like using my so-called amazing gift to find your sister's body. I finally starting to learn about you, and I want to know more."

She takes the fortune cookie, splits it open, and removes the slip of paper.

"I guess I need this after all," she says with a fake sigh, "Mr. Mindboggle can find the deceased but not discern the living?"

She reads the fortune, wads it up, and tosses it in the ashtray.

"Not to your liking?"

"It said `True Love is Within Your Reach'. What does yours say?"

I make elaborate show of opening the cookie.

"Wise is the man who toasts KGO Radio with Hamms', the Beer Refreshing."

She's incredulous.

"Hamms Beer? In a fortune cookie? KGO? That's in San Francisco."

"Yeah, I know. When I was in San Francisco several years ago I actually had a fortune cookie at Johnny's Kan's Restaurant that said that."

"And this one, today?"

"The same as yours, you know, `true love'."

I do exactly what she did – wad it up and toss it in the ashtray. She arches her eyebrows. Fair's fair. True love is like true crime. More people appreciate fiction.

A moment of self-consciousness stalls us both. We acknowledge it with simultaneous throat clearing followed by honest laughter.

She speaks first, and it's the serious question.

"Do you ever think about life after death?"

"Everyday."

"I'm sure."

"No. Fact. Just twenty four hours ago I was wondering if dogs went to heaven."

"Do they?"

"Does it matter?"

"Maybe. At least to dogs."

"Do you want dogs in heaven?"

She toys with her cookie.

"I'm not concerned about dogs."

I take her hand. She lets go of the cookie.

Here is where I show off my astonishing audiographic memory. If I hear it, I remember it. If I read it out loud, I've got it between my ears forever. Years ago I read aloud from the book

HEADLOCK

Paris Talks, a collection of short talks given by renowned spiritual philosopher and humanitarian Sir Abbas Effendi, better known as 'Abdu'l-Bahá. Words first uttered in Paris on November 4th, 1911 are appropriate to this discussion; I need only speak them in more contemporary parlance. I consider this the elocutionary equivalent of colorization. It may be offensive to purists, but it brings the art to a new audience.

"A person can be physically weak, but spiritually strong, right?"

She agrees.

"Well, then its quite apparent that spiritual strength is something very different from physical strength. The two are not the same, and one is not dependent upon the other."

"I'm with you so far," she says encouragingly. I keep going.

"The spirit or soul is changeless, indestructible. The progress and development of the soul, the joy and sorrow of the soul, are independent of the physical body."

"Give me another example."

I let go of her hand so I can gesture.

"If we're caused joy or pain by a friend, if a love prove true or false, it is the soul that is affected. If our dear ones are far from us, it is the soul that grieves."

"I still grieve for Sarah," she admits.

"That's a perfect example." I take her crumpled fortune out of the ashtray. "Good fortune and misfortune can affect the body or the soul, because each has its own individuality. If some guy breaks your heart, it's not your physical blood-pump that's in pain, is it?"

"Nope."

"We agree," I say confidently, "when we find true love, we're happy; but if we meet with lying, faithlessness, and deceit, we're miserable. This misery is obviously not of the body, but of the soul. My client, Richard, for example, is sick of being emotionally mistreated. He is miserable because of lies and deceit."

"And when people are murdered?"

My first thought is of Richard's father, but I realize she means Sarah.

"As body and soul are different and distinct, what happens to the body does not necessarily touch the soul. The soul isn't in the body like water in a glass, or," I take a sip of tea, "tea in a tea cup. I think it's more like light in a mirror."

She likes that and nods.

"If you're looking at your reflection in a mirror," I continue, "you can break the reflection without hurting yourself. If a cage containing a bird is broken, the bird is unharmed. After all, when is the bird freest, in the cage or out of it? The same thing applies to the spirit of human beings. Death may destroy the body, but it has no power over the person's reality, which is spirit."

She manages a smile.

"Gee, Jeff, you're better than a fortune cookie after all. So, what happens after you're dead?"

"Me personally? Well, I'll take around my resume and try to get a gig."

"Why," she asks with a much-needed laugh, "is there unemployment after death?"

"Could be. After all, you can't get a job without experience. I think the trick is to develop spiritual qualities and attributes here and now – you know, `Plan for a stable future after you're gone. It beats on the job training.'" I say that in my best radio voice.

"Do you mean that if I don't have experience being spiritual, I might be on welfare?" She's getting into it, intoning her question as if she's the amazed and easily impressed token female sidekick on the 700 Club.

"Maybe in the Afterlife, what we call `welfare' is termed `mercy' Hopefully, after the soul is freed from the body it is plunged in the ocean of Mercy."

"What if it can't swim?"

"I guess it gets ethereal water wings, or a numinous inner tube." I make dog-paddling motions with my hands, and get wide-eyed like a scared puppy.

She looks at me — those blue eyes are darker and more beautiful than ever — and bounces a piece of fortune cookie off my forehead.

"You a minister or something *and* a private eye *and* an author?"

"My mother wanted me to be a Rabbi"

"Rabbi Reynolds? Reynolds doesn't sound like a Jewish name."

"I said my mother wanted me to be a Rabbi; I never said we were Jewish."

"So, you've never been a real Rabbi?"

"Only like the Great Impostor – you know, I 'd show up in

some small town in the Midwest where the community desperately needs a Rabbi, and I get away faking my way through Yom Kippur."

She almost believes me.

"I'm kidding, Randy. It's more of a hobby like stamp collecting or searching for Bigfoot. It's fun to think about spiritual things. As for the fun ratio of life after death, centuries ago the great Rabbis said that you should imagine every physical pleasures you ever enjoyed, and then cram them into one minute. Then you take that one minute and add it to all the minutes of everyone who ever lived, and compact all of that into one minute of unbelievable pleasure."

"I'd wet my pants."

"Thanks for sharing."

"You know what you need, Mr. Rabbi Reynolds, Private Eye Author?"

"I bet you're going to tell me."

"Amazing, you *are* psychic. Listen..." she averts her eyes and pokes at a few cookie crumbs on the table. She's about to change the subject, and you don't need to be psychic to sense it. That's OK. Conversations of a spiritual bent are so content and concept heavy it's like swallowing an entire pan pizza.

"I've read tons of mysteries at the library," she continues, "and what you need if you're gonna crack your latest case – this one you were telling me about, Richard Tibbit and the murdering step-mom, is a psychotic side-kick."

Bingo.

She's not the first fan to point out that the hero of my previous two books was a loner while many modern mystery heroes have sociopath pals who do their "dirty work." These characters are either exceptionally complex or dangerously two-dimensional. The best authors, of course, create the best psychotic second bananas.

"You mean I should have a Gabby Hayes or Huntz Hall wannabe with a .45 in his waistband or a straight razor up his sleeve?"

"Well, at least in your books if not in real life. Like in your last book..."

I hold up my hands in protest.

"Never say `last book,' say `most recent'."

She rolls those magnificent eyes.

"Ok, your most recent book, the one where your hero cracks the case of the ex-mistress of the Prime Minister found floating face down in Walden Pond."

"*#10 Drowning St.*"

"Stupid title"

"It sold"

"Fine, but I think it would have been better if he had a sidekick or two."

"Now it's up to two?'

"Leo Waterman has all those homeless guys."

"Leo Waterman is not a real person. He lives in a word processing file. Jerry Ford's computer is a time-share condo for the fictionally homeless. And speaking of Jerry, he's the one who tipped me off where to find that damn Nazi cripple who beat me up."

"You were beat up by a cripple?"

"Yeah, and then I was assaulted by Quakers."

She shrugs. "It's the oats."

"Actually, Quaker Oats isn't owned by Quakers."

"I know," she winks, "and the Amish don't make Amish Cigars either."

"They don't even smoke, the Amish."

"You're avoiding my advice."

She's right.

"Yes. I've though of using a psychotic sidekick or creating one. The fictional ones are easier to manage. I don't need one. Really. My clients meet all the requirements."

"You mean Richard Tibbit?"

I sip more tea. It's cold.

"Less than two days ago, I knew next to nothing about Mr. Tibbit and his plethora of paranoid delusions – today I know that he's probably not that deluded at all. When he says this Violet Langness murdered his father for the insurance money, I don't doubt it – that's not the question. He hired me to find out who all was involved, and `if its over.'"

"You going to find out?"

"I'm not giving back the money. Besides, one of the other significant characters also hired me."

She looks confused; I tell her about Jake "Dickhead" Livesy and the rumors about his lifestyle.

"How could you take him on as a client too? If he's a sicko

and in on it, isn't that conflict of something?"

"Interest, yes, conflict of compounding and confounding interest, but I wanted to keep him on the sidelines until I got back."

"A stall."

"Exactly, and a spur of the moment move."

"Is that legal?"

"My folks wanted me to be a Rabbi, not a lawyer."

"Then, is it ethical?"

I don't answer, I shrug. Another stall of dubious ethics.

The waiter returns and scoops up the black tray and my my credit card. In the old days, I'd pay Mr. Woo on the way out. Jimmy's been gone a long time, and his little boy is now a grown man.

Paid up and exited, we're walking from Jimmy Woo's front door to the adjacent parking lot. Two men walk by arm in arm singing an old drinking song, and a beautifully restored old Pontiac eases out of the lot. Chief Pontiac was an Indian so big that they named a city in Michigan after him, and an entire line of automobiles. The big Indian's driver is careful not to dull the shine by hitting pedestrians.

Traffic on Broadway is heavy, the air a cacophony of conflicting car stereos and full-throated engines. Adding to the aural ambiance are the sidewalk-stationed boom boxes of panhandlers.

There is one nestled against the brick wall next to the Jade Pagoda. He's wearing the obligatory vet's outfit with a cardboard sign around his neck reading "Homeless Hungry Vet: Please Help. God Bless You." Crouched next to him is an enormous white canine, fluffy as can be.

"Help a vet?" he asks, looking up hopefully.

"Eat the dog," I say warmly and Randy about faints.

I don't give to beggars. Period.

Just out of Mr. Hungry's earshot, Randy expresses her disapproval.

"I can't believe that! How could you be so cold? This poor homeless...."

I cut her off.

"Simple. The dog is healthier than half the kids in America – shiny coat, good teeth, obviously well fed spotless and well-groomed. Now, check out his hands. They're dirty. So are his clothes. If he's so poor, hungry, and dirty, how's he supporting a dog who eats more than a teenager? And why is the dog so damn clean? He's in costume Randy, in costume. That Army jacket is used Vietnam era, and unless he was in Saigon at the age of ten, he's never even been to boot camp. Get it? He's a hustle."

She doesn't buy it.

"What if you're wrong? What if he's for real? What then? It wouldn't hurt to give him a dollar. I thought you had compassion." She's finding me more disgusting than I find the beggar.

It's not about compassion, it's about justice, and here's where I wrestle with the Jewish law of *Tzadakah,* which is different from Christian charity. The Christian basis of charity is love or compassion; Jewish *Tzadakah* is based on justice – giving is the right thing to do. You give even to the most offensive and disgusting beggar because compassion has nothing to do with it. I grasp the concept, and for the community at large, I agree. I give to charity, and how much is none of your business, but I refuse to personally give a dime to beggars, *Tzadakah* or not.

"He should sell a pencil."

"What?"

"He is begging, Randy. Even if he was offering to sell me a five-cent pencil for twenty dollars, at least he wouldn't be begging."

She's squinting at me, and fumbling with her purse. I bet she's digging out a dollar.

"The *Kitab-i-Aqdas* says..." I'm attempting to explain.

"Never heard of it."

"It's The Most Holy Book."

"Wouldn't that be `The Holiest Book'?"

"Yeah, but Most Holy sounds more formal. Anyway, it says, `It is unlawful to beg, and it is forbidden to give to him who beggeth'."

"That sounds awfully cold."

"Not at all. You want to help this guy who, if you ask me, doesn't need help at all, then we'll set him up in business."

"What?"

I take her by the arm and return to Mr. Hungry and his well-fed pooch. I take three Classic Wax pens out of my pocket and hand them to him.

"Here. You just became an entrepreneur. Sell the lady a pen."

Randy hands him a dollar, he give her a pen. The dog is sniffing me in a private place. Cats have enough class not to do that.

"Excellent, now give me a dime."

"Huh?"

"She gave you a dollar for the pen, right? So, pay me ten cents for the damn pen and you just made yourself one hell of a profit, became a business man and stopped being a beggar."

He looks at me like I'm an asshole, but he gives me the dime.

"Perfect. Now I'm advancing you those two other pens. I'll be back someday to collect twenty cents. When you sell those, go over to RiteAid and buy a bag of pens. I think they cost $1.49. Sell 'em at a buck each and you'll make money."

"Yeah, like I wanna go get a street vender's license."

Figures.

So, the point of this story is this: I figure the dog is the more innocent of the two. After all, the animal is just a prop in his little charade. To show I am not such a jerk, I smile at Randy and together we reach out to pet the animal. As we lean forward, the damn thing jumps on us, its massive paws whacking Randy and I off balance and out of the way.

Thwap!

A bullet smacks the dog right in the center of the forehead. Randy gasps, the dog drops dead, and Mr. Hungry spills his pens.

"Oh Jesus,. Jesus, Jesus, Jesus!" The beggar, shocked, is babbling. "Jesus, Jesus, Jesus, Jesus."

I don't think the dog's name was Jesus.

"You're in heaven now, Jesus," moans the beggar holding the dead dog's bloody head, "You're in heaven now."

The dog's name *was* Jesus, for Christ's sake.

The sidewalk crowd hasn't noticed a thing yet, Randy is chalk-faced, and I'm already grabbing her by the arm and propelling her towards the parking lot.

"C'mon were getting the hell out of here."

Her eyes are still on the dead dog, but her feet obey my command. She fumbles the keys out of her purse and soon the Subaru is heading west on Roy Street.

"Who would want to shoot that beautiful dog?"

"Gangs, Randy. It's gang related intimidation."

She's incredulous. She's also driving a bit erratically.

"Gangs? Drive- by dog-shootings?"

"It could've been more brutal - drive-by-vivisection. Beggar turf wars. They've been going on for decades," I explain, adlibing furiously. "Kill the dog; take the location. That spot by Jimmy Woo's is the Park Place of panhandler real estate. I'll bet you anything Mr. Hungry and his four-legged Jesus were squatters on some other gang's turf, or hadn't paid their Beggars'Gang protection dues."

Her fingers tremble on the steering wheel.

"Scary stuff," she says. "I mean, one of us could have been shot."

No kidding. I wonder if I was the intended target.

"We were never in danger," I say this as if I really know what I'm talking about, "it was a pro-job by a canine kill specialist."

It's a short drive to her Capitol Hill apartment on the 100 block of East Thomas. There's no underground parking nor car port. Like battling panhandlers, drivers compete for street space. She squeezes the Subaru in between a battered orange VW bug and a metallic blue Volvo 1800E.

Randy's regaining her composure, and I'm doing my best to act cool. In truth, my adrenal cortex is going berserk. I'm pumped, primed, and brain synapses are lit up like Vince McMahon's Titantron.

Having checked out of the hotel, my sacred possessions are stuffed in the Subaru's micro-trunk. I drag them up the four flights of stairs, Randy fumbles with her keys, and soon we're inside.

She calls the apartment building "Aardvark Arms," but it doesn't really have a name. It's older, the rooms warmed in winter by heavy metal radiators and wheezing space heaters; cooled in winter by open windows and portable fans. The inevitable upgrade to high priced condos hasn't transpired, so she resides in the drafty luxury of a "cheap" apartment with a million-dollar view of Lake Union, downtown Seattle, and the Olympic Mountains.

She immediately chug-a-lugs several ounces of Pepto-Bismal, and scurries off to change her clothes while I flop on the couch. There are pictures on the wall, but I'm not looking. I'm sure there's at least one of Sarah up there with the Parrish prints. A remote control pokes me in the rear. I dig it out from between the cushions and aim it at the 1980's era rosewood Sony. The picture comes on; the sound is low. I flip through the usual re-runs, cartoons, earth-shaking news updates, and stop when I hit TNT.

Wrestling.

It's WCW, Ted Turner's high-powered and well-funded federation, now populated by former WWF performers. Even the commentators used to be with WWF. Names, identities, and gimmicks have mutated —heels are babyfaces and babyfaces are heels

— but it's the same old faux grudge fueled alliances, shouted posturing, and illegal objects.

"I can't believe a grown man would watch that stuff unless he had a ten-year-old with him," says Randy as she walks back in carrying two real glass bottles of Coca-Cola. She looks adorably comfy in faded jeans and fuzzy black sweater.

She hands me a Coke and pulls a joint out from behind her ear.

"Wanna smoke some pot to calm down?"

"Vomiting doesn't calm me down," I remark pleasantly. "Tried pot a few times and discovered it makes me violently ill. You go ahead if you want."

"Naw," she sits down on the couch, "it's against my religion to get stoned alone. I think of it as a social lubricant."

She says "lubricant" as if drenched in 30-weight oil. The prohibition on solitary stoning is apparently one of the more obscure secular doctrines.

I sit up, take a big drink of Coke, and it nearly fizzes all over my lap.

She laughs, I sigh and rest my head on her shoulder. I'm staring out the window thinking about canine killers, Richard Tibbit, Dickhead, Verna, and big Indians.

"You wanna go back," asks Randy, "and tell that homeless vet that there are no dogs in heaven?"

I chuckle but it's not funny.

"No. Let him have his Jesus waiting for him in the realms beyond."

A comfortable silence passes, and the only sound is the muffled commentary from the hyperbolic WCW announcer.

"Now, Mr. Mindboggle Private Eye Rabbi," she teases, "you said you wanted to know more about me – by traditional methods – so you sit right here and I'll show you my photo album. By the time we're done, you'll know the story of my life."

This is where men feign interest and women share. Of course, I'll listen to anything and she knows it.

Her big book of little memories is remarkably shy of any endearing childhood photos, nor are there any sisterly shots of Sarah. It's mostly cockeyed Instamatic photos taken from the front row of rock concerts – pop singers with absurd hair, and obvious erections straining against the too-tight fabric of their ridiculous stage pants. I don't ask how many of these guys she slept with, but

I figure that's why these icons of post-pubescent eroticism are immortalized in treasured K-Mart jumbo prints.

As the pages flip, the photo quality dramatically improves.

"I took a photography course," comments Randy, "I'm not bad at it, either."

Quite good, actually. Quite good indeed.

We've just admired several silly shots of some poodle band – – all coif and costume — and she cracks up looking at a shot of herself, obviously drunk, with three backstage groupie pals. Two of them are similarly attired clones, and the third looks older and more weary as if she not only took on the band, but every roadie who ever dragged an amp off a truck.

Randy taps her finger on the haggard one's face.

"I could tell you something about her, boy," she says with nasty intonation, "she can do some amazing tricks."

"Like stamp out her age with a hoof?"

"God, you're cruel."

"Ok, what – she spins plates?"

Randy looks at me with conspiratorial delight.

"She has the biggest, fattest…"

I finish the sentence for her.

"…longest tongue you've ever seen in your life."

Her jaw drops.

"You've been with her? You?"

"Her name is Riki, and I've never seen her before in my life."

She slugs me in the shoulder right where Sullivan's brace connected.

"You being a psychic-pudding again?"

"No," I tell the truth, "she has an aunt who lives in Walla Walla on one of the `uh' sounding streets – Valencia or Bonsella."

"You've met her?"

"No, Richard did about fifteen years ago. She saved him from getting the crap kicked out of him by some big Indians."

"Well, you know what Walt Disney said…."

""It's a small world after all?"

"Nope, `That's Goofy.' She beat up the Indians, did she? I guess she could have given them a tongue-lashing. I mean, that thing is *huge*."

"She didn't beat up anybody. She simply warned them that he used to be a wrestler."

"How'd she know that?"

I have to laugh.

"Listen, if this case becomes my next novel, I'll give you an autographed copy and you can read it from page one and get up to speed."

She sets aside the scrapbook, and feigns affront.

"Well then, Mr. Edgar Award winner, why don't you write the ending to the novel now, read it, and thereby solve the case? I have a pencil and some paper if you want to get to work right away."

Despite her intended absurdity, its makes perfect sense.

"Ok, then. You wanna be the sidekick, we have to get busy. You have 3X5 cards or a large dry-erase board?"

"Cards I got — Uno, Skipbo, pinnacle – maybe some three by fives... "

"Get 'em."

She's up, off, and rummaging.

"What's the deal on the dry-erase board?" she's hollering from inside a closet somewhere. "If you're planning an AMWAY presentation, I'm outta here."

"How tragic," I call out while moving over to her old oak dining room table, "I thought you wanted to replicate my success by being `the detective's downline.'"

"Well, I do wanna go down on the detective, does that count?"

I don't comment, but save the information in my mental ego-boost file. While she rummages, I stare at the TV. If brains had gears, mine are spinning, meshing, and whirring like crazy.

Returning, Randy notices my blank look of distracted consciousness.

"Watcha thinkin' 'bout, Mr. Private Eye?"

"Wrestlers."

"Oh, that's romantic. You ever notice that wrestlers shave their armpits?"

True. Most people never notice that.

"Yeah, I noticed. Not sure the reason. Must be aesthetics."

"You an aesthetic supporter?" She says it like she's positive it's incredibly clever.

"Yep. Big supporter. I've spent more money on records, tapes, and CDs..."

"Oh!' Randy interrupts, "My new old Moody Blues album. I forgot all about it. Where 'd I put it?"

She could be the polyphasic poster child. First she was rummaging for cards, now she races in search of the lost chord. I swivel my gaze to the tube. Some fat guy in a tuxedo is interviewing Nature Boy Ric Flair. Fans never wear tuxedos to the matches, and neither do the wrestlers. Why in hell would they stuff the stupid announcer into one?

Randy dances back into the room holding the Moodies aloft in one hand, the cards in another.

"Tah-dah! I found it right where I left it. I hope it's not warped," she's joyously prattling on as if she didn't just watch a dog get its brains blown out, "I hate when that happens. It skips all around and you miss stuff. Makes you crazy."

Maybe crazy enough to tear your clothes and sleep in a graveyard.

My brain synapses are firing in random patterns.

I ask a peculiar question.

"When did you first notice that wrestlers shave their armpits?"

She looks endearingly chagrined.

"I had a teenage crush on a TV wrestler. I memorized every available inch of his incredible, muscular bod."

Cute.

"Which one?"

She smiles wickedly.

"Which inch?"

"Which *wrestler*."

"*The Total Package.* I had good taste."

She slides the record on her Gerrard turntable's silver spindle.

"He was also called `the Narcolepse' or something for a while…"

She means "the Narcissist." He did the self-worship act on WWF. He's the Total Package, all right. Blond, handsome, and wears stars and stripes on his minuscule trunks.

"That's him on the TV right now," she says, glancing at the choreographed grappling, " I used to think he was the hottest thing in the world. Then I found out he was married and had a dozen kids… well, three or four."

We both look at the screen, and say his name at the same time.

"Lex Luger."

"I used to sit in front of the set and chant his name," she admits, "Luger! Luger! Luger!"

HEADLOCK

Wham! Lightning!

I'm off the couch, on my feet, and coming towards her.

"Say that again."

Her eyes blaze with excitement, misreading my enthusiasm for passion. She jumps into my arms.

"Luger! Luger! Luger!" She raves, hooking a leg around my thigh and pressing herself hard against me. "If I knew that's what it took to get you hot, I would have yelled it first thing this morning."

I kiss her quickly on the lips and pull back, her tongue is chasing after me.

"Easy, easy, slow down honey," I insist, "I don't want to lose my train of thought."

She gives me a good hug and a lovely grind, but my mind is two hundred sixty two miles and years ago in Walla Walla's Rooks Park.

On TV, Lugar wins by disqualification. The fatboy used an illegal object.

"An illegal object..."

"I know, I can feel it..."

The expression on her face is spectacular. She's becoming unleashed. My lower nature is becoming ascendant, but I maintain my eroding standards. I hold her at arm's length. She's lovely; I'm smiling.

"What's it about me yelling Luger that's got you goin'?"

"A confluence of coincidence — the combination of your little comment about the warped record, me thinking about Richard Tibbit, and the electronic arrival of Lex Luger."

"So?"

"Richard skips. Richard's warped like an abused classic rock album. All the notes are there, it's just that I'm not getting them all at once. There're gaps. Some stuff just goes by because he's so damn content heavy when he's spewing it out. Anyway, what you said..."

I decide against giving her the gory details.

"...helped me see things more clearly."

"Well, that's why I'm such a good psychotic sidekick."

The poor kid in the park *was* there to kill Richard, and I know who the gun belonged to, where it came from, and how the kid wound up with it. When she chanted "Luger," I could feel the fire, smell the cordite and see the body fall. One bullet to the head. His brains exploded. As for the second shot, I have a theory. And there was another image – half obscured behind the trees – it looked like the logo of a power company or an electrical firm.

She pulls me close again and poses a question.

"How does your gift work, when you use it, I mean, like when you knew who I was"

"It's not a gift, and it works like this: I clear my mind and ask questions. Anyone can do it, the trick is `say it, don't weight it.' People get intuitive guidance all the time, but more often than not, they block it."

"Do you hear voices?"

"I'm not a schizophrenic, thank you. No, I see pictures mostly. Sometimes they're perfectly clear, other times the scenes look like an out take from a Fellini movie."

"What's a Fellini movie?"

"Weird images that I have to figure out."

"Do you figure 'em out."

Not always.

I don't answer.

"Can you tell something about me, something I haven't told you?"

We move back to the couch, and I slide my hand up under the fuzzy sweater and rest it on her soft belly.

I'll do it, just a little.

My eyes close, and I ask.

I open them again, and kiss her cheek.

"Well?"

"This morning, when you thought we'd had sex and you didn't remember it…"

"Yeah?"

"You said `a girl could get pregnant….'"

She turns her face away.

"You're not that girl."

She sighs.

"Nope. Not since I was sixteen. Thanks to an abortion gone bad, I'll never be anyone's mother. Strange, of all things, that you would pick up on that."

Maybe it was because my hand was on her belly. Maybe. Or it was the one thing she most wanted concealed at this stage of our relationship.

"If you really want kids," I offer helpfully, "there are thousands waiting to be adopted."

"I'm not ready for Mommyhood," she says crisply, quickly shifting subjects. "You ready to play with the cards?"

"In a minute," I flip out my cellular and dial Richard. He's home. That's the one nice thing about knowing a recluse – you seldom get their answering machine.

"The Luger, Richard, the Luger..."

"What about it?"

"Your Dad's, right?"

"What'd I tell ya?"

"You didn't tell me."

"Well, not in so many words, but it was obvious. Dad brought it back from the war – a 9mm untraceable memento - kept it in a box up in the cabin. I told ya about the cabin, right?"

He never mentioned a cabin.

"No, you skipped that."

"Well, I told ya I wasn't gonna tell you everything at once. I mean, I know I'm a pain in the ass."

I realize what I'm dealing with. His head's full information, suppositions, suspicions, unwarranted inferences, and it's been fermenting for years. I bet he doesn't know what he's told me and what he hasn't.

"I'm gonna ask you one very specific question, Richard, and I want a very specific answer."

"Yeah, well, I'll do my best."

He sounds mildly irritated.

"Can you think of any reason why you haven't been bumped off, any reason at all. I mean, if they really wanted to kill you, you'd be dead."

He thinks it over.

"Well, maybe the letters. I wrote three letters, ya understand. I laid it all out, right? In case something happened to me, okay?"

"When was this?"

"Hell, it musta been when I got fed up. Years ago. I mean, I've kept my mouth shut, okay? I know how to keep my mouth shut. 'till now, right? They know I've kept my mouth shut. I mean, ya don't want things happening to your wife or kids, ya understand."

I understand.

"Where did the letters go?"

"One went to an ex FBI agent, another went to a lawyer, and

the third one went to another buddy of mine. I told them all that if I should die all of a sudden, open the letter."

Randy is sitting on the couch giving herself a pedicure. She smiles and winks. I think I'm infatuated.

"The only way those letters would keep you alive would be if the `bad guys' knew about them."

"Well, I made sure they did. You see, they would send snitches up to my house – different shady characters I knew from around town."

Snitches

."…They'd drop by with all manner of excuses of things to talk about. I didn't trust anyone after things started to go down. So, I made sure one of them at least knew about the letters. I didn't let him read 'em, but I made sure he knew about 'em. I'm not stupid and I'm not crazy."

No, he's not stupid and he certainly is not crazy.

"There's only problem with those letters, Richard. They don't protect *me*."

He hacks out a rueful laugh.

"Yeah, well I told you to be careful. Study all that stuff I gave you. It'll all come in handy, you being a private eye. You may have some travel expenses, legwork, whatever, and that's why I gave you so much money, you know, just in case. Listen, the wife and I are going up to the pen to visit our kid. Come by for coffee when you get back."

"Cut down on the coffee, Richard, trust me."

"Coffee doesn't bother me. Besides, that was a test."

Another perfect Jack Nicholson.

"Test?"

"Yeah. You're supposed to be psychic, so I sent you the mental image of a big cup of coffee."

Swell – a broadcaster. That's what we call them. They know how to send. Some are also receivers. If he's really a sender, he's had practice and plenty of it. Otherwise, he wouldn't know what he was doing. If he's an amateur, he can moderately mess with me by simple signal interference. Because of his unique mix of insights and suspicions, I wonder just how into this mental stuff he really is. It's slippery ground, rife with superstition and ego temptations. If you doubt it, just ask me.

"Oh, one more quick question, Richard – does the Power Company or an electrician have any part in this?"

Silence.

"Power company?"

'Yeah, or electrician."

"Nope. But hell, ya never know. I mean, I hired you to find out who all was in on it, right? "

"'And if it's over.' I remember. I can tell you that one right now: had you not contacted me, the answer might have been, 'yes, it's over.'

"Well, I can understand that. Listen, one more thing, no matter what people say I'm not some sort of goddam gangster. The only shit I ever pulled was when I was a teenager."

"What about the bank robbery?"

He bangs his Zippo on the table loud enough that I can hear it over the phone.

"I never robbed a damn bank in my life! I told you I can explain that, and I will, but we're on our way out the door."

"Have a nice day."

An acknowledging grunt, a quick click, and he's gone.

"I bet you have one hell of a cellular phone bill," comments Randy, "you could have used my Princess rotary with the light-up dial."

The Moodies album, despite the repetitive scratches that validate its authenticity, doesn't miss a single groove.

She joins me at the table, a pack of three by five lined index cards in her hand. We each have a pen.

"What're we doin'?" she asks.

"Pretending we're novelists," I explain helpfully, "this is what some writers do when they construct a novel, and it's the same thing detectives do when cracking a complex case." I deal out the index cards.

"Do you use this technique when you crack complex cases?"

I've never cracked a case more complex that a twelve-pack of Pepsi. Remember that business about the drug cop Verna mentioned? Even on that case, which was a big deal, I didn't have to crack much – mostly verification of unsettling details. You know, like that blond detective guy on Perry Mason who would walk in the door and tell Perry what he'd found out. You never had to watch him actually find it out, you just heard about it when Perry did. Well, what we all found out didn't make much of a bang. In fact, I doubt it made the front page of Walla Walla's prestigious daily. It is, however, making one hell of a dent in the City's insurance budget.

Here, in a nutshell, is what happened.

Mrs. Robert Escarrega, originally from Tacoma, Washington, found herself in Walla Walla while her hubby was completing a tour of duty in our armed forces. The little woman, whose first name is Lilith, also found herself developing a few bad habits – alcohol and drugs. Realizing she was getting out of control, and not wanting her beloved to come home to a wife in active addiction, she turned to the local 12-Step meetings of AA and NA – Alcoholics Anonymous and Narcotics Anonymous. Same sort of programs; same style Big Books. Plenty of meetings, fellowship, and other addicts and alcoholics helping her stay clean and sober one day at a time.

Happy story, right? Not so fast.

Also attending these meetings was Arvid "AA" Armstad. This young man was so white, he was almost albino – that's why his pals called him "AA." Arvid was – no kidding — nearly translucent.

Attending the 12-Step meetings, he shared his experience, strength and hope with the fragile Mrs. Escarrega. He also gave her free room and board, use of a car, and set out systematically to destroy her life. He was an undercover police informant attending 12-Step meetings to get leads on people to arrest for drugs. The only easier way to find drug users would be to take down the license plate numbers of folks checking themselves into rehab clinics and then wait for a relapse.

He didn't wait that long, not Arvid.

Her confidence gained, he told her about a dear friend who really needed to get clean, come to meetings, the whole nine yards. One problem: the good buddy lacked the confidence to walk into that church basement and hear the message that he too could live a life drug-free. The solution: give him twenty dollars worth of cocaine to snort ten minutes before someone reads, "Why we are here" and he'll come for sure.

She says that's the most stupid thing she has ever heard.

He insists she score the dope for this humanitarian effort.

She refuses. He nags

More refusals; more nagging.

At length, she agrees to get the twenty.

When they deliver it to the good buddy, surprise!

He's Thomas H. Carter, aka THC. The drug cop.

HEADLOCK

She's busted, but not hauled downtown for booking. Oh, no. Instead, she's told that now she must work off her legal obligation by luring others who attend 12-Step programs to relapse so they can be arrested too. An easy harvest.

Now, Mrs. Escarrega really gets mad.

She tells THC he can go to hell and take his lying see-through buddy with him, so they jail her, and she's prosecuted for delivery of cocaine. The judge, amazingly enough, finds her guilty and sentences her to thirteen months in prison. Wonderful.

At sentencing, however, the judge comments for the record that "Mrs. Escarrega was not predisposed to commit this crime, but only did so at the insistence and urging of Mr. Arvid Armstad."

Bingo. Classic entrapment.

Well, Mr. Escarrega gets out the service just in time. He hires a real lawyer instead of trusting her fate any further to a rubber-stamping public defender. Proving there is justice, she wins her appeal and files a multi-million dollar law suit against the city for civil rights violations. Of course, this took a few years to play out, but when all was said and done it was a slam-dunk. She can take that to the bank, and I believe her and hubby will soon be vacationing in Cancun.

What did they do to Arvid and THC?

Duh.

Nothing.

Not a damn thing. Once it was in the lawyer's hands, Carter was out of the loop. Unless he made a point of following the case, he might not even know the outcome. After all, the loot isn't coming out of his paycheck. This isn't unusual. Cops and cities get sued all the time. This is why God invented liability insurance.

My part in that little soap opera was simple legwork and interviewing on behalf of Mrs. Escarrega's attorney, hence I know more than ever appeared in the paper. Once the word was out on little Arvid, he was conveniently "relocated" in our valiant so-called War on Drugs.

Keep this story in mind if you ever attend an AA or NA meeting and feel an urge to share. When you hear them say, "We are never under police surveillance at any time," remember it may be wishful thinking.

Someday, when I'm long-gone from the little town with the funny name, I'll make a three by five card for Arvid Armstad, and another for THC.

"What's the deal on these cards, smarty-pants?" asks Randy.

"Each character in the story, or the case, gets one," I explain while writing names across the top of the cards, "one for Richard, one for Dickhead, another for the dad, the step-mom…."

Each card crammed with available data, I shuffle and deal.

"What's this called?"

"Playing mix 'n' match."

"Does this help."

"Maybe."

I study my hand, moving names and details into diverse relationships.

Randy eyes me intently.

"Well?"

I rotate my shoulders, crack my back, and lay my cards on the table.

"Leviticus 19:14"

"Was that World War I?"

Sweet.

"Bible quote, Randy. `Thou shalt not put a stumbling block before a blind person'."

Her eyes do that funny squint thing.

"The first commandment in that same verse says `You shall not curse a deaf person'."

She pokes at the cards.

"I don't get it. If you curse a deaf person, they're not gonna hear you anyway."

"Exactly. That's the point. The *Midrash* says that each time you embarrass another person you also diminish God Himself."

"God shrinks?"

"Let's not get literal. Anyway, even though the deaf can't hear the curse, God's image is diminished, for we are created in the image of God."

She rests her chin in the palms of her hands, elbows on the table.

"What does that have to do with all this?" Her eyes indicate the content heavy three-by-fives.

"Well, by the same reasoning, a person may not curse himself. To curse oneself is to curse the image of God."

"Who's cursing?"

"I am."

She looks sad.

"Because of me? Because I sort of tempt you?

"No, not because of you, for heaven's sake," I take her hands in mine, "because of the way I'm approaching this case. You see, this is a weekend and I didn't plan to do anything except have fun and then start in on this business when I got back. Plus, I figured I could sort of suspend time…"

Her head tilts sideways as if she's auditioning for *Lassie Come Home*.

"What I mean is, I got Dickhead on hold – I hope – and I can't do too much investigating into Violet Langness until Monday when I can get on the Internet. I'd just relax and have fun except an old fart Nazi tried to beat the shit out of me and on top of that, Jesus the Wonderdog got his brains blown out in front of my favorite Chinese restaurant…."

"Yeah, gross. And?"

Luger.

"My mind keeps wanting to go where I don't want it to."

Her eyes brighten, and she pulls my hand to her lips.

"Like my bedroom?"

She never gives up. Tenacity is an admirable quality. So is commitment, and that's what this case takes. That, and no fear. Fear is only useful when you're being attacked by wolverines.

Here's the deal: it's one thing to play private eye for plots, it's another to play it for real. I know the difference. If I have to leap into the fray with an automatic stuffed into a shoulder holster and a snub nose .38 strapped to my ankle, so be it. Jeff Reynolds PI can bust a nose bone with the hardboiled best of them. Just ask Dickhead about the lump on his noggin. No, I can play it rough, I can crack the case, I can do all that.

And more.

If I follow the pull, going all the way in requires both remarkable detachment and emotional vulnerability. Anyone mastering that balancing act belongs on Ed Sullivan – the show, not the journalist. Hurkos could do it. Paramedics, ambulance drivers, ER nurses, and trauma unit specialists do it as well. They put their heart and soul into the experience and sleep at night knowing they did their best even if a child dies in their arms.

Randy pokes the end of my nose with her finger.

"Having visions, little boy?"

Ooops. I was staring into space, looking through her as if she were translucent vapor.

She gives my hand an affectionate squeeze.

"If you were a surfer, Jeff, I'd wax your woody," she intones playfully, "In fact, I've got a surfboard in my bedroom I'd love to show you."

What the hell is she talking about?

"C'mon…" she tugs insistently, "you can hang ten."

"I don't hang that far. You'll be disappointed and reject me."

Laughing, but not dissuaded, she leads me down the hallway as if we're on a magnificent adventure. The bedroom door swings wide and, were I more emotional, the sight would take my breath away. Give you a hint. It's not her baseball cap collection. It's also not the heart-shaped bed, nor the mirror above it.

"Is that swoopy or what," asks Randy happily, "it does everything but brush your teeth."

Swoopy indeed. Situated in an ergonomically designed workstation is a multi-media PC with all the bells and whistles, including a DSL connection to the World Wide Web.

"I'm a real surf bunny," she announces proudly, "and I'll tell ya, those sex chat rooms on AOL are incredible."

I'll take her word for it.

"Nice baseball cap collection." I say, glancing back at the far wall.

"Hey, I'm one hell of a pitcher," she says proudly, "both underhand and overhand. Now, Mr. Morose God-Shrinking Detective, you have the three by five cards *and* your Internet connection. Happy?"

God bless Randy Nussbaum. I get my bag and dig out Richard's care package of Xerox copies, my hand-held recorder, and the tape of our phone conversation. Randy and I pull up two chairs in front of her 17" monitor and log onto the Internet.

I'm rapidly keyboarding and mouse-clicking. God bless Richard Tibbit. His carefully folded copies contain the all-important primary identifiers: social security numbers, birth dates, the works. I doubt Richard envisioned me doing my PI work on the Internet – he's not exactly Mr. High Tech – but modern times call for modern methods.

My face is almost pressed against the Verbatim anti-glare screen; Randy's hand strokes my thigh.

"This is exciting," she says, "Is this how real private eyes do it?"

Real private eyes, mind you. Real ones. What am I? Chopped

liver?

"Yes, my dear, this is how the real ones do it. They sit and stare at computer screens until they go blind."

"I thought guys went blind from…well, you know. I figure every time I make love to a man, I'm improving his eyesight."

"You've never looked better, trust me. Now, this is gritty realism, Randy, the kind that we leave out of our pulse-pounding blood and thunder adventures once they make the transition from mean streets to quiet bookstalls."

"Is this going to come out in paperback? I like those because they're cheap and you can bend them all up without feeling guilty."

"I'd prefer hardback first, if you don't mind, but a trade paper edition from a reputable niche publisher such as Deadly Alibi Press is perfectly acceptable. Knowing you, you'll borrow it from the library and return it on time to avoid a fine. Besides, this is the best plot I've stumbled on in six months, Richard's counting on it, my cats need Friskies, and my agent's been after me to start a new one. I'll heavily fictionalize it, of course. Instead of surfing the net, we'll be dodging bullets and dangling from balustrades."

"I'm in it, right? The drop dead gorgeous sex pot psychotic sidekick?"

"'natch, and in the book we have sex about a hundred times – and that's before we even meet."

"For real?'

"Yeah, we practice a lot when we're alone."

I'm now accessing a custom database that will tell me virtually anything and everything about someone based purely on his or her social security number. Face it, you have no secrets. With just your name and address, I can find out what you do for living, name and age of your spouse and children, the make and color of your car, the value of your home, credit information, your employment records, family tree, military records, which web sites you visit, I can even find that long forgotten drug bust you had in college.

Your private life is public domain.

"Numbers 24:5."

"Chicago, *25 or 6 to 4*," Randy counters with an oblique musical reference

"How good is the tent of Jacob."

"I give. How good is it?" she responds eagerly.

"The question isn't *how*, but *why*. The important thing is why it was good. The tents of Jacob's people were always set up so the doors didn't face each other. By intentionally doing that, they demonstrated their sensitivity to privacy, as they could not and did not want to see what was happening in their neighbor's tent."

"Cool. So what things were going on in the tents anyway?"

Say goodnight, Gracie.

Actually, according to the Talmud, you're not even supposed to enter your own house without knocking first, lest you discover something private that your spouse wouldn't want you to know about.

As we say in the trade, "them days is over."

It was much easier to be a criminal in the old days, so much seedier to be a private eye. As for fiction's gritty realism, here's the quick translation: sex, violence, negativity, and foul language. In the true crime genre, include graphic photos of blood soaked bodies. A major publishing house rejected *Finding Sarah* on the grounds that the author needed more sex. I'm sure they meant the story, but I took the issue under advisement and showed the rejection to my wife. She responded with one of her own.

Today, the realism of America's mean streets is found in drain grates on the information super-highway. I cruise with all the ease of Martin Milner on *Route 66*.

Let's get the goods on Violet Langness Tibbit.

I key in her social security number, and the screen fills with detailed information of every job under every name she's had.

"Here we go, Randy, the facts are flowing."

Hot damn.

Violet Tibbit was indeed formerly Violent Langness. She had also been Violet Hodgins, Violet Hoffman, Violet Schmidt, and, for less than six months, Violet Sullivan.

"Did I ever tell you I had five wives?"

Born Violet Faron in Portland, Oregon, her employment history reveals career paths as diverse as her monikers: nurse, cook, psychiatric receptionist, insurance agent, hostess, dancer, and home caregiver. Her gig on the tugboat when she snagged Richard's dad was her second tour of duty – she'd worked for them before. Maybe she quit 'cause she couldn't find a qualified victim.

"Wow," Randy exclaims, "what a piece of work. She's giving Liz Taylor a run for the money in the husband department. Why would she marry an alcoholic geezer like Richard's dad?"

"He wasn't a geezer in those days, and about half a million

dollars in death benefits, according to Richard, is good reason enough for the likes of her. But I want to know about these previous husbands."

"Hey, in the mood for some popcorn?"

"Sure, plenty of butter…wait, I'll get your keyboard greasy…"

"I know how to take care of that," she says, and blushes.

While I meditate on the blush, she scurries off to the kitchen, returns with Saran Wrap, tears off a filmy sheet and stretches it over the keyboard.

"There ya go. You can still type, but the keys stay clean just like at McDonalds."

Because of the blush, I suspect her affinity for computer sex-chat rooms is inexorably linked with Saran Wrap, but discretion and propriety preclude questioning.

Randy gets to work on the popcorn: I multi-task into the death benefits data base, the master death index, and use a purloined authorization code – a trick of the trade -- to sneak into a comprehensive arrest and criminal charges data base.

Bingo. Some fancy cross-referencing reveals that dear old Violet was the heartbroken recipient of death benefits from not only Tibbit, but Langness and Hodgins as well. Schmidt and Sullivan miraculously survived matrimony, but I'm willing to wager their bank accounts didn't.

Her arrest record dates back decades – two arrests for prostitution in Portland when she was twenty, one charge of insurance fraud, and here's the best one: charged with murder in the death of her husband, Thomas D. Hodgins.

This is fun.

Now we check the Nexis news feature file for the Portland Oregonian at the time of the trial.

My, my, my. Accused of bumping off Thomas Hodgins by poisoning his nightly ration of Tapioca pudding. She was acquitted thanks to the brilliant defense tactics of Leonard Goldstien. She also married again less than two years later.

So far Richard is on target about dear old step-mom, but it gets better – or worse.

The corn is popping, and I can hear Randy banging cupboards.

In a separate window, I run quick check on Randy Nussbaum. One arrest for possession of pot five years ago, and a small bust for being an independent "escort."

Oh boy. I won't have to fictionalize this one bit.

The popcorn is perfectly buttered, salted, and served with flair by the effervescent Ms Nussbaum who shoves handfuls into her kisser with all the enthusiasm of a ten-year-old at a slumber party.

"Learning a lot?" she asks, undeniably attractive with her mouth stuffed, "here, it's really, really good."

I lean back, stretch, and scoop a handful from the Tupperware bowl. I poke at the senior Tibbit's death certificate.

"It doesn't say his brains exploded, but it does say he died of complications from diabetes. So, if Richard is right, ex-nurse step mom probably spiked ol' dad's vein with an insulin overdose for convenient brain death. Not the first hubby to die on her, so to speak. More of them are dead than alive, and she was actually indicted in the death of. Hodgins, an accomplished if eccentric broadcasting entrepreneur. Acquitted by a well-hung jury..." Randy brightens at the expression, " she immediately disposed of his country-western radio empire."

"I'd dispose of anything country-western, dead or not," offers Randy.

"He also held controlling interest in several hit-music stations, and she liquidated those assets faster than she liquidated Hodgins. Each deceased hubby left her significant loot, and each living one was probably looted before discarded. "

"Wha' di' sh' do wi' ta..."

Huh?

Randy swallows.

"What did she do with the money?"

"God only knows. Maybe it went into her arm, up her nose, into a slot machine in Nevada, or on the ponies. Got a blank disc? I want to save this."

"Sure. You done already?"

"The wrong thing to ask a man in your bedroom," I quip, "and no, I'm not done. We're going to have ourselves a little on-line infoparty."

"What fun!"

She's easily amused, a sign of affable flexibility or her thought processes are in the "no diving" end of the pool. My intuition tells me it's the former. Randy is no dumb bunny. She's more than good looking, she's a comfortable companion. This amazes me, and it didn't dawn on me until now. I've been accustomed to feeling self-conscious and defensive around women for so long, I forgot what it was like to feel at ease with one. I savor the moment of simple, unaffected interpersonal comfort, the resultant smile is imp-ishly contagious and Randy is soon smiling as well.

"Whatcha grinnin' about," she asks, matching my joyful expression with her own.

"I like you. I like you a lot."

Her cheeks get pink and she actually says "Thank you!"

Back to work. I save my searches on floppy as I go. It takes some fancy finger work and adroit manipulation, but eventually I'll know more than I care to about the evil step-mom. I begin working my way from beginning to ignominious end.

"With all those hubby's, did she attain mommy hood?"

Good question. More searching and cross-referencing.

"Seems she had a daughter, Blanche, who died very young...and...let me double check something here..."

Oh, Jesus. I don't like what I'm thinking.

"You thinking what I'm thinking?" Randy's voice is hushed.

"Yeah. Can't help but think it – murdered her own child for the insurance and the death benefits."

Except for the clicking of keys and the whir of the hard drive, everything is supposition and silence.

"There was also a son with her maiden name. Maybe the father is unknown. He'd be about the same age as Richard, actually older, Derek Bane Faron."

"Is he alive?"

I close my eyes, open them, look up and blink rapidly. Smart private eyes avoid private eyestrain. More searching and cross-window examination.

"Yep. Let's see if we can find him."

Were scooping butter-soaked kernels from the bottom of the Tupperware bowl. She calls them "old maids."

Interesting. He's alive, all right, and has an address in Weston, Oregon. Get out your map. Weston is the mailing code for an entire area that includes Tollgate, a rustic ski area. Folks have cabins there. It's also less than a two-hour drive from Walla Walla.

"I told you about the cabin, right?"

I have an idea, and access the "ultra" phone directory – even the unlisted numbers are here – and check for Faron in Weston, Oregon, and Walla Walla, Washington.

Bingo. Nothing in Weston, but a Luther Faron in Walla Walla. It's not a Derek or a DM, but one Faron is better than none.

"You gonna call him?"

"No, Randy my dear, you are."

I give her the number.

"Put on your front office voice, say your calling from Social Security. Simply ask for Derek Faron."

"What if I get him on the phone."

"Tell him you're trying to verify the benefit mailing address for his mother."

Randy picks up the phone and starts to dial.

"Wait a sec'. Isn't she buried in Nevada?"

"The odds are better in New Jersey."

She completes the dialing procedure, clears her throat, and plays the part perfectly.

My ear pressed against the receiver, I follow the conversation with intense interest.

"No, Derek Faron doesn't live here, thank God," mumbles the aggravated respondent. "I ought to change my name. We're not even related. If I had a dime for every person who called here looking for that flake, I'd be rich."

"Well, do you know where we can contact him?"

I'm expecting a vague, negative response. We get more than I could have hoped.

"Try McFeely's."

The conversation abruptly concluded, Randy and I gaze at each other with mutual bemusement.

I move from the chair and stretch out on her heart shaped bed. She brings over the three by five cards, stands next to me, and fans them in front of my face. Images flow over me like a cartoon waterfall.

"What did you mean `the odds are better in New Jersey?'"

"She isn't dead."

Her jaw drops, and an adorable jaw it is.

"And," I continue, "as Mark Twain wrote…."

"*Reports of my death have been greatly exaggerated*?"

"No," I slap the mattress, "*Jump on the raft, Jim.*"

She backs up away from the bed, almost to the door, and rubs the palms of her hands together with mock glee. Scraping her foot on the floor like a bull, she makes an elaborate show of her intentions. She takes an exuberant run at the bed, launches herself into the air, and descends towards me like a flyboy ready for the pin.

I've got to trust her.

She land on me perfectly, her body giving the bulk of her

lightweight impact to the mattress, her lips finding mine with adroit and flawless dexterity. She kisses me and it's every bit as engulfing and passionate as that first one in the elevator, except it has an added dimension I can only describe as "personal" – she's not just kissing, she's kissing *me* and we both know the difference

Delicious.

"What now, Mr. Handsome Kissable Detective?"

"We relax freely."

"You mean we're done with our infoparty, you've learned everything you need to know, and you've solved the case?"

"Quite possibly I have."

"Based on what you learned on the Internet, from the clues, the cards, the phone call, and your amazing psychic powers?"

I tousle her hair.

"Nope. Actually, as with most mysteries, the answers were right in front of the detective the entire time, or obvious by omission."

She puts her nose against mine.

"I'm right in front of the detective, and I think I need to be more fully explored. I'm not asking you to violate your morality code, whatever the hell that is, but I want you to kiss me, and kiss me, and kiss me some more, and hold me and hug me and squeeze me more than you have already, and if you don't, I'm gonna make a Federal case out of it."

Never argue with a woman threatening indictment.

"Thank you, Ms Psychotic Sidekick, you just identified the major plot point. Except for obligatory action, exposition, and dénouement, I've got this one solved. Now the only trick will be keeping the hero and his client alive."

"Are you toying with me?"

"My pleasure."

Perhaps this is easy familiarity; perhaps it's erotic brinkmanship. Either way, it's fun. Her moves are spontaneous, fluid, and honed to perfection by years of practice. I keep up my end of the bargain, occasionally watching the action reflected above me with spectator sport detachment. No, we don't go "all the way," at least not inserting tab A into slot B, but suffice it to say we have no anatomical secrets anymore and neither was denied release from palpable sexual tension.

In snuggle mode, I glance over at her bright computer screen. My data downloaded long ago.

"I wouldn't be good at it, but I could give it a try," I whisper thoughtfully.

"You're great at what you've done so far," purrs Randy, "you referring to making love? Can you go at it...so soon?" She sounds more curious than hopeful.

She called it making love, not having sex – a noteworthy distinction.

"No, I mean playing the punchboards at McFeely's."

"Oh."

Mild dissapointment.

"Randy?"

"Yeah?"

"Would you consider accompanying me to Palm Springs for a weekend?"

She sits bolt upright, eyes wide, and a big grin on her adorable visage.

"Does that mean yes?"

She swoops down and kisses me with unabashed enthusiasm.

V

"You stink."

She says it loudly, emphatically, and he better not argue.

"Do not!"

He's arguing, the idiot. He's twice her size, but she's the bartender, this is McFeely's and, by God, the guy does stink.

"Listen, you stink and the customers are complaining. They can smell you and they don't like it."

He raises his arms in protest. Wrong move. We all wince.

"I just took a shower this morning at her house," he bleats plaintively, pointing towards a bleary-eyed woman with hair the color of shoeshine polish. Hell, it might be shoeshine polish. She grins stupidly as if taking a shower at her house is second only to tractor pulls in entertainment value.

"But did you change your clothes?"

"Well, I took a shower..."

"Next time change your clothes," she is firm, but polite: staunch and unyielding. "You stink and you have to leave."

"Can I have a beer first?"

"I'm cutting you off."

"I'm not drunk yet!"

"But you stink. Get out."

He walks, stops half-way to the door, turns around and gives her the finger.

"See if I ever come back into this fuckin' place again."

She shrugs, half the customers laugh, the rest are too absorbed in their ninety-nine cent Heidelberg's and inconsequential conversation to even notice.

To the left of me is a tall redhead who, at one time, must have had all the boys agog. Buxom, slender, with legs all the way from here to there, she's clean, freshly made-up, and you could play connect the dots with the needle marks on her arms and hands. A statuesque bit of babbling local color, her name is Loni and she graduated from Walla Walla High School short of twenty years ago. The mother of two children by different fathers, her list of former husbands includes the deceased, the diseased, and the currently incarcerated.

Her life isn't easy; her pain is obvious. No matter how many times we've bumped into each other it's as if we've never seen each other before. Perhaps it's a side effect of her self-medication, a biochemical condition, or a social affectation. If you have no interpersonal history, you always start fresh.

Honestly, in a town this size, you can bump into everyone, including shut-ins.

"How ya doin'?" That's me asking.

"Okey-dokey," her voice is megaphone loud, her smile is broad, and half her teeth are elsewhere, "I'll have some heroin at five o'clock, then I'll be even better. I was just calling about getting some pot. If you give me a ride, I'll give you a bud."

I can't believe she's bellowing about illegal drugs in public. The public pays no mind.

"Uh, no, actually, I don't smoke that. Makes me puke."

"Yeah, well, I'm gonna have another wine cooler then go get the pot. Maybe I'll just walk over, it's not far. I got time to kill before my job."

"What job?"

She laughs.

"A head job."

No comment.

It's almost 11 am, and the place is well populated. Don't get me wrong – not everyone at McFeely's is a wet head, hooker, or drug addict. The 24-hour phone number for Narcotics Anonymous is posted by the front entrance should anyone have the need, desire, or inclination to get clean and sober. Perhaps they know their odds of getting busted increase if they try to get clean, so they play it safe by slow death. Mostly it's lower income regulars killing time with convivial conversation, low-key card games, neighborhood camaraderie, and the ever-popular punchboards. Many of the peculiar characters crammed into the miniscule booths are harmless souls recently re-located to the neighboring McFeely Hotel from various institutions.

"We don't have many problems here," confirms the friendly bartender, "and I hated having to toss that guy out, but he really did smell bad. The regulars are well behaved. That's how come they're regulars, ya know, they get along."

She checks on an order of hard-boiled eggs. Not quite ready.

"We do get some people with mental problems from next door. It's sort of the first place they live on their own after leaving a halfway house. Sometimes we get a paranoid schizophrenic or two, but folks are fairly tolerant in here. People tend to be nice to each other."

I light up an Old Gold.

"You have a guy come in here called either Derek or Bane?"

I wait while she takes care of the egg order.

"What was that name again?"

"Derek or Bane. Maybe goes by both. Maybe in his late fifties, thin..."

She shakes her head.

"Could be, I've only been working here for a couple years."

When a place has a fifty-year history, two years is a clocktick.

I check my watch, look at the door, and get a slight adrenaline rush when the phone rings.

"Is there a Jeff Reynolds here?"

"That's me."

I move down to the small green phone at the front of the bar. There is a tin can next to it with a small sign requesting twenty-five cents per call. I've never seen anyone make a voluntary contribution.

"Yes, hello?"

"You out of your mind?"

It's Richard.

"Nope. Trust me. I was expecting you by now. C'mon."

"Man, I don't know. I haven't been in there for ages...I mean it's like ...I don't know..."

"Listen, Richard, we talked this out. All you have to do is show up, be civil, maybe even play the punchboards..."

"I'm not playing the damn punchboards."

"You said you'd be civil, Richard. You said you could do it."

"Yeah," he says with a sigh, "I can do it. You're sure you know what you're doing?"

"Positive."

The redhead is pouring a fresh wine cooler down her throat without so much as an obvious swallow.

"Well, alright then. I'll trust you. I'm on my way."

I check my watch again. Good thing everything in Walla Walla is so close. I cooked up this little plan after returning on a mid-evening flight from Seattle preceded by innumerable good-bye kisses from Randy and a serious discussion about her coming with me to LCC in Palm Springs. I bet she looks incredible glistening with #2 SPF suntan oil.

Arriving at the Walla Walla airport, I left my Buick in the parking lot and cabbed it back to Snob Hill. As long as that lead sled sits in front of the airport door, I'm obviously out of town. I'm never, however, out of vehicles. Tucked away behind the garage was my seldom used but always reliable Volvo wagon – not the Volvo I want, the Volvo I need.

The cats, mad as hell at not being able to shed fur all over my furniture, ranted at me as I let myself in. I wasn't in a hurry about anything, not even phone messages or mail.

Take my advice — don't get sucked into an exaggerated sense of urgency. There are two kinds of problems in this world: those that solve themselves and those that will wait for you. In Walla Walla, problems have a tremendous half-life. The smaller the town, the slower the pace. In the hustle bustle beehive world of over-crowded impersonal urban areas, folks rush around in 911 mode twenty-four hours a day. Not here. Time and crime wait for you like Pumpkin Pie after Thanksgiving dinner. Unless you're actu-ally dodging bullets, there's seldom need to break a sweat.

Here's another insight for you: you can easily spot the whackos, the troubled, and the addicted because, for them, every-thing is always urgent; everything is a crisis. Humans who func-tion most efficiently retain the polished veneer of practiced tran-quility. It is my calm, reasoned opinion, and my current, unalter-able conviction, that I don't want to wind up dead before the final chapter, and I don't want Richard pumped full of lead either. But we need not be rushed.

As I told you before, meditating on spiritual matters is the contemporary crime-buster's secret weapon, and a relaxed approach nets the best results.

So, I put on Dylan's *Blood on the Tracks*. I sat in the living room's red art-deco chair, Pooter wheezing on my lap, and gave serious, thoughtful consideration to various concepts seemingly disconnected from this case's considerable number of conundrums. In reality, nothing is disconnected. Suffering and selfishness are universal.

Just as the earth attracts everything to the center of gravity, and every object thrown upward into space will come down, so also material ideas and worldly thought attract us to the center of self. Anger, passion, ignorance, prejudice, greed, envy, covetousness, jealousy and suspicion imprisoning us in the claws of self and the cage of egotism. When trying to escape from one of these invisible enemies, we will unconsciously fall into the hands of another. No sooner do we attempt to soar upward than the density of the love of self, like the power of gravity, draws us to the center of the earth.

That's not all bad news, especially for someone in my line of work. Once I discern someone's center of gravity, I know where he or she's going.

After a good mental workout and another play of *Tangled up in Blue,* I checked my phone messages. There are two, and both are fairly recent.

Well, well, well.

Verna.

"Uh...this is Verna...uh...I'm calling from McFeely's. I guess you're still out of town like you said...I need to talk to you...you can find me at McFeely's or the Pastime when you get back..if I'm not there, you can call me...I'm in the book."

In the book? Is she in the Yellow Pages under: **Hookers – Big Hair**? The next message was, I admit, a surprise.

"Hey. Uh. Listen. God on a skateboard, man, I owe you an apology. I was out of line. I mean, Reynolds isn't a Jew name anyway, right? Sorry I called you one. I just saw that pen and lost it. Christ in a headlock, pal, I mean that damn Dean owns that record store. I sued his ass, ya know. I saved the coaster, though. Anyway, I'm not so big that I can't apologize. I mean, we Kafabes gots to stick together. Besides you pack one hell of a punch, and I respect that. So, anyway, I figure what could have been a friendship got fucked up. Next time you're in town lets get together and have some drinks and let's just forget about our misunderstanding."

He didn't mention his name, but he didn't have to. Lighting Rod Sullivan. Amazing, but not as amazing as the readout on my caller ID.

It didn't say Sullivan. That isn't a surprise. Most wrestlers, like disc jockeys or your new favorite author, adopt fake names and use them socially as well as professionally. His real last name, or the name of the phone number's registered owner, showed up on caller ID along with his area eode 206 number.

Hodgins.

I'll accept most coincidences easily enough, but this one was a stretch, even for me. The world may be small, but not that small.

Let's call him.

"Hey, Lightning," I say as if he's my best pal in world, "this is Jeff, your sparing partner from the J&M and no hard feelings, man, none at all," I talk fast, then faster, avoiding the disaster of any misunderstanding – I figure I'll sell him a non-existent relationship immediately, "you pack one hell of a whollop, yourself. But it's cool. Friends right?

He burps, an indication of inebriation and an audio signal that he might, if possible, punch me right through the phone

"Hey, God in a boxcar, man. We gave the customers quite a floor show, didn't we?" He laughs and wheezes and coughs.

Thank God, and thank the boxcar He rode in on.

"Yeah, we sure did. Hey, man, well get together for a good time, I promise, and I'm buying."

He likes that. I can tell. He hacks out a joyous expectoration and spits.

"There's somethin' I gotta know, Lightning…"

"Yeah?"

"Were you related to, or have you ever heard of a guy named Tom Hodgins, a radio guy in Oregon?"

"Shit. Yeah. He was my uncle when I was a little kid. How did ya…oh, God in a neck brace! You got that caller ID, right? Well, hell. Yeah. I bet I know your next fuckin' question…"

I don't

"Was he murdered? Hell, yes. My folks talked about that 'till they day they died. That bitch poisoned him, and got away with it. Hell, my dad would have probably inherited those radio stations if Uncle Tom hadn't been married to that miserable cooze. God on steroids! She had a damn Jew-boy lawyer, too. Fuck her and her goddam Tapioca pudding and the mother-fucking Jew she hired. My family always hated Jews. Dean was a damn Jew too and he fucked me good. Big surprise, right?"

Yeah, right.

"Well, Rod, old pal, I got a piece of news for you…"

"I'm all ears and dick."

"After she killed your uncle, she married…"

"A guy named Sullivan, I know. That's just a coincidence. I just liked the name. You know, John L. Sullivan and all that."

"No, even more. She eventually married and murdered the father of Larry Large — you know, that asshole Richard Tibbit."

"What?"

He about drops his braces.

"No shit, Sullivan. You and Tibbit have more in common than a step-over toe-hold – you've both had family members murdered by the same bitch."

Another PI tip – mirror the language.

Sullivan, dumbfounded into silence, throws something against a wall. I hear the crash.

"God in a fuckin' coffin," he moans. "How the hell did that happen? When did she do that?"

"About fifteen years ago. Collected almost a half-million in death benefits. They were married longer than any of her other victims, which leads me to believe she tried to kill him a few times and failed, or she was waiting for the big payoff."

"She'd wait for the payoff, the miserable bitch. But how the hell did she get into his family, for Christ's sake?"

"She was cookin' on a tug…"

"Shit. A Merril/Stroum, right?"

"Yeah, so?"

"Well, that's who she was workin' for when she got hold of my uncle. Met at some party or somethin'. He was a party kind of guy, from what I hear, and she was a party girl. God in Hell! What about Tibbit?"

"The story I hear is that a local cop was in on it with her – and maybe the snitch you know from the pen"

"What? That's goofy."

"No, it's a small world after all, my friend, a small world after all."

"Bane, the iron-pumping wrestling mark?"

"The same."

"God in a trench coat! He's the guy that told me Tibbit robbed a fuckin' bank."

"And I bet that was about five years ago, right?"

"About, yeah."

I wrapped up our little confab with false promises of shared dissipated nights and re-confirmation of our mutual distaste for "them damn Jews." I hope he gets hit by lightning.

A quick phone call to McFeely's reveals that Verna has scooted over to the Pastime, leaving only moments ago.

The Pastime, owned by another brotherly branch from the same Fazarri family tree as McFeely's , is an affordable family restaurant on the West End of Main Street. Not fancy, but flavorful. You can get a big delicious breakfast, impressive lunch, or filling spaghetti dinner. The bar runs the entire length of the building, features wide, comfortable booths, and there's a self-contained card room for friendly games and relaxed conversation. Robert Fazarri and I share more than a nodding acquaintanceship, and we're both pals of Travis Webb. Once a notorious teenage computer hacker, the youthful Mr. Webb taught me almost everything I know about Internet back doors and other unshared surfing secrets.

The Pastime's most unique and wondrous aspect is the wall shrine to Marilyn Monroe. Everywhere you look, Marilyn looks back. Classic photos, Life Magazine covers, the works – if it's Marilyn, it's on the wall. Should her body turn up missing, look for it at the Pastime.

I found Verna sitting alone in a booth glaring at her drink. Lord only knows how a beverage pissed her off. She nods when I walk in and motions me over. I slide in across from her.

"You called?"

"Yeah. You asked about big Indians. Not the one's that cut me, the ones that hassled Richard. Well, I wasn't gonna say nothin', but now I'm ticked and I don't give a shit. You know her?"

Her eyes blaze towards the card room. Sitting, drinking, and talking to an obese, balding man in a white T-shirt, is Loni the leggy redhead.

"Neither one of them looks Indian to me."

Again, Verna gives me that look.

"She's not. You're sure stupid for a detective. I hate her. She's a whore, the bitch. I was hot on some guy earlier and was already spending the money in my head, you know, and then she muscled in with her long legs and big tits."

Do we sense professional jealousy? We now know Verna's center of gravity.

"I mean, just look at those boobs of hers. They're practically hanging out right in front of God and ..."

Mary Higgens Clark?

"...everybody. Besides, she only comes in every other day. It's not fair," she continues with increased bitterness, "this is my only way to make a living, and she's got like a real job on the side. Can you imagine that?"

No clue what this has to do with Indians, but I roll with it.

"Loni has a real job? You mean where someone pays her to do something responsible?"

She nods as if confirming the redhead's key role in the World Trade Center bombing.

"Get this," hisses Verna wickedly, "she doesn't want people to know it, but I found out that she works three days a week. Oh, she's hush-hush about it, but it's a goddam fact."

"Forgive me for being slow on the uptake, Verna, but why would she be so secretive about it?"

She rolls her eyes, shakes her head, and takes a drink.

"If you were her – all fucked-up acting, strung out, and a hooker — would you want your customers knowing you had a normal job on the side?"

A unique perspective, to be sure.

"It makes me sick," grouses Verna, "She really pisses me off. I mean, it's like she leads a double life. One day she's stoned and hookin', the next she's being Florence Fucking Nightingale for God's sake."

Let's all visualize long legged Loni strutting about in nurses' shoes and white nylons.

"I bet she has one hell of a bedside manner," I offer pleasantly. "Is she state licensed?"

"Yeah, as a whore!"

"I mean as a nurse or caregiver or whatever."

"Oh, who the fuck cares. She's has my money in her pocket and it's not fair."

113

"Forgive me if I missed something, Verna, but what does she have to do…"

"With the Indians?"

"The Indians."

"Ask her to show you that picture of her sick-ass criminal husband she keeps in her purse," she snarls, "and that damn photo is as close as she can get to him for the next eight years, 'cause his fat Apache ass is in the slammer where it belongs."

"I take it you two aren't pals."

She glares. 'nuff said.

"You telling me that her dearly beloved spouse was one of the Indians that hassled Richard?"

"What's a spouse?"

"Husband."

"Yeah. I wasn't gonna say nothin', but things change. I kept my mouth shut, okay?"

This is beginning to make remarkable sense.

"Let me guess," I say thoughtfully, "the guy who put hubby away was Dickhead, right?"

She nods.

"And prior to that," I continue, "the big Indian was not to be trusted anyway."

"No shit. He was a snitch, if you ask me."

I can't resist.

"Like Bane?"

Before she can answer, she spies Loni leaving her overweight companion and striding towards the bar. Leaning over and stretching her legs behind her, Loni rotates her butt in a seductive, grinding, and mocking rhythm.

Verna leaps from the booth like an enraged lioness and heads right for her.

While Marilyn Monroe looks down from a framed endorsement for Luster Creme Shampoo above them, Verna and Loni exchange words, and I doubt they're pleasant.

Proof is immediately forthcoming.

Wham!

Loni, clutching a handful of big hair, slams Verna's head into the bar.

Screaming, swearing.

What a floorshow. Sullivan would love it.

The redhead, obviously in control, repeatedly bangs Verna's

noggin on the hardwood. Some little guy at the bar grabs his soup bowl and scurries away. Like me, he prefers watching from a safe distance.

Summoned by an excitable waitress, the Pastime's elderly night manager shuffles towards the fray, attempting authoritative, fatherly, intervention.

"Loni, Loni, stop it," he insists, "stop it right now."

"It's not my fault," wails Loni, giving Verna another whack, "she called me a whore!"

"Loni, you *are* a whore," he states flatly as if appealing to her reason, "let her go."

Verna, paralyzed with anger and anguish, yelps like an inbred Pomeranian as her taller, younger, and stronger adversary shakes her by the roots.

"Okay, I'm a whore," admits Loni tearfully, "but she *called* me one!"

"Let her go right this minute, I mean it." He's old enough to be her grandfather, half her size, but he's the room's only authority figure.

"Not 'till she says she's sorry!"

Verna, perhaps fearing involuntary baldness and another painful reunion with the bar, complies.

"I'm sorry, I'm sorry, I'm sorry!"

Loni releases her. Verna, clutching her traumatized follicles, hurries back to the booth. Her eyes as red as her forehead, she's sobbing horribly.

The redhead, breathing heavily, braces herself against the bar. Faced with reprimand and punishment, she pleads for leniency.

"Please...listen...she started it..."

Hands on hips, his eyes scan her from scuffed boots to limp curls. The room is dead quiet save for Verna's sniveling.

"First of all, you two make up. I never want a scene like that in here again, you understand?" A look tossed to Verna includes her.

"When you've done that, and I mean do it now, we'll decide what happens next."

Detention? Extra homework?

Loni studies the floor, sighs, and allows a tear to stream down her cheek.

"We better talk, Verna," says the redhead, and Verna squeaks a weepy reply. Loni slings her purse over her freckled shoulders,

BURL BARER

comes towards the booth, and I slide over. She unhitches the purse
and plops it in my lap as she sits down.

"I've got some cool pictures of my husband and kids," she
begins as if everything is normal, her voice cracking with emotion, "wanna see?"

I realize she's addressing me, not Verna.

"Sure, love to."

She pulls a packet from the purse and tosses it on the table.
Verna sniffs and wipes her eyes with the backs of her hands.

Apparently if I'm looking at Loni's beloved family photos, I
cease to exist. She and Verna have their heart to heart.

"We're liable to be tossed out for good this time," moans
Loni.

Verna bobs her head like one of those rear window car toys,
gasps air between sobs, and chokes out a wet apology.

"I'm sorry I called you a...a... whoooore."

"I am a whore," laments Loni.

I'm staying out of this.

"I'm a whore tooooo," confesses Verna tearfully.

"We're both whores," sniffs Loni in absolute agreement.

"I'm just a bitch," admits Verna.

"We're just a pair of bitches and whores," asserts Loni sadly.

They both sob foolishly for about fifteen seconds.

"Bitches and whores; whores and bitches..." Verna recites
her repetitive litany as if it's a nursery rhyme. They're holding
hands across the table in a Pastime séance of social status dismay,
commiserating their mutual martyr's misery at being bitches and
whores.

Where are the social scientists when we need them? This is a
classic Milton Layden situation.

Layden.

What a smart cookie.

Unlike Hurkos, Milton Layden, M.D., never fell on his head.
When he began his psychiatric residency at John Hopkins Hospital in 1945, he discovered a single, simplified approach to treating
hostility and resentment. Clear, succinct, and quickly forgotten.
Except, of course, by me. I have a hard time forgetting anything.
In fact, I can recite Layden's formula by heart. As it means nothing to Loni and Verna, our prime examples of the formula in action, I'll keep this between us.

$I \rightarrow A + Ob + H + S + Mar.$

HEADLOCK

Cool, huh?

What does this have to do with anything?

Plenty.

When I walked into the Pastime, Verna was already steamed. True hostility only occurs when humans feel disrespected, suffer a loss of personal status, and feel inferior. Verna felt it with a capitol "I" when a potential trick tossed her aside for the younger Loni, This, in turn, generated anxiety. Just as pain signals a threat to personal well being, anxiety signals threats to emotional well being. Sadly, for Verna and everyone else, anxiety doesn't identify the underlying conflict any more than pain provides a diagnosis of the ailment.

Feeling inferior, anxious, and obsessed with self, Verna over-compensated by the mirage of superiority. By putting Loni down, she hoped to feel better about herself. In the process, she began martyring - blaming others. Then, of course, Verna leapt for validation of intrinsic superiority by calling Loni a whore directly to her face.

Insulted, Loni went through the exact same stages and capped them by whacking Verna's head into the bar.

Who's fault was that? According to Loni, the credit goes to Verna. By the end, they both were martyrs.

See?

First Verna, then Loni, followed Layden's model perfectly. Were Milton Layden, M.D. in the Pastime, he'd feel vindicated indeed. I'd mention this to my wet-eyed booth-mates, but my amazing psychic abilities tell me they couldn't care less. Hell, they might even punch me.

The manager, shuffling around behind the bar, mutters to himself about the women's lack of decent, common sense. He's martyring, too. Can't blame the old guy. Make a scene on his turf, in his bar, and you're gonna give him I -> A + OB + S + Mar., too.

As for me, I'm thumbing through Loni's collection of candid photographs - shots of a skateboarding teenage boy, a younger girl losing her baby teeth, some middle aged women playing a board game, and a Polaroid picture of a big, naked, Native American.

Real big; real naked.

He may be nude, but he doesn't look delighted. Talk about your wilting gaze.

I'm meditating on Mr. Nude Apache; the little manager shuffles over. Verna buries her head in her hands; Loni fidgets and chews her lip.

He just stares at Loni, hands on hips. Then he takes his index finger and wags it in her face. No words, just a wagging finger.

She can't take the tension.

"For God's fucking sake," bleats Loni, "just tell me what you're gonna do. I mean it's not like I hit an employee or a food customer - it was just Verna."

"Yeah," confirms just Verna, "it was only me, and I'm a whore and bitch."

He holsters the finger. "I'm both too, honey," acknowledges Loni.

"Enough of that," he interrupts.

Ooops.

"Did you two make up?"

"They certainly did," I interject happily, "they've rekindled the flame of friendship, become united in their views and thoughts, and their purposes are joyously harmonized. The three of us were just admiring this delightful photo of Loni's buck naked husband."

I hold up Mr. Nude Imprisoned and wave him happily. The women, slack jawed in surprise, are amazingly silent. He stares at me for a moment, then unholsters his finger and wags it at me.

"Hey, aren't you...."

"Yes, and I have been for years. Nice to see you again."

He hasn't seen me, or talked to me, in ages, but this is Walla Walla. Unless you isolate, you see everybody. Of course, my moderate fame proceeds me amongst those who read. At least twice a year the local paper, desperate for feature stories, recaps my brilliant career complete with color photos.

He holsters the finger.

"Really, I should come in here more often," I say as if he and I are the only two in the room, "the food's good, the drinks affordable, and you've got the best Marilyn Monroe collection I've ever seen."

He likes that.

"Thanks. Nice to see you again, too."

I nod and smile the social signal that the conversation has concluded, then give him an almost imperceptible wink.

He sort of smiles, looks at the women, and has only one thing left to say as he walks away.

"Have a nice evening.... and behave yourselves."

Glee reigns supreme.

Giddy at not being expelled, they shower me with idiotic affection. Verna forces her ample abdomen over the table, almost spills her drink, puckers up, and smooches my cheek. Loni goes to plant one on my lips, and I check her quickly for cold sores before I allow even fleeting impact.

I wish I were with Randy.

"That was soooo cool," enthuses Verna, "you got him to just forget it."

"Wow, thanks man," Loni adds, "I guess I owe ya something. Wanna drink?"

"Actually," I answer, being remarkably blunt, "I want some direct answers to a few simple questions."

"You a cop?" Loni pulls back and wipes her lips. God forbid she should kiss a law enforcement officer.

"Naw, he ain't no cop," explains Verna, "He's a stupid private detective. You know, like fuckin' *Magnum, PI.*"

"You here all the way from Hawaii?" asks Loni seriously.

"No, but I am working on a real case, just like on television. I can't arrest anybody, of course, because I'm not a policeman. I'm just a private eye. But you can help me solve the mystery."

"Oh," Loni brightens, "this is sort of like *Diagnosis: Murder* except you're not a doctor."

"Nor do I play one on television," I add helpfully, "Right now, you're in a mystery. I'm the handsome private eye..."

"I'll go for that," the redhead says, and gives my thigh a slow squeeze.

"And I'm gonna ask you a few question. You give me answers, and that's that."

"Okey-dokey," agrees Loni.

"I've already told him some stuff," reveals Verna timidly, perhaps worried about a resumption of hostilities once Loni finds out how much I know.

"First question is for you, you adorable redhead," I say, laying on charm with a trowel.

"Shoot!"

Well, sometimes you have to take risks.

"What's wrong with the old lady in Weston, the one Derek `Bane' Faron hired you to take care of?"

Stunned is an understatement. When she responds, it's in a hushed whisper.

"How the fuck did you know about that? I mean, one or two

people know I work out there a few days a week, but that's only because I've needed a ride a few times. But no one knows.... I mean.... shit...you know..."

More than a lucky guess and I bet you were one step ahead of me.

In a town of twenty-seven thousand, you have simple circles of social familiarity – little universes unto themselves in which the players seldom shift spheres. And as a dog returns to its own vomit, and Violet returned to the tug boats in search of a new victim, Bane the snitch turned to the repertory players of the west end's watering holes - McFeely's and the Pastime - when he needed a little help around the house. Specifically, help that could keep her mouth shut, do the job, and is paid off under the table or with contraband chemicals.

That's who'd hire Loni, all right. Makes sense. Her incarcerated hubby and she had been in the loop for years. All the addicts and rip-off artists know each other, feed off each other, and when they're not whacking each other's heads into the bar, help each other- for a price

"Well, what's the answer?'

She digs a Doral out of her purse, lights it, and blows more smoke towards the ceiling's burnt apricot glaze of aged nicotine.

"Some sort of brain cancer, I guess. I just keep her clean and....comfortable." She puts an almost immoral spin on the last word.

"Morphine?"

She smirks.

Heroin?

She nods.

In 1898 the Bayer Company introduced its new miracle drug with the trade name, "Heroin" and advertised it as a remedy for a wide variety of ailments. Ironically, it was initially offered as a cure for morphine addiction.

"You get some too, I trust."

Another nod.

"How bad is she?"

"Oh, she's out of it most of the time. But sometimes she talks to me, but she talks all sorts of weird shit."

"Like, for instance?"

"Two things she says over and over - how she hates Jews, and that were sittin' on the shit."

120

"Did you ask her what shit?"

"Yeah. Asked her what Jews, too. I thought Jews were the people in the Bible."

Another prompt for details.

"She just says she hates all Jews and that were sittin' on it. Crazy old bitch. It's the brain tumor that makes her talk like that, right? . Or maybe the smack. I dunno. I just take care of her when he doesn't."

"And where is he when you're there?"

"I think Pendleton or LaGrand, maybe Portland or Spokane if I'm there more than a day. He does somethin' there, I guess. Something religious sounding."

"I beg your pardon?"

"He don't seem the type, and he don't act like a church guy, that's for damn sure," Loni elaborates, "mostly he babbles about wrestling. That's his big thing. Got a satellite dish for watching all the Royal Rumbles, ya know, and shit like that. But then he says he's doing things like it says in the Bible, and his mother is real proud of him. Maybe he's getting' ready for the priesthood, like some sort of Catholic."

Maybe he's sarcastic.

"Then again," she adds, "most Catholic priests don't have a handy supply of smack."

The lady's got a point.

I take a different tact.

"Nice place, is it?" That's me asking.

"The trailer?"

Damn. I wanted her to say "cabin."

"Trailer? I figured it was a cabin."

Loni digs a stray chunk of mascara out of the corner of her left eye.

"Well, there's a cabin, but she's in the trailer."

Whew.

"So, is it a nice place?"

"The cabin or the trailer?"

Who's on first?

"Either."

"Yeah, not particularly. I mean they both got beds, heat and lights and a kitchen, toilet and big screen TV sets. It's convenient for when she dies, too."

"Why's that?"

121

"Hell, it's right next to the grave yard."

I can't resist.

"You ever sleep in a grave yard?"

She thinks it over. Verna scowls. She's out of the loop in this conversation and that's bound to tweak her hostility switch.

"What kind of weird-ass private eye question is that?" interjects Verna testily.

Loni shrugs and answers.

"Just once, but that's because I was drunk and passed out. Does that count?"

I shrug too.

Verna rises to leave; Loni takes back the photos and stuffs them into her purse.

"I'm gonna scoot over to McFeely's before someone baldheaded changes his mind," she says, and Verna agrees.

"Listen, don't be telling people what you know and what I said, okay?"

"Okay."

"Do private eyes pay for information?"

"I got you off the hook, remember?"

"Oh, yeah, I forgot, thanks."

My mind, once again, is calculating odds and eventualities. Weston.

Hell of a drive, especially at night. If Loni is here, that means Bane is in Weston with his beloved not-dead murdering mother. I wonder what shit they're sitting on. Am I going? Perhaps, but not now. "Hey…I've got a swell idea," I say as we hit the back door, "I've got plenty of money…"

They stop in their tracks like hunting dogs sniffing quail.

Loni's eyes run over me like I'm gravel and she's a monster truck.

"I don't do doubles, understand? You can have me or her but I ain't getting' naked with Verna."

Verna can't decide if this is an insult or a compliment, and her fat little hands form preparatory fists. If she loses one more customer, she's gonna break Loni's nose.

"Let's put it this way, ladies," I explain as I open the door, "I'll pay you both good money to help me on this case – more money than you'd make gettin' naked."

They look at each other and nod.

My next line is especially for Loni.

HEADLOCK

"And I promise you more money than you're making from Bane as long as you keep close to me and follow what I say, and allow me to give you a ride to work."

Agreed.

In this end of town, loyalty follows the cash flow.

"Where to now, Mr. Money?" prods Verna.

I flip out my cellular and punch in a number.

"Richard, this is Jeff. Put on the coffee, you're about to have company."

When it comes to hospitality, you can't beat a recluse.

Always happy to have company, Richard and Lynette Tibbit treated we three like long-lost family. The Mr. Coffee dripped an aromatic welcome, a fresh bag of Oreos was torn open in our honor, and hellos and handshakes were passed around like cheap party wine.

Their home – as cozy, comfy, cat-friendly, and unpretentious as its owners – sits on a quiet side street in a normal neighborhood. The couch is overstuffed, the easy chair s deep-seated, and a Rent-to-Own home entertainment center takes up half the living room wall. Lord only knows how many times over how many years the Tibbits have sat here with their coffee and cats while Pat Sajak gave the Wheel of Fortune another spin.

The wheel is certainly spinning tonight.

In the bright florescence of Lynette' kitchen, Loni's makeup looks as if it were applied by Barnum and Bailey. Catching a disconcerting glimpse of her reflection in the kitchen's small mirror, she asks directions to the washroom. A few minutes later, she returns several layers lighter.

As for Verna, there was initial awkwardness when she recognized Lynette as the nurse who cared for her dying mother several years ago.

Soon, the consultation's primary participants huddle around the Tibbit's kitchen table, the Zippo getting one hell of a workout. Lynette doesn't smoke, but the rest of us are going at it like Brown and Williamson.

Richard, remarkably comfortable with recent revelations – he recognized Loni's lesser half immediately — offers additional color.

"Oh, she tried to kill him more than once, you understand.

She was far too impatient to wait it out, hope for natural causes and such. In fact, one time she tried to rig a propane tank to gas him and another time she tried to drown him – all supposedly accidents, of course. I knew what she was up to, and she knew I knew."

"And you told your father, didn't you."

"Hell, yes. But he didn't want to hear it. When she tried to drown him in Medical Lake, it was so obvious. There was only one life preserver, and he let her wear it. Now, he would never be away from his bottle, because that's what he did, okay? She was wearing a life jacket, he wasn't, and he was drunk. She stood up, overturned the boat, and she grabbed him and held him under –- my Dad told me this himself. I mean he admitted that he had to slug her to make her stop holding him down, but he chalked it up to panic on her part. Think about it! She's got a goddam life preserver on!" Richard's voice rises with emotion. "I warned him, I warned him, I warned him! He was in complete denial about it. He insisted that she loved him and it was all a misunderstanding on my part."

"You ever tell anyone else?"

"Damn right," he responds eagerly, "my wife and I went to a family reunion up in Idaho. I got a cousin that used to work for the damn FBI, honest to God. So, I approached him and told him what I thought. And he said, `that's what your dad said,' meaning my dad had already told him what I believed. And I said, `God damn, man, she's gonna kill his ass. You used to be in the FBI, do somethin' 'cause Dad won't listen to me!'"

He shakes his head in dismay.

"He just walked away, never said another word. That ended that."

He pauses, stretches, and then offers a warm Jack Nicholson smile.

"I get kind of wound up on this, you understand. Let me get you some more coffee, okay?"

Sure, I could use a warm-up.

My attention riveted on Richard, I hadn't noticed Loni picking absentmindedly at a few tiny arm scabs, and looking longingly towards the night's darkness. Out there somewhere are more drugs. Not tonight, Loni. Not tonight. Part of my evening's duties include keeping her clean and sober 'till morning.

Verna, assured of money and happy for inclusion, plows her way through the Oreos, mumbling agreement by the mouthful as black crumbs tumble into her coffee.

As for me, I'm watching, listening, thinking, and ultimately hatching an absurd one-act for *Theatre McFeely*. If all goes well, this whole happy hootenanny will play itself out by mid-week. By the weekend, Richard will be free from fear, and I'll be rubbing Randy down with minimal sunblock. After Left Coast Crime, I'll devote eight hours a day transforming this into a novel. When I get to this placid "Oreo and conversation" scene, perhaps I'll insert some unexpected outburst of vindictive violence. Maybe I'll shred Lynette's gingham kitchen curtains with a fusillade of fire-power, shatter her salt and pepper shakers with hot blasts from a .357 Magnum, or send Richard's Borgward Isabella coupe arcing skyward in a bright ball of yellow flame.

"There's a book in this, right?" asserts Richard at one point, "I mean, when all is said and done, this should really be one of your books."

"Oh, it's a book alright, Richard," I concur, "with plenty of action, adventure, sex, intrigue, and..."

I almost say "big Indians" but catch myself when I notice Lynette staring at Verna's scar.

"...explosions."

"Explosions?" Verna likes that idea, and reaches for another Oreo; Lynette brings her some milk.

"Yeah, we were gonna blow up your hair," offers Loni, "but it was already as big as it gets."

Richard chuckles, Loni laughs aloud at her own joke, and Lynette assures Verna that big hair makes her look exactly like that country singer that won the Grammy, whatever her name was.

"Oh, yeah, her," says Verna, and smiles about it.

"It's not money I'm after, honest to God," insists Richard.

"I like money," offers Verna.

"Damn straight. That's the only reason I'm sittin' here," admits Loni, "no offense intended, of course."

"Of course, dear," says Mrs. Tibbit on cue.

Damn. This is like *Leave it to Beaver Goes to Hell*.

"What I'm trying to say," continues Richard, "is that if Jeff here can give me some peace of mind, and then writes it up like one of his novels, then folks in this town will at least have some sort of idea, okay? And someone, maybe, will understand."

Who says folks in this town read my books?

"We've been through it, haven't we honey?" says Richard

to the Mrs.

Lynette nods.

"God bless you, Lynette," he says seriously, "I couldn't ask for a better wife. Really." He reaches out and takes her hand. "When people are married, really married, they go through everything together, as if they are one soul."

In who's life? Not mine, pal. Maybe not Loni's either.

She digs through her purse and hands Mrs. Tibbit the infamous Polaroid.

"Here's my husband, Lynette."

"My, Loni, he certainly is…."

Lynette's vocabulary hits an understandable snag

"Naked," states Verna flatly, "big and naked."

"Yes, he certainly is both of those," Lynette agrees.

"That's the big Indian I told you about, Honey," explains Richard graciously, "you know, years ago when he was a young buck…"

"Buck naked now," asserts Verna, "and probably getting' butt-banged by Raul the Transylvanian Cross Dresser up there in cell-block four."

Loni looks at Verna in drop-jawed disbelief.

"I can't believe you said that, and what do you know about Transylvanians? You a vampire or something? Lord knows you get enough practice sucking…"

"Now ladies," interrupts Richard, "remember you're guest here, okay? We're all after the same thing, more or less…"

"I'm here because this guy…" she points a bright red fingernail in my general direction, "is paying me, or so he says."

"Me, too" pipes up Verna, looking in vain for on Oreo refill. Lynette checks the cupboard and retrieves a bag of low-fat Fig Newtons. Verna thinks it over, then daintily pops one in her mouth.

"What about the bank robbery, Richard?" I ask off-handedly. "We're talking Frontier Western Bank about five years ago, right?"

"Oh, that." He gives his wife a quick glance; she nods almost imperceptibly. There's something going on here. "It wasn't me. I mean I could have been involved, you understand, but it wasn't me."

"Explain."

"One day, see, I just get sort of fed up. You gotta understand that I knew they wanted to push me into something, give 'em an excuse to whack me or put me away, right? Well, I'm not about to give 'em the pleasure. Oh, there was a time when I would have just gone ahead and killed 'em – Jake, the snitch, even that bitch herself – but I resolved to stay cool, keep my mouth shut, not react. Well, one day I just go ahead and go over to the snitch's house, knock on the door and walk right in. He's sittin' there and doesn't even look surprised to see me. The first thing he says is: `Richard, I wanna rob a bank.' Hell, you could have knocked me over. He offers me a cup of coffee, just like we're old friends. So, I play along. I know banks, all right? I never robbed one, but I got a thing for banks. I walk in one and I can tell you exactly how many cameras they got, everything, okay? So I tell him that if one were really gonna do it, the one bank to rob would be Frontier Western."

"Because?"

"Response time. You see, the cops go on their little patrol routes, and they are supposed to not get into a routine, but they do. Well, there is one time of the day when all the cop cars are just far enough away all at the same time that you could hit Frontier Western with a quick in and out and get away clean. Now, ya gotta keep tabs on the patrol cars for about a week to analyze the routine but once you know, you could do it."

"And that's what happened?"

"Yep. About a week after that it came down just like I laid it out. Now, you think that's a coincidence? And another thing, right away – like within a few days —I get a call from my son in Seattle and he says, `Dad, are you robbing banks now?'"

Richard smiles and gives that expansive hand gesture.

"See? Once it starts, it spreads. Of course, the local boys in blue about wet their pants having a real honest-to-God bank robbery right here in Walla Walla, Washington. So, you figure out how the rumor gets going that it was me."

Not too difficult.

The snitch makes sure it gets to his kid. From there it moves on in ever widening circles. Naturally it gets back to Sullivan via his own incarcerated ass-hole son, and Sullivan tells everybody in the wrestling network who ever worked with Tibbit and one thing leads to another. The rumor mill goes full throttle. As the old expression goes: if you want to send a message, you can telegraph, telephone, or tell a wrestler.

"Now, with the snitch in bed with Jake, naturally the bank robber's trail is cold as ice, right?"

Verna raises her hand to speak as if she's in third grade.

127

"I used to watch The FBI on television. Robbing banks is a Federal offense. If they get you, they send you to a Federal Prison, not the State one like they did to Loni's big ass naked Apache husband."

Loni, either immune to, or tired of, Verna's sarcastic remarks, simply says, "That's right. Federal prisons are a lot nicer, too."

Richard rips the top off a fresh pack of Bel-Airs.

"It may be a Federal case," he explains, "but it's the local cops who respond to the scene, and the local detectives who handle the investigation. They just send a report on to the Feds. Face it, the Feds are always happy to let someone else do the work. And can't you guess who was the detective on the case?"

"Jake Livesay?"He gives me a look he must have learned from Verna.

"You see, I know how to keep my mouth shut. Let 'em start a rumor that I was the robber, what do I care? No one even questioned me, and if they did I wouldn't tell 'em anything anyway. Just one more thing to keep me quiet. They already murdered my father, blew that kids brains out, I mean, hey, I got a wife, right? And kids, okay? I say the wrong thing and someone else gets hurt."

Maybe I'm that someone else. Maybe it's Jesus the Wonderdog.

I notice the look on Lynette's face, and it's dismay. Maybe I should alter the topic, but there's something I want to know.

"Richard, if you don't mind me asking, why would this snitch assume you'd know about robbing banks?"

He gets this pained expression, leans back, gives out a long laborious exhale, and shakes his head.

"I've never robbed a bank in my life, and I've never planned one for anybody else. But you gotta understand that I know people, okay. I've done things in my life that I'm not proud of, I'll admit that, but I'm no gangster. I just, well...remember George Raft?"

"Never heard of him," insists Loni.

"Me neither," adds Verna.

"Yeah, I remember George Raft," I say, "hell of a dancer. He also never watched his own movies, and I get where you're going."

Loni wipes her nose on her hand, and lodges a complaint.

"You guys have fuckin' lost me here. Who's this George guy dancing on a raft?"

"He was a movie star and a dancer," I explain, "He played

mostly gangsters in the movies, and lots of his pals were crime figures and gang bosses. In fact, his buddies were irked with him because he played a Federal Agent in a movie. They took it personally."

"Don't blame 'em," says Loni, "who wants a pal turning into a fucking cop?"

Richard smiles and nods.

"George Raft wasn't a gangster himself, he was an actor, but he knew people, okay? I know people too, and for some reason they kept coming back into my life. I mean, I'm a standup guy and even if I don't agree with you, or what you do, I can just let it go. I don't pass judgement, and I can keep my mouth shut. There are some things I just won't talk about."

"Sullivan said you broke a killer out of jail, will you talk about that?"

I'm taking a risk here, okay?

Richard and his wife give each other another look, and Loni is suddenly interested.

"Yeah, talk about that," she insists encouragingly, "maybe we can pull the same stunt for my husband."

"It's a simple story of basic stupidity on my part," admits Richard, "coupled with me doing what I felt I had to do at the time."

Lynette nods a go-ahead signal. She's obviously the primal force in this family.

"When I got drafted into the service, Lynette lived in my folks' basement rather than live at home with her own family. I won't elaborate the details, because that gets into things about her family dynamics that are really none of your business, but let's just say I didn't want her livin' at home, okay? So, she's living in the house and I get a letter from her while I'm in basic training at Fort Ord. She writes me and tells me that my step mother doesn't want her there, and that she has to move back to her own folks' house."

"That's the shits," offers Verna.

"Yeah, well, I couldn't let that happen," he continues, "now, I had two weeks left of basic training. So, I go to get a pass to come home and they tell me, `you don't have nobody but the army.' That was the mentality. And I told 'em that I had to come home and take care of personal matters and that I would go through basic all over again if they would just let me go home to take care of an important family situation. Well, you can guess…"

BURL BARER

Loni can guess.

"They wouldn't let you do it, would they?"

"No, they wouldn't, so I went friggin' AWOL. I just took off, came home, got Lynette an apartment, and basically didn't go back. Just figured `let 'em come get me.' Shit, I've screwed up my life every time I've done, ya know, well, so they come and got me, put me in jail right down town, and guess what I did."

"You broke out."

"Yeah, damn right. I broke out. And to insult them just a little bit worse, they had a killer on hold for the penitentiary right across from me. I let him go. We basically took off and were together the whole day. Then he says he's takin' off, and that was fine with me. They got him easy enough – a roadblock at the Oregon border. As for me, I went to a service station, called the wife, and told her to come get me. So, she comes down and I jumped in the car and took off. Remember, Hon?"

She remembers.

Richard stretches, digs out another Bel-Air, and completes his tale.

"So, there we are, and I'm thinking to myself, `what the hell am I doing?' All I'm doing is burying myself more. I got a wife, I'm making her life hell, so I just went and turned myself in. They put me in the county jail for a while, and the Army decided that since I was two weeks away from being done with basic, they'd just forget the whole damn thing and just boot me out. Not exactly honorable discharge, but at least I was back with my wife and could get on with my life. Anyway, that's the lamebrain story of me breaking a killer out of jail. That's the way I used to be – highly reactive, okay? Now days, since I learned meditation and gave my life to God, I don't behave that way, you understand. I mean, I have done some things in this town to actually improve law, order, and justice."

I help myself to a Fig Newton. I forgot how good they taste. I must remember to pick up come the next time I buy Friskies.

"What did your snitch buddy do after the robbery?"

Before answering, Tibbit gets up and pours himself a fresh cup of coffee. Another glance goes between him and the Mrs.

Damn. What the hell's the subtext here?

I put my mind on cruise control while Richard makes his way back to the table, and my mental screen fills with the newspaper story about me, the one that prompted Richard's initial contact.

130

Richard sits and looks directly at me, as if speaking to me without moving his lips.

Oh. I get it. He's going to broadcast.

Go for it.

Wham!

One hell of an explosion, and over it is the same image that came to me at Randy's – the Power Company or an electrical contractor logo. What the hell is he trying to say?

Just that fast, the image is gone. I don't even blink.

"Getting' rusty?" asks Richard with a slight smile. This goes right by our hooker tablemates, but Lynette gets it.

"Now, as for the snitch, no sooner is the bank job history than he's outta here. Takes off for Nevada probably to gamble, or maybe just goes up to Spokane or Idaho to chill out. Anyway, he just sort of makes himself more than scarce."

Loni suddenly bangs her hand on the table, and makes a dramatic pronouncement.

"Phineas!"

Verna about chokes on a Newton.

"What you yellin' about, woman?" objects Verna. "You having some drug reaction?"

"No, Phineas is the guy Bane goes to see. I was trying to remember that damn name all night, ever since this guy asked what he talked about and I said it was religious or something, remember?"

Richard pushes back his chair, obviously uncomfortable, but Lynette leans in like this is some sort of payoff.

"Who's Phineas?'

"Well, it's a Biblical name," drawls Richard, "I got my own ideas about God, but I keep 'em personal."

End of subject.

There's a quiet moment, then he adds a throwaway line: "It was just a rehearsal."

Rehearsal? From the look on his face, I'm not supposed to request clarification.

We all sit there in awkward silence for moment. I tune in, but Richard's not broadcasting a thing. The transmitter is shut down tight. I'm not gonna push it. Nope. Not going there.

It's Lynette who finally speaks up.

"I still have that nice newspaper story about you, if you need another copy."

My immediate response would be to pass, but I sense more than courtesy in her offer.

"Sure, that would be great."

She excuses herself to go get it, and I decide to get Richard back on track.

"One more thing, Richard…well, actually two more, but first things first."

"Yeah?"

"Tell me everything — maybe even draw me a picture – about the cabin your Dad had up towards Tollgate."

"That's where the Luger came from, you know." he remarks ruefully.

I bet it's still there somewhere.

He tells all he can recall about the little house in the big woods near the small cemetery. The last time he was up there was long before dad married Violet Langness.

"Not much too it," says Richard, "I don't know about now, but back then there was a big old trunk against the wall and inside were a bunch of old photographs and stuff like that, but underneath was his war memorabilia – the Luger and some German knives with those designs on 'em, okay?"

"I saw that trunk when I was in there," remarks Loni proudly, "he piles dirty clothes on top of it. I remember that."

Richard tells a bit more, and Loni says it all sounds familiar to her, except for some of the other details about inside the cabin because Bane doesn't let her in there. Mostly she stays in the trailer with the old lady. In fact, she says, the cabin is padlocked from the outside. She's was only in there once or twice, and then briefly.

I'm not surprised.

"Now, last but not least," I say, rising to the occasion and stretching up to my full height, "it's time to teach these girls a few tricks about flyers and fatboys."

Suddenly, I grab a handful of Loni's red hair with my left hand and bring my right elbow crashing down full force on the top of her head. My right foot stomps the kitchen floor a mili-second before the elbow harmlessly lights atop her hairdo, and the room shakes with the loud vibration and Verna's screams of disbelief.

"Hey!" Loni laughs. "You 'bout scared the poop out of me. That didn't even hurt. That's what those wrestlers do on TV."

I grab Verna's nose with my left hand and bring my right

down with a loud slap. Sort of a Three Stooges Meet Hulk Hogan move. She blinks.

"Huh?"

Richard is vastly amused.

"Ya gotta sell it, Verna," he says.

"I do sell it," objects Verna.

'Not sell *that*," advises Richard, "sell the action. He made it look like he slapped your nose almost all the way off your face. You're supposed to act like he really did."

"Why?'

"Yeah," agrees Loni, "why are we doing this?"

"Because you're going to be very very good at it," I explain enthusiastically, "because I have a plan that involves you using these skills, and most of all because you are getting paid to learn a new talent."

"How much?"

"Talent?"

"Money."

"Think hundreds."

Loni jumps up.

"I used to watch this shit on TV all the time. My first husband, the one who died of AIDS, really liked The Mountie. I called him the Mounted because I bet the other wrestlers rode his ass all the way to Canada and back."

"Well, you get the idea, Loni. This is just like WWF, except its gonna be the MWF – McFeely Wrestling Federation."

Loni and Verna look at each other a start to giggle.

"You're not gonna put us in tights and masks or nothin' are ya?" Loni asks sheepishly, as if her current costume of skin-tight jeans and mammary exposing sequin studded blouse isn't already absurd.

"No, you can wear your normal get up. Richard here is gonna teach you some basic tricks of the trade, so to speak. Then, Loni, I'm going to have you sleep over at my place so I can drive you bright and early to Weston."

Loni checks her watch.

"Yeah, no shit. Morning comes around awful early on workdays. Hell, I can't believe I'm almost sober."

"Me neither," agrees Verna, "and I don't have a real job, so I can get just as drunk and stupid as I damn well please."

"Well, it pleases you a lot because you sure do get stupid

when you drink," Loni says, then decides to soften her tone, "but I'm the worst of the bunch, no doubt about it, Verna. I'm just a bitch and a whore."

Verna, pleasantly surprised by Loni's convoluted peace making, actually gets some real color in her puffy white cheeks.

Richard runs his hands through his thinning hair.

"Hell, Jeff, I'm surprised the wrestlers trusted you, what with you knowing all those moves."

"Whatcha mean?"

"That's why they didn't trust me. When they were teaching me, I already knew the moves from my army training and simply from watching a lot of wrestling on TV. They think they have so many secrets, but when you put that stuff all over the television, anyone with more than half a brain can figure it out."

Verna brightens and becomes animated.

"Did you guys see the steel cage match between Cactus Jack and the Undertaker? Cactus Jack should have won. He was robbed. Bang bang!"

There's your half a brain.

Lynette stands in the kitchen doorway holding a newspaper page. As she doesn't approach the table, I decode that as a signal that I'm to get up and go to her. As I do, she steps back into the living room. I follow.

"Here. This is what inspired us to contact you," she explains, "I saved the entire page. Did you, or did you just clip out your story?"

"I keep a file of clippings, but I seldom go back and read them."

She looks me right in the eye.

"Oh, you really should."

I fold it up and put it in my inside pocket.

Richard and the girls are up from the table and coming into the living room.

"Help me move this chair aside, Jeff," he asks, "I'm gonna teach these adventurous women some new moves."

A car engine slows to an idle outside the window, and the Tibbits freeze where they stand. Lynette turns stoically and lifts back a corner of drapery. She exhales and her shoulders relax.

"It's just the neighbor's kid, Honey."

Richard shakes his head, shrugs, and looks sheepish.

"Hey, ya gotta forgive us because you gotta understand,

134

right?"

Right.

"I mean, we've been jumpin' at shadows for fifteen years, right? You never know, okay? A guy could get killed around here. If they want you dead, you're dead."

VI

"Damn it, Loni, you're hooched."

Despite my best efforts at enforced sobriety, Loni greeted the new day spread eagle naked on the bedroom floor with an empty bottle of Nyquil in her hand.

Delightful.

Here's the deal: leaving Richard's, we returned Verna to her haunts, making sure I knew how to contact her without searching every bar in Walla Walla. Then I sped Loni by her current crash-pad to grab her "other work clothes." Her residence of the week is a tiny, respectable looking house on Bonsella, or maybe Valencia – one of the "uh" sounding streets. She wouldn't let me go inside because the people she's staying with are, according to her, "real uptight" about anybody they don't know coming to the house.

She insists she'll only be a minute. Twenty of those later she stumbles back to the car, reeking of pot.

"I had to take a few bong hits," she explains. In her social circle, bong hits are an unavoidable imperative.

"Life without choice must be difficult," I agree, and we motor up to Snob Hill. She sits slack jawed and red-eyed while I explain my plans for the following morning, then I send her off to the upstairs master bedroom.

There are more bedrooms, but the cats and I share cramped space on the downstairs couch so I can guard the door. I don't want our addicted houseguest sneaking out for further chemical refreshment.

She outsmarts me by simply raiding the medicine cabinet. One well-drained bottle of green, licorice flavored goo later, Loni's statuesque form decorates the bedroom floor like an alabaster lawn ornament.

When morning arrives, I walk into the bedroom to wake her

up. There she is, very naked.

Not a pretty sight.

Light green bruises and deep blue needle marks stain the near-translucent skin; twisted stretch marks mar both breasts and belly.

Pooter follows me in, wheezes, and sniffs her indelicately.

"She's not edible, stupid. Let's have a little human dignity here."

Well, I wake her, drag her to a precarious upright position, and pilot her into the bathroom.

It's been a long time since a woman showered in my house, and non-specific memories deplete faster than hot water.

I'd already showered, shaved and put on fresh clothes before waking Loni, and prepared plenty of hot coffee and juice. She accepted both when she stumbled down the stairs and shuffled into the kitchen. Heavy lidded, she slurped down two quick cups before stepping outside to hotbox three Dorals in rapid succession. I offered her a toaster waffle with turkey bacon, but she shook her head furiously at the thought. She managed to choke down some buttered 7 Grain Wheat Berry toast.

"Don't you have any real bread?" she objected, "You know, with red, yellow, and blue balloons printed on the wrapper?"

My daughter used to ask the same question.

Damn, I can be so paternal.

Mr. White Knight.

Dr. Laura would spank me.

I fed the cats, put them out, and we took off.

The ride to Weston, augmented by the aural backdrop of the Volvo's low hum and Loni's world-class snoring, offered ample opportunity for mental reflection

Phineas.

In the Bible, his name is "Phinehas," and his big scene is in Numbers 25:7-8. The same scene is in *Friday the 13th, Part II*. In the movie, two lusty teenagers copulate like wild weasels while our crazed killer, Jason, sneaks up and runs them through with a javelin-like object. Swoosh! Right through the guy's back, her belly, the mattress, and into the wood floor. The director shot the scene looking down on the couple from above. In reality, the actress was sitting on a chair with the actor on her lap. His "back" was a realistic latex replica. Much time and money went into that back, especially the way it split and bled when Jason rammed that poker through it.

Turns out it was a waste of money. It was too realistic for the censors, the ratings board, and someone's mother. The gory details never made it past the cutting room floor. They did, however, make it into Numbers 25.

Phinehas, says the Bible, raced into the tent where Zimri was having sex with Cozbi, a Medianite prostitute, and ran them through with a javelin. Sadly, for Zimri and Cozbi, neither was made of latex.

This is not all bad news. Because Phinehas was so zealous, God made with him an everlasting covenant of peace, and bestowed priesthood upon his descendents. As for Zimri and Cozbi, this is the really amazing part. Their deaths were taken as atonement for the Children of Israel's sins. Imagine that. I've never heard anyone preach, "Cozbi the whore died for our sins," nor have I seen a church feature a copulating couple icon as a focal point of prayerful reflection.

Maybe you have; I haven't.

Snoring all the way to Weston, Cozbi on Nyquil.

As for Lynette's advice to read my newspaper clipping, I did as she suggested. In fact, I read the entire page, both sides.

Sharing equal space with me on one side is a photo feature about the new Beef Princess; the other side has regional crime news. One item concerns counterfeit bills passed in Yakima, another notes recent car-jackings in Wenatchee, and another recounts the similarity between last fall's bombing of a Women's Clinic in Spokane, an S&L robbery in Louisiana where a pipe bomb was tossed, and the aborted bombing of a Texas newspaper.

"Authorities see no direct link between the Spokane incident and those in Tulsa and Shreveport," states the article, "although Ted Olmstad, Federal Prosecutor, has not entirely discounted a connection between the clinic bombing and the same day robbery of a Spokane Valley Bank."

Nice guy, Ted Olmstad. We met during the Sarah investigation when he was the new kid in the King County Prosecutor's office.

A bank robbery.

Explosions.

"It was just a rehearsal."

Swell. Remind me to call Ted.

When we hit the Weston exit off the two-lane highway, I

wake up Loni. From here on, this woman is painfully important.

"C'mon. Snap to, kiddo, I need directions."

She sniffs and snorks her way to consciousness, rolls down the passenger side window, then hacks and spits out something Sullivan would be proud of.

"Just keep driving," Loni says, "it's closer to Tollgate."

She rummages in her purse, pulls out a small triangle of torn newspaper, and carefully unfolds it.

"Wanna toot?"

Toot.

Cocaine.

"No thanks."

"You sure? Look, you can tell it's good 'cause it's `cop dope.'"

"Cop dope?"

"Yeah, there's blue die in it. The cops test it for purity by puttin' somethin' on it that turns it blue. When you get the blue stuff, you know it's `Cop Certified Okey-Dokey'." She laughs, scoops some up with her fingernail, and sniffs it up her nose.

"Damn," she enthuses, "this will help me wake up."

"How do you get `cop dope?'" I ask innocently.

"Verna's right, you're sorta stupid."

"Thanks."

"I mean I like you alright, but you don't know much. Cops basically bust the competition, or users that piss them off, or Mexicans. Take THC, for instance. He's the big drug cop, right? Well, how much of the drugs he takes off dealers when he busts 'em ever makes it back to the cop shop, and of the drugs that he does bring back, how much stays there?"

"I give up. Not much?"

"No shit. This stuff right here is from THC," she says scooping up a nail-full for her other nostril, "not directly, of course. He supplies it to another guy who's *never* been busted. Oh, every so often a customer gets popped, but that's only if they get squirrelly or cause problems."

I'm not as dumb as she thinks. A major drug bust thins out the competition, raises prices, and assures increased profits for cop-connected dealers. I'm sure THC reaps a commensurate financial reward.

Is this "official policy" of our local law enforcement?

Of course not.

The honest cops in Walla Walla disdain the likes of THC, but unless they're in the loop, they don't know and/or don't want to know. I gleaned these insights during the Armstad investigation. You can't point an accusatory finger at the Chief of Police or the Captain of Detectives. They probably are, if you'll pardon the expression, clueless.

I heard on NPR one day that in 1994 the retail value of illegal drugs exceeded international trade in oil, and was second only to the arms trade. How can any commodity, with trade of that magnitude, remain the exclusive domain of criminals?

We're talking "dangerous drugs," right? Got news for you: one hundred forty six thousand people die each year from taking the correct legal drugs for properly diagnosed illnesses as prescribed by responsible physicians.

Loni re-folds her paper triangle and tucks it away.

"I always save a bit for later," she says with slightly renewed animation, "I'm not like some coke head who just snorts the whole damn thing at once."

No, she just guzzles Nyquil.

I'm not saying she's psychic, but Loni's electrified brain made the same synapses leap.

"The only reason I drank all that was because I was havin' trouble sleepin', and I didn't want to come to work without being rested."

She giggles.

"I bet you were surprised to find me all naked and everything."

"Yes, it was not an anticipated sight."

"Did ya wanna jump me? Huh? Didya?"

She serious?

"I mean, were you tempted to just stick it to me for a morning wake up call?"

I ease down the driver side window a crack, and light an Old Gold. We're winding up a two-lane blacktop leading, eventually, to mighty fine skiing. The outside air has that freshly chilled feel.

"The thought never crossed my mind."

She laughs, fidgets, and drums her fingers repetitively on her thigh.

"Yeah, but I bet it crossed your dick."

She's awake now. I long for the previous nasal drone.

At length, she directs us down a wooded turn off.

"It's just a ways up now. The cemetery is just ahead."

HEADLOCK

The terrain reminds me of Issaquah, and Issaquah reminds me of Sarah Nussbaum.

"Stop."

I stop near the first row of tombstones. The cabin and trailer aren't far.

"I never let anyone drive me right up to it. He won't allow that, okay? So, you just hang out, sleep, or pretend your praying at a grave until he's gone."

"How long does he stick around?"

She thinks it over.

"Depends," she says opening the Volvo door, "ya never know."

"Remember, get her drugged as usual but not so much that she goes completely under right away."

Loni nods. Her bony shoulders hunched against the crisp morning air, she strides purposefully towards the plot of property once owned by Richard Tibbit's father.

I drive the Volvo down a bit further, and turn onto an old, rutted lane running past pitted headstones. I park, pull the seat's side lever, and recline. You know what I'm going to do, don't you?

That's right.

Sleep in a graveyard.

The full-throated roar of a revving Monte Carlo brings me back from the dead. The red Chevy, parked beside the cabin, exudes a blue exhaust cloud. The killer's keeper prepares for departure.

I'm cold. No wonder they put a ski resort up here. Maybe the chilled atmosphere accounts for my weird dreams – Phinehas and Jason on drugs, blowing up the tents of Jacob. Remind me never to read Numbers 25 again.

I exit the Volvo, and walk reverently to the nearest gravesite. *Ian Dickerson Age 27.* No date of birth; no date of death.

Sixteenth century mystic Isaac Luria believed it was beneficial to meditate while lying prostrate on the grave of a saint.

Was Ian Dickerson a saint? If so, should I lie prostrate on his grave in order that, as Luria insists, our souls be bound together and, thusly fused, ascend together?

I have no intention of finding out. No grave flopping for this shamus.

I recite a prayer for the departed, invoking God's hospitality towards this favored guest, Ian Dickerson.

Graveside praying for total strangers is another quirky pastime I've cultivated over the years. Not that I do it daily, mind you, but an old grave, untended or long forgotten pulls at my heart. This person I've never met, perhaps long deceased before I was born, was someone's beloved. If there is life after death, Mr. Dickerson probably gets a kick out of this screwball private eye/ author pausing in mid-mystery to pelt the Lord with prayers on his behalf.

My prayer completed, I watch the Monte Carlo blast down the highway. I've got my "black bag" of PI tools in the trunk, and enough curiosity to kill every cat in a twenty-mile radius. There's considerable distance between the trailer and the graveyard, but I'm not about to leave tire tracks in Faron's driveway.

Loni's peeking out the trailer door as I approach. She looks nervous; I credit the nose candy.

The trailer is no dump. We're talking a decent mobile home, the kind that is only mobile from where you buy it to where you park it. As for decor, it's early WWF, WCW, and NWA. The wall's resident artwork consists various pull-out posters from Wrestling World magazine, and the ever-popular painting of what I call "The Scandinavian Jesus" – long blond hair, blue eyes, Roman nose. As Sullivan would say, "Jesus in Oslo."

A large bed, positioned directly in front of a 32" television, takes up most of the living room.

Loni points to the bed's bulky occupant.

She's huge. I mean this woman must weigh in at close to four hundred pounds. Loose, buttery flesh hangs off her like melted lard. Her eyelids are shut, but her eyeballs are slowly rolling around behind them like greased ball bearings.

"You're a mess, honey," I comment softly, "You've been eating too much candy. And as for muscle tone…"

"Yeah, she don't much exercise," whispers Loni.

The massive behemoth beneath the sheets heard not a word.

The hi-8 camera, a fresh tape, my little micro-recorder, and a cute little digital camera come out of the bag. I'm documenting everything, and not just because I'm thorough – I'm covering my ass here.

"Has the old dear been injected?"

HEADLOCK

"Yeah, shot her up right after he revved up that Monte Carlo. Not enough to put her under too deep, just enough to, you know, what you asked me to do, you know…"

I know.

"How long is Faron gonna be gone?"

She bites a nail.

"Said he'd be back tonight. That's the way it usually goes. Then he'll pay me. Sometimes he'll drive me down into Weston, which he doesn't particularly like to do 'cause he has to leave her alone, but mostly it's up to me to get a ride back into Walla Walla. No problem, though. I got friends who'll come pick me up over at the graveyard 'cause they know I got money to spend."

Nice friends.

With my equipment set up, I send Loni to a neutral corner, lower the lights, pull a chair up to our semi-conscious patient, and practice my bedside manner.

Okay. Relax.

I set my little tape machine on her pillow. This isn't for recording, it's for playing a specially designed tape of white noise – waves slowly rising and falling; a slow, steady heartbeat, and some cute little electronic boings that seem to lob gently back and forth.

I lean over, my mouth by her ear. The trick here is voice modulation – not quite a monotone, not too animated – a sine wave pattern. Easy, beguiling, trustworthy, intimate. I learned these techniques ages ago – guided relaxation and visualization exercises to induce altered states. This subject is already drugged and vulnerable, so it should be easy. The Amazing Kreskin has nothing on me.

I slow my heart rate and blood pressure, relax my larynx, and direct my brain waves to hover between the Alpha and Theta states – Alpha is dreaming; Theta is anesthesia or shock. I'll link with her brain waves, get on the same frequency, but I've got my mental wall reinforced. I'm have no desire to plug directly into her drugged and deviant consciousness

Here we go. Roll tape.

"Feel a warm wave of relaxation flow slowly over your entire body, from your toes all the way to your head. With each breath, you enter a deeper state of relaxation, more relaxed and at ease than ever before."

Her rapid eye movements are less rapid; her breathing deeper. It's part technique, part drugs.

BURL BARER

The tape plays, and every ten seconds I verbally encourage progressive relaxation. Soon, I'm adding references to safety, trust, and candor. Word by word, phrase by phrase, I'm creating a mental world where she is so safe, comfortable, and open that she'll say whatever crosses her mind.

Loni, fascinated, stares.

Time to take risk number one.

"You are so clever, " I intone softly, "yes, you are so very, very clever."

Pause.

"You are the most clever woman, especially when it comes to men."

I'm bathing each word in thick syrup of soothing resonance.

A slight smile pulls at her thick, leathery lips.

"And you're proud of your accomplishments, and here, where it's perfectly safe, you express yourself freely. You have complete freedom to say whatever you please, however you please. Whatever   you   say   is...perfect."

Keep your fingers crossed. I'm going for it.

"The Tapioca pudding was brilliant...you were so clever with that pudding..."

No response

"It must have been fun watching him eat himself to death. Did he die soon enough, or did he last too long?"

She smiles.

I repeat the question, matching the first time's intonation perfectly. It sounds more like internal replay than outside persistence.

"He took too long to die," she replies effortlessly, her voice a soft conspiratorial whisper.

My heart about stops, and, if you'll pardon the cliché, my skin crawls. I can't lose it now, must stay relaxed and in tune.

"But you got off..." I prompt.

"Yes...I got off when he died, and got off watching him die."

Loni gasps, then covers her mouth with a needle marked hand.

"You're so good. You're so good...you got away clean. Smart to hire a Jew."

"Jew lawyers are best," she replies slowly, "even the Klan hires Jew lawyers."

She finds this amusing and almost laughs. I'm not pressing this mental button again for a while. I don't want excessive jocularity disrupting the hypnotic state. The seductive aural atmosphere

144

envelops her, subtly offering additional relaxation cues every ten to fifteen seconds.

"Tibbit was a tough old bird..." I begin again.

"A stupid drunk..." she slurs.

"You did your best to drown him..."

"Bastard hit me..."

"But you tried..." I say it as praise.

"Held him down best I could, just too tough..."

"The insulin injection worked perfectly, didn't it?"

"Killed him dead as nails. Brain death."

"Smart. Very Smart. You are the best."

She smiles.

Loni is chalk-faced.

I'm going for details.

"And what about that Jake, isn't he somethin'?"

She says nothing. Perhaps she's going too deep, drifting into unconsciousness.

"Dickhead," she rasps, "dickhead Jake. I like his wife."

Not exactly an incriminating statement, so I may have to press her.

"Of course all he wanted was..." I leave it hanging.

"Boy's butts and blowjobs," slurs Violet, "...and money, he always liked money."

Maybe Richard's right about Jake.

"Richard must have been a challenge..."

She stirs, massive bulk rippling under the bedcovers.

"Crazy little shit. Retard. No one listens to him."

"You're right. No one ever listens to Richard."

I allow her to drift a bit before broaching a new topic.

"All the money. What did you do with all the money?"

Silence. Maybe the question's too complex, considering the plentitude of husbands and diversity of raided assets.

Let's get specific.

"The insurance money from Tibbit. What did you do with it?"

"Spent some. Partied..." her voice is weaker now, "Helped my son, Derek...." I can hardly hear her. "... help....Phineas."

She snores.

Jesus.

Phineas.

I look at Loni and Loni looks at me.

Realizing I've been holding my breath, I loose a long exhale. I need a smoke. Pressing video recorder's stop button, I motion to Loni, and she joins me outside while the white noise tape takes Violet to deeper levels of serenity.

"Holy shit," says Loni, "I didn't know you were a fuckin' hypnotist."

"Yeah, well, I can also do a razor blade edit on quarter inch audio tape that would leave a digital-dependent recording engineer drop-jawed in awe." I can't believe I said that. It's true, but Loni couldn't care less.

"You're weird."

"Me?" I look at her. "In that bed is a serial killer, and you think *I'm* weird?"

"Yeah, but she's old, ugly, and got brain cancer, so ya gotta expect problems."

I flick ash on the ground.

"Loni, just so you'll know, that woman murdered several innocent people. She did it coldly, with full knowledge of what she was doing, and she did it without the slightest trace of regret --you heard that yourself. Even dying of brain cancer, she delights in her own evil."

Loni thinks it over, takes a deep drag off her Doral, and shudders.

"Sick fuckin' bitch," she states flatly, "and she looks like Jabba the Hut."

"You got it, princess. She's evil and she'll be evil 'till the day she dies."

"And burn in hell for it, too, I guess," adds Loni softly, " I mean, if you believe in that stuff, you know, heaven and hell and life after death."

There's a distant sadness in Loni's eyes, and it's her own life that has her worried.

"Loni, you have a good heart, and you're doing the best you can with what you've got."

"I'm a bitch and a whore," she says, but she smiles while she says it, "and I don't know if there's bitches and whores in heaven, but I never killed anybody. I mean, I may be killing myself, but..."

She stares at her Doral's glowing tip, her eyes wet with rising tears. Spare me. Damn. I'm such a softie.

So, here we are. The psychic/author/private eye and the needle-marked hooker holding each other close while a multiple

146

murderess snores in drugged repose beyond the trailer door.

Loni's tears, warm and wet, roll down the side of my neck. While I press her against me, I look at the cabin.

The front door is padlocked.

I'll get past that easy enough.

Loni's still holding me as if her life depends on it, but I'm thinking about Phineas. When Loni first exclaimed the name, I quickly discounted the immediate twinge of fearful significance. Once inside the cabin, I'll know for sure. What if I'm right? What the hell will I do then?

Loni eases herself off me, wipes her dribbling nose on the back of her hand, and composes herself.

"You're okay," she states, feigning more emotional strength than she manifests, "weird, but okay. In fact, if you want, I'll give you head and not charge you for it. I mean, the trailer has a bedroom if you'd like that. Wanna?"

I'm speechless.

"Ya know," she says off handedly, "it might help you relax."

I wipe a tear from her cheek with my thumb.

"It's the thought that counts, Loni, and I'll always remember you made the offer. Maybe I'll take you up on it sometime, but right now I've got work to do."

I assure you that "sometime" does not exist on my event planner.

"You gonna get her to say more shit?"

"No, I'm going into the cabin and look around."

"It's locked up tight. Always is," she insist worriedly, "I've never, ever, seen it unlocked...except one time when he had me in there. You can't just bust in 'cause he'll know and..."

"Easy, take it easy. I'm not gonna bust anything. He'll never know anyone was in there. Trust me." I make that last statement as an absolute imperative, because it is.

She looks at me as if she's evaluating a scientific formula or discerning the relative quality of a new batch of dope.

"Okay," she says evenly, "I'll trust you. Hell, I *hugged* you for God's sake. That must mean something 'cause I never really hug anybody the way I hugged you, except maybe my husband when he wasn't hittin' me.."

She goes back inside; I prepare for simple breaking and entering.

Padlocks only keep out honest people. Honestly, there's nothing stopping me. Yes, I pick locks with the professional expertise of Lawrence Block's beloved mystery hero, Bernie Rhodenbarr. That's me, *The Burglar who hugged a Hooker.*

It's strange the things one thinks about while preparing a burglary, especially if I'm the one thinking. Any normal guy would process Violet's disturbing confession, the implications of Phineas, or the possible duplicity of Jake Livesay and Derek Bane Faron. Not being that normal guy, I'm thinking about Block's *The Burglar who admired Mercedes McCambridge.*

Purchased at Fan Night, I didn't crack the cover 'till the ninety-minute flight back to Walla Walla. Larry's best yet, it's even better than *The Burglar who Played Bar Mitzvahs*, or *The Burglar who Sampled Scampi.* The delightful plot has Bernie coerced into stealing rare out-take film footage originally shot for Orson Welles' classic "Touch of Evil" from a film collector obsessed with actress Mercedes McCambridge. Our hero discovers an entire sub-culture centered on McCambridge's performance as a pot-smoking S&M biker chick. As a leather-clad gang leader, McCambridge looked more Green Lantern than McFeeley's. She's the same actress that did the demon's voice in *The Exorcist* and had to sue Warner Bros. for credit.

One other reason you'd never find Mercedes McCambridge at McFeely's is that she's a recovering alcoholic and former honorary chair of the National Committee for Education on Alcoholism. Amazing how I remember this stuff but can't remember to buy Friskies. As for Ms McCambridge, her 1971 statement about alcoholic women is forever embedded in my long-term memory bank:

"We alcoholic women are on the best-dressed list, the most-admired list year after year, we are the social butterflies, the wittier darlings of the `in' group. We hold office, we sit as judges, we have large families, we teach Sunday school, we offer you coffee, tea, or milk on an airplane, and we administer vital sera into your veins."

Well, alcoholic Loni administered vital sera into Violet's veins, that's for sure.

Wait a second. What was it Loni said?

"I've never, ever, seen it unlocked…"

Uh-oh.

I stop short of insertion for the second time in two days. Bad joke, okay, but my hearts pounding like the drums in Max Steiner's score for the original *King Kong*. I ease my hand away, and the little wire trembles between my fingers.

Whew.

Any fool stupid enough to pick this baby is gonna get his head blown off – the padlock's wired to an explosive charge.

Prudent.

Obviously, our sly cabin dweller doesn't diffuse this device each time he enters or exits, and I bet he doesn't crawl through a window, either.

A cleverly disguised back entrance, unwired and easily violated, leads me in via a cluttered closet.

The cabin's layout is exactly as Richard described it: one big room with everything in it. It's been fixed up since Richard's time. No doubt the insurance money and/or ongoing death benefits paid for the big screen television, digital satellite receiver, fancy stereo, laser disk player, VCR, and one hell of a fancy computer set-up. The bed's nightstand features a few "Spotlight" newsletters, and a lovingly displayed scrapbook.

Could it be newspaper clippings saved for gloating purposes?

No such luck. The scrapbook contains photos and memorabilia from the old days of Northwest Championship Wrestling – Instamatic snapshots taken ringside and "backstage." Unlike Randy's memory book, the photo quality remains consistently poor. Faron never took a photography course. Here's one of Lightning Rod Sullivan looking twenty years younger and several buff guys with arms around arena rats. One has her tongue lolling out of her mouth. It's huge. Hello, Rikki. In addition to the fading photos, there are schedules for "upcoming NWA matches," circa 1970's, and an original, authentic, AWA booking sheet autographed by Lightning Rod Sullivan and other notables of the decade.

The cabin's furniture is *Elvis in Las Vegas*, but the décor is one hundred percent professional wrestling. Pullout posters from WWF magazines line the walls, and shelves display an astonishing collection of WWF action figures. He's got them all. Big Boss Man, Papa Shango, the Mountie, Nasty Boys, Bushwhackers, Hawk, Animal, Ted DeBiasi, Hulk Hogan, Bret Hart, Jimmi "Superfly" Snuka, Yokozuna, Lex Luger...

Luger.

Where's the trunk?

There it is. And yes, it has laundry on top of it.

Move the laundry. Try the lid.

Not even locked.

Bingo. It's open.

Big surprise: old wrestling magazines spanning decades and federations, embracing every fatboy, flyer, and colorful character in squared circle history. Here's one with Luna Vashon on the cover. What a sweetheart. Her dad or uncle is Mad Dog Maurice Vashon. Like father like daughter. She shaves half her head, draws purple lines on her face, and wears a spiked collar. My kind of woman.

Okay. I'm nervous. The bulbous half-dead bitch smacked out in the trailer didn't exactly put me at ease with her sweet memories of premeditated murder, and that wired padlock gave me a definite adrenaline rush.

I remove the magazines, carefully placing them in perfect order on the floor so I can put them back exactly as I found them.

The trunk has an obviously false plywood bottom with a convenient finger hole for easy removal.

Insert finger; lift plywood.

My, my, my. It's absolutely empty.

I repack the trunk, move to the computer, and boot it up. When it requests my password, I type "Phineas."

Rejected, I try the alternate spelling. That's not it either.

Let's attempt something subtle.

"num25."

Bingo. I'm in. Sometimes I amaze even myself.

His hard drive holds mostly games, Internet access, and Word documents. A quick click on the Internet icon triggers automatic log-on. Only a man who lives alone uses automatic log-on.

His "favorite" web sites, from what I can tell, are hard-core porno – both gay and straight — and ultra far-right politics. These sites, sadly, I can't access because he's linked directly to the "members oniy" page — the secret access code provided by the site administrator, not the customer. Reading his private email is absurdly easy, if not unethical. How vulnerable are the tents of Jacob. Faron's cyberpals use anonymous remailers and prefer "Ovrlrd11," "TopCat," and "Drgn3K" to real names.

As for content, here's a sample:

"The USA will be in chaos. No phones, no mail, no services, and no roads. The public will be fed up, and once civil authority completely breaks down, they will turn to us in droves."

I'm so sure. What a load of crap.

HEADLOCK

I lean back, stretch, and think things over.

First of all, there's no law against reading or believing this bullshit. Second, I've found absolutely nothing in here more exciting than a trunk load of wrestling magazines. I also haven't found the Luger, and it's increasingly obvious that I've been lured into overstepping this case's original parameters: find out if it's over, and who all was involved.

It's obviously not over with Violet still breathing and Jake sweating bullets. Nope, not over at all. As for who was involved, the old lady's whispered confession, illegally obtained and inadmissible as evidence, confirms most of Richard's so-called delusions.

Before copying the computer's contents onto disk, I scroll through the documents folder. There's one big file named "Manual." Maybe it explains how to repair a Monte Carlo.

Nope. There are fourteen parts, and only one remotely concerned with Chevrolets. The manual includes instructions on converting legal guns into fully automatic weaponry; "legalizing" stolen cars, forging money orders and cashier's checks; buying military equipment, gas masks, surveillance and explosive devices; and monitoring local and federal law enforcement agencies' radio traffic.

Extremists.

For some it's a fantasy, for others it's a lifestyle. For both, it's some sort of mental illness.

In the past thirty years, dozens of these movements have built separatist compounds, settlements and training grounds in the United States. Some are now defunct, while others still operate. Many adhere to far-right and white supremacist ideologies, such as the Christian Identity religion, and have stockpiled weapons. Others are religious sects of a less aggressive nature.

Some analysts believe these groups reflect the increasing alienation, fear and hostility in America that have driven them to isolate themselves from society and government. Since when do armed robbery, counterfeiting, and bombing qualify as isolation?

While the data transfers, I check out his video tape collection. Predictably, there's plenty of porno and action movies, plus a few with hand written labels.

Well, well, well. Between two hard-core classics, here's one called "Phineas on TV."

Let's get a look at this Phineas guy.

Into the VCR it goes.

Roll tape.

I'd know those graphics anywhere — "Hot Story," America's most garish and aggressive tabloid television program. Gripping news footage of the smoking rubble and bloody victims of the Oklahoma City bombing fills the screen while the announcer informs us that today's investigate report concerns hate groups "at war with America."

The camera cuts to the hard-bitten features of an unsavory character locked behind bars. Serving a thirty-nine year sentence for armed robbery, this unlovable chap is also identified as a proud member of a violent, radical group calling itself "The Priesthood."

The show's host looks more like a GQ model than a trained broadcast journalist, but his voice is perfect.

"I understand," prompts our well-dressed MC, "you consider to what happened in Oklahoma City to be killing but not murder."

The special guest thug nods in thoughtful agreement, then gives his assured response.

"Absolutely. The only thing that would make it murder is if we weren't at war against an elite group behind the scenes who are manipulating us into a one-world government."

How many worlds does this nut think we have? Unless he's got that spare planet in his pocket, one world is all we've got.

"Concerning this so-called elite group," probes our clean-cut anchor man, "do you have any idea…"

"Who they are? Of course. I would say 90 to 95 percent — are Jews."

The program cuts to film footage from surveillance cameras showing masked gunmen, supposedly of The Priesthood, robbing a bank. With this on-screen, the MC's voice-over tells us the characteristics common to these criminals and other similar groups are "hatred of the federal government and fear of a united world – a world in which Blacks, Jews, and other minorities are treated as equals."

In case you're wondering where these thugs come from, "Hot Story" is pleased to provide their special guest's glorious family history – he was raised a "fundamentalist Christian" by his preacher parents.

I bet mom and dad were delighted to see their son on national television.

His "political awakening," as he puts it, began in the 1960s when he joined various conservative political organizations, moved to the radical ultra-conservative edge, formed a tax protest group, quickly progressed to counterfeiting, then graduated to robbing banks. Not exactly a logical progression, but a progression none-the-less.

"This man is the offspring of not one, but two, ministers of the Gospel," remarks Mr. GQ with appropriate disgust, "how in the world did you get from there to here?"

He expects a sensible answer?

"By very simply analyzing the situation and realizing that we are at war," states the right-wing poster-child "at war with the Jews, Niggers, Catholics, Mexicans, and anyone who wants to take America away from white Protestant Christians and turn it over to the United Nations. Make no mistake, this is war," the camera moves in for an effective close-up, "and any military man or sincere clergyman will tell you that God uses war to cleanse the earth from wickedness. When it's time for a war, God allows certain evils to be exterminated, and I'm here to tell you it's a privilege to engage in God's wars."

I thought he was here to serve thirty-nine years.

"You feel good about it then," says GQ, restating the obvious.

"Absolutely. The righteous are called by God's law to exercise holy violence against the wicked, thereby manifesting God's wrath."

Click.

Enough.

Do these criminals have agents?

The Priesthood.

Phineas.

God made with him an everlasting covenant of peace, and bestowed priesthood upon his descendents.

I'll be damned.

Fighting Missionaries.

The Phineas Priesthood must have forgot the "covenant of peace" line. They also forgot Phineas is Jewish.

I fast-forward the tape, checking the production credits for familiar names.

"At War with America." Producer: Chet Rogers.

I rewind the tape, eject it, and return the video to its place of ill-deserved reverence between *Cynthia Sucks Seattle,* and

153

Backdoor Big Boys.

All document files and correspondence are successfully copied. I must be missing something. After all, Derek Bane Faron wired his front door with explosives, for God's sake.

I sit down at Faron's table and close my eyes. I'm just going to clear my mind and ask for a hint, that's all, just a hint.

All I get is wrestling, wrestling, and more wrestling.

I'm having a real Milton Layden Moment – I'm feeling hostile towards Richard because he hasn't been up front with me. What the hell does he mean his life was normal once? When? Damned if it sounds normal to me – jail breaks, knowing gangsters, being on a first name basis with every two-faced snitch in town.

Perhaps Richard hasn't been honest with me, and maybe he's formulated sufficient justifications for his prevarication.

I'm really getting irked and I know it. I'm moving from Milton Layden to Sissela Bok.

Sissela Bok.

Isn't that a cool name? She writes books about lying, smartly observing that all deceptive messages involve self-deception.

Lie: an intentionally deceptive message in the form of a statement.

Richard's made many statements, and right now I'm not so sure I trust their unvarnished veracity.

I flip out the cellular. No, I'm not calling Dr. Laura or Sissela Bok.

"You awake, Richard? Well, you are now. Listen, I'm sittin' here in the cabin. Yes, *that* cabin. I had a friendly little chat with a massive blob of blubber that admits killing your father. In fact, I got the admission in living color on video tape."

Richard is momentarily speechless, and I don't wait for a response.

"You were right, but let's hope you're not dead right. You hired me to find out if it was over and who was involved. I can tell you right now who all was involved: your step-mom, probably Jake, and the snitch who turns out to be Violet's son. Got that? Either Jake or the snitch set up for Indians and that other jerk to harass you exactly as you suspected. As for the kid shot in the park, I can't say for sure, but I bet you're right about that too- he wouldn't go through with it so he was offed rather than run the risk of the kid talking."

"That's what I told you in the first place."

"I know you did Richard, and you've spent fifteen years fantasizing about paybacks – the great American myth of Redemptive Violence. You knew they wanted you to step over the line, but you refused. Of course, if you could find someone else to step over the line for you..."

"Hey," he interrupts, "I told you the risks right up front. Hell, you got it on tape. I warned you very early on."

That's true. He's warned me repeatedly, even at that first conversation in the Red Apple.

"But you didn't say a damn word about the Phineas Priesthood."

"The Phineas Priesthood? What the hell is that, for God's sake? I've got my own ideas about religion, but whatever snitch is into, I don't know and I don't care. Besides, I haven't even seen that little bastard since before the bank robbery. You gotta understand why I called you. I mean, it all was there at the same time."

"What was where?"

"Your picture, the news story, the conversation I had with my wife..."

"You're losing me here, Richard. Get clear. Be specific before someone burns a cross on my lawn."

"Okay. Lynette and I were talkin' about the situation – me just pacing around wonderin' – and then we saw the story about the bank robbery in Spokane. Well, the way that robbery came down was almost identical to the one in Walla Walla. It couldn't be a coincidence. I mean, I wouldn't say that the same guy did both, but I bet he knows who did or is connected in some way, right? Well, Lynette's holding the newspaper up reading it, okay, and there's your face showing through the robbery story."

I'm dumbstruck.

"You mean to tell me that if the Beef Princess's picture and mine had swapped positions on the page, you would have called her instead?"

"No," he explains wearily, "It was ...now, this may sound stupid, but he took it as a sign. I mean, there you were showing right through the page. I had just said to Lynette that the bank robbery in Spokane is probably connected somehow to the snitch, and we was holding up the page, ya know, sorta toward light there in the kitchen, and your face just sort of.... well... we turned it over, read the story, and that's when she said to call you. You looked honest, had the credentials."

"Do you realize, Richard, that had you waited just a while longer, it really would have been over?"

Silence.

"Richard?"

"I'm here, I just don't understand what you mean."

"It's not about your dad's murder; it's not about the kid in the park, or the damn big Indians."

"Of course it is." He insists.

Agitated, I'm pacing around the cabin.

"No, it isn't," I counter," and I'll tell you why. You never had one shred of evidence that would stand up in court, and you said yourself that she took care of your credibility – you don't have a gram, let alone an ounce. Sure, had you crossed the line, you'd be in some institution or dead. You didn't, but I did. I'm sure Jake is wetting his pants waiting for me to get back, and I can't wait to hear what's he's got on his mind."

"I still don't get it."

"For God's sake Richard, get a clue. There's a five-year statute of limitations on bank robbery. The time is almost up. No one has ever been charged – hell, no one has even been investigated. You couldn't go to the authorities, but I can. That puts me either in deep shit or a position of power – hard to tell."

"Jeff, I paid you and I warned you, and I've opened up more to you than anyone except maybe my wife, okay?"

Okay.

"Yes, Richard, I know. I just needed to get this off my chest, and to talk, okay?"

Jesus, I'm starting to sound like him.

"I understand, pal," he says, and he means it.

"Derek Faron isn't just connected to that bank job in Spokane," I elaborate, "he's also connected somehow to a bunch of damn whacko's. I'm liable to be in hot water with every far-right neo-Nazi from Walla Walla to..."

Uh-oh.

To where?

I grab Faron's wrestling scrapbook and flip through the pages.

Damn.

"Jeff, you there?

"Yeah, I'm here Richard. Uh, listen...you know that newspaper feature about Spokane, remember how it also mentioned Tulsa and Shreveport?"

"I guess. So?"

"The FBI and the BATF seldom consults old AWA booking sheets."

"AWA? What you talkin' about?"

"I just found the missing link, Richard. You better be sittin' down, cause this will rock your socks – Derek Bane Faron is more than mildly affiliated, he's the chief executive planner of domestic terrorists' criminal itinerary. He's using an old AWA booking sheet as a template, for God's sake. I can tell you which cities are next and in which order."

He also has an old NWA schedule. If they hit Spokane first, they're starting mid-schedule. Hell, Yakima is having a little counterfeiting problem right now, as a matter of fact."

"Hmmph."

What kind of response is that?

"Richard?"

He's still there; I hear the Zippo click.

"Jeff, you gotta look at it from my point of view. I've been seething inside for years. They murdered my father, you understand, and that eats me alive inside. I want to kill 'em, all right, but I can't do that, or even try it because they want that. I thought that – now, no one says this makes sense – that you could put my mind at ease by proving, at least to me, that I'm not just some crazy paranoid retard with a damn head injury, okay? "

I told you before, guys like Richard seek vindication or cash.

"I honestly had no idea that the bitch was alive, that Derek or Bane or whatever he calls himself was the son of the bitch, or that this bank robbery business was so..."

"Genre-bending?" God, I'm thinking out loud.

"What?"

"This started out a mystery, Richard, but it's becoming a damn thriller. Do I look like Dean Koontz?"

"Who?"

"Oh, never mind. I'm ranting. I do that, okay?"

"No problem."

I put the scrapbook back where I found it.

"Richard, when I was over at your place last night, you broadcasted, didn't you?"

"Yeah," he admits, "just one image. Did you get it?"

"Tell me exactly what you sent."

"An explosion, the kind used in the bank robbery and in Spokane."

"Nothing about a power company?"

"You've asked me that before."

Faron's phone rings and I about crap.

"Jesus, Richard, Faron's phone's ringing. Call ya later."

I sit down and stare at the black PhoneMate. The ringing stops and the answering machine kicks in.

"Talk to me," snaps Faron's voice, then the tone.

"Listen up. That prick Reynolds is back. He was seen talkin' to that babe with the big tits..."

Tony Fennelly?

"...the drug slut you've got workin' up there last night at the Pastime. That may not mean shit, but we can't take chances. I'm supposed to meet with him when he gets back. I think he's trouble, but we got that covered, don't we?"

What the hell does he mean by that comment?

"I'll see where his head's at. As for her, maybe she's shot up one too many times, you think?"

Click.

Dickhead.

Swell.

Oh, what the hell.

I pick up Faron's phone and punch star-69.

"The last number to call your line was...509-382-..."

A 382 prefix means Dayton, Washington. It would take Dickhead two hours or more to get here if he left right this minute, and he's not coming here at all, so to hell with him. What's he doing in Dayton? There's not much there except some excellent Queen Anne, Italianate, and Gothic architecture. During Dayton's peak period, businessmen and farmers built large and impressive homes.

I always liked Dayton — *Dorsey's Café* served the best hotcakes in Eastern Washington. The town, named after founder Jesse Day, was a flourishing community until the smallpox epidemic of 1881. So frightened were people that no one was allowed to enter or leave town, and all mail and supplies were left at the edge of town. If that weren't bad enough, the following year was the "great fire" and the "great flood" – while the city was engulfed in flames, they opened the local mill's water raceway to flood the streets. Gone were the two newspapers, seven churches, flour mills, lumber mills, city hall, telegraph company, and the brass band's musical instruments.

Things change. Each town has its time, each nation its Prophet, every cause its Priesthood.

I re-play and erase the message – no need for Faron to ever hear it.

I take several quick digital pictures of the AWA and NWA schedules, collect the computer disk, and make sure everything is exactly as I found it.

Damn. I know there's something eluding me. I close my eyes.

"Give me something, here," I plead aloud, and get nothing but wrestlers.

If you keep getting the same answer to the same question, and it's not the answer you want, what's the answer you expect?

Well, let's assume these wrestlers are the answer.

Which wrestler?

Directly across from me is a matted and framed poster of the Ultimate Warrior.

"This is war..."

The wall safe is traditionally behind the Renoir. Faron has no Renoir.

Down comes the Warrior. Behind the muscular madman is an unguarded cubbyhole – you don't need a safe when your front door is a bomb — crammed with bag after bag of white powder. I don't think it's CoffeMate or Oxydol.

Cop dope?

Could be, and plenty of it. I'm no expert on so-called street value, but it must be a king's ransom – a small Balkan king, but a king, nonetheless.

I'm not touching this stuff, no way. The Ultimate Warrior re-hung in his place of honor, I nose around one last time and pull open the nightstand drawer.

Hello — the Luger, the knives, *The Turner Diaries,* and a motel edition Bible. Hey, I'm not Richard Diamond, okay? Besides, everything is always in the last place you look.

Holding the Luger in a handkerchief, I check it out. It's loaded. Hmmm. If I take it, Faron will absolutely know his space was violated. Tempting, though.

What would you do? Not exactly a moral conundrum, but a tactical one.

Exiting the cabin, I return to the trailer via the back way. As I approach, I notice smooth dirt by one panel of trailer skirting.

I should be a detective. The dirt is smooth, I surmise, because the panel swivels out like a hatch, scraping the ground.

What was it ol' Violet told Loni?

"We're sittin' on the shit."

Well, you can't be a private eye without getting your hands dirty and your knees too. Flashlight in hand, I crawl under the trailer.

Not a pretty sight. Amid the obligatory spider webs are enough explosives to make this mountain a molehill, cases of ammunition, a metal suitcase, and leaflets bound by the hundreds. They guy is obviously into bulk buying. I grab the suitcase and snag a sample flyer before crawling back out.

So, here I am, standing behind the trailer, reading this stupid pamphlet. The front cover proclaims: "Race War Coming: Are U Ready?" The illustration shows ape-like and rat-like creatures running through the streets. The rats wear Yarmulkes and prayer shawls; the apes have boom boxes and tennis shoes.

The inside text is a rant against Jews, Blacks, Catholics, and our fine Federal Government. In essence, an incitement of racism, Anti-Semitism, and sins of social disruption – and they link it all to the beloved Bible. There should be laws against Spiritual Malpractice: using Sacred Texts for immoral purposes.

The first sin mentioned in Genesis is incitement to commit wrongdoing. You know the story: Eve and the serpent. The little creature does a swell sales job. His idea, not hers.

That's no excuse. Saying "I was only following orders," or, "it was his idea in the first place," is not adequate defense. In fact, so heinous is incitement to wrongdoing, the *Mishna* states that a person can't repent for it. I doubt the pamphlet's author gives a cartoon rat's ass about the *Mishna*.

Disgusted, I shut the pamphlet and flip it over. The back panel features another cartoon – a guy made of electricity, sort of like Ready Kilowatt, wearing a hard hat with "WP" on it.

White Power.

There's my Power Company and elusive electrician. On either side of him are stylized lightning bolts — the logo is that of Hitler's *SS*.

Nazis. I really hate those guys, I really do.

As for the suitcase, it has a little swivel combination lock. If Faron is consistent, the combination should be 2578 – Numbers 25:7-8.

God, I'm brilliant. Open Sesame.

Loot, and plenty of it. I'd say tens of thousands in twenties, fifties, and hundreds.

Now, obviously this isn't my money. I'm willing to wager that it isn't Faron's either. Bank loot from Spokane? Maybe, maybe not. Counterfeit? Could be.

Who cares?

For the sake of argument, let's say I'm putting it in protective custody.

I haul everything back to the Volvo, put the suitcase in the wayback, and then return to the trailer. The big old bitch is out cold; Loni watches *Jerry Springer.*

"Everything okay?" asks Loni nervously, "I was kinda worried. I think this place has rats or something. There's creatures crawling around down there," she says pointing at the floor, "you didn't fuck anything up, did you?"

I hope not.

"No. I'm not that kind of guy. That was I crawling under the trailer..."

"An eye? Yuck!"

"Me, me, me," I explain helpfully, "it was *me* down there, that's why *I* look a bit dirty."

She scrutinizes my appearance.

"Naw, you're on of those guys that looks clean-cut no matter what."

Let's hope that's a compliment.

"Listen Loni, if anyone for whatever reason – Faron, for example, mentions you and me being together last night, it's simply because I hired you for sex."

"Was it good for you?" She asks, showing me the gaps between her incisors.

"Yeah, I'm still drained. You know nothing about me, what I do for a living, or anything like that. Okay?"

"Okay. Besides, I don't know much except you're kinda stupid for a private eye, but cute in a clean-cut sort of way."

"I'm not stupid, Loni, I'm just...inexperienced. Now, has your scumbag employer ever crawled around under this place like I did?"

Her brow furrows as if she's thinking. It may be learned behavior.

"Not when I'm around," she says, "I mean, today was the first time I ever heard weird shit going on down there, ya know?"

An outburst of on screen inter-familial violence on *Springer* captures my attention. Some guy in a tank top is wailing away on a woman with hair even bigger than Verna's.

"Is this what you do all day, watch *Jerry Springer* while the lady lies there?"

My question comes off unintentionally harsh, and she shoots me a lethal look.

"I happen to be a trained professional," objects Loni.

Professional what? Whore? Damn. I should be ashamed. If that's what she chooses to do with her life, I'm not going to judge her.

"I keep her clean too," she elaborates defensively, "you want responsibility for her bed pan, do ya? This job isn't as easy at it looks."

Her eyes reflexively dart towards the cache of hypodermic needles.

"You stay clean while you work?"

She stands hands on hips, glaring.

"Damn straight! What kind of professional caregiver would shoot-up on the job? You must think I'm a real dip-shit," her voice rises angrily, "and what the fuck are you doing anyway? Snoopin' around, causin' trouble, I'm liable to be fired or killed or get the shit kicked out of me if he finds out..."

Swell. Erratic mood swings are bundled free with every addict's mental hardware.

"I'll show you exactly what I'm doing," I interrupt while pulling two crisp one hundred-dollar bills from my wallet, "I'm giving you money..."

Her anger evaporates into the distant mists of history.

"...and maybe I'll take you up on that head-job some other time. Just remember you offered, okay?"

"Okey-dokey," Loni agrees happily, "when ya comin' back? I'll chew gum for exercise till ya' get here." She laughs uproariously at her juvenile joke, her mood elevated by the influx of cash.

"There a phone here?" I ask.

"Yeah," she says, pointing to the white wall phone, "so I can call a hospital or ambulance if she really takes a downturn. He don't like me yakkin' to my friends on it, though."

'He calls you on it, does he?'

She scratches her rear with unladylike enthusiasm.

"Yeah, sometimes he calls and tells me when he's on his way, or calls to check in."

"Know the number?"

"Sure, it's on it. Unlisted, but the number is on the phone."

It's on it all right. I copy down the number, then write my cell phone number on a piece of scratch paper and press it firmly in the palm of her hand.

"The minute his car pulls in, or when you know he's on his way, call this number and a ride will be on its way. I'll arrange it. Make sure you tell him that you have a ride picking you up over by the cemetery, but for God's sake don't mention my name. That's for your own protection. Whatever you do, don't let him offer to give you a ride to Weston."

I'm not about to have her vanish forever somewhere between Faron's lot and the Weston intersection.

I collect the remainder of my gear, and as I'm heading for the door, Loni raises another topic.

" Wait, I wanna tell ya something. You know Verna was making rude jokes about my husband, right? Well, she thinks he doesn't get out for eight years. Well, he gets out real soon, and I mean any day. In fact, I'm sorta expecting maybe even... well..."

"Well, what, Loni?"

"He's not gonna be in more trouble right away because of you and that Richard and all, is he?"

So, the big Indian's coming back. Return of the native. One more chip in the cookie, one more joker in the deck. This could be fun.

"Never fear, Loni. None of this reflects poorly on your dear hubby. In fact, we may be able to put him to good use."

On my way back down the mountain, I deem my behavior rather amusing. One moment I'm mentally spouting Talmudic ethical/moral observations, the next I'm violating numerous legal ordinances. A private eye license doesn't authorize committing burglary, hypnotizing drugged up murder suspects, nor cruising down the highway with a small fortune in someone else's loot sliding around in the wayback.

I don't require authorization, only justification. Yep, we don't need no stinkin' authorization.

Look at it this way: Richard hired me. Richard believed people were plotting against him. Violating Derek Bane Faron's privacy and confidentiality – his personal email correspondence now resides in my black bag – validated Tibbit's suspicions. This puts me in an entirely different moral/ethical arena. According to Jewish law, and I can provide documentation if you insist: if you know that people are plotting against someone, you have an obligation to divulge any and all information, even if that information was initially confidential. This comes under the prohibition of standing by while a brother's blood is spilled. Of course, how much and how immediate the harm comes into play when experts offer their opinions. As there are no experts in the Volvo, my justifications will suffice.

The drive home winds me down to Weston, on to the main highway, through Milton-Freewater, Oregon, and back into Walla Walla. Once you hit the city, the highway becomes plain old 9th Street. At the corner of 9th and Plaza Way, I hang a right towards Dairy Queen. I'm positive a Peanut Buster Parfait has been communing psychically with me for the past ten miles.

Just my imagination, as the Temptations would sing, running away with me. The DQ is closed for remodeling. I turn left at the intersection, drive past the far end of the Southeastern Washington Fairgrounds, and through a pleasant residential area. In the rear view mirror, I see a blue cop car. On any other day, I wouldn't give it a thought. This isn't any other day. It follows me all the way home, staying about a half-block behind.

I pull into the driveway, and I'm about to yank that suitcase out and get it in the house when the squad car arrives.

VII

Two plainclothes cops, one dog. I'd know the one cop anywhere – THC.

"Hi Carter," I call out cheerily, "have I a got a tail light out or something."

He ignores the question. After all, his car is emblazoned with a Narcotics Detection Team logo, not Traffic Safety Patrol.

"Need to talk with you for a minute," he intones seriously. His affably smiling partner is about a quarter inch above minimum height requirement, and looks vaguely familiar.

"Sure, I'm in a public spirited mood, what can I do for you?"

Leaning against the Volvo, I fish out an Old Gold, and try to recall where I've seen the little guy before.

"We notice you've been spending time with Loni the redheaded hooker. Isn't she a bit out of your usual social circle?"

"I'm broadening my horizons, so to speak," I offer pleasantly, "she's a lovely lady with a unique perspective on contemporary social issues."

He fakes a smile and looks at the pavement.

"We have pictures of you waiting for her by a known dealer's house last night."

"On one of those `uh' sounding streets, right?"

"Bonsella," he affirms, stating the exact address, "glad you admit it. The neighbors are sick and tired of that sort of activity, so we've kept an eye on the place, notified the property owner over in Seattle of what we think the renters are up to, and that sort of thing. We've noticed Loni crashing there lately," he continues, "of course, the welcome mat is always out for her type at a dope house."

"Of course," I'm Mr. Agreeable.

"Well, we watched her get in that wagon of yours," he says gesturing towards the Volvo, "and the two of you took off. We have a nice, clear picture."

"You want me to autograph the photo?"

He looks at me as if I'm scum. I smile.

"Carter, I'm delighted you're documenting my night life, but I don't know either the vocation or avocation of her current land-lord, and it's really none of my business. What's the point?"

He shrugs, puts his hands in his pockets, and attempts look-ing casual. I'm positive he doesn't make these house calls on ev-eryone with whom Loni spends time.

"She's trouble, a drug addict with a notorious history, a hus-band who's a convicted felon, and most of the people she hangs out with are pretty much trash. So, when a respectable citizen such as yourself…"

He glances over at my snob hill home.

"…a man with a nice home, good career, fine family…well, we get *concerned*."

I bet.

He just stares at me. His diminutive partner remains silent, a silly grin on his face.

"Well, I appreciate your concern," I reply, "Actually, I'm using Loni as a character in my new book. What I'm getting from her is plenty of authentic dialogue and some fascinating stories – local lore. And yes, before you ask, your name came up in conver-sation. But like I said, I'm writing fiction."

I got balls, okay?

He tenses and tries to hide it.

We three stand there like actors who've lost our place in the script. I flick ash on the concrete.

THC breaks the silence with an ominous request.

"Mind if my dog sniffs your car?"

"If your dog has a license he can *drive* my car," I enthuse, "Ol' Fido can rub his wet little nose all over the car, the house, the garage, the wife, the kids, the cats…"

THC looks at shrimp.

"Whatch think?"

Shrimp shrugs.

"Even if there are no drugs in there now," THC states flatly, "we could tell if there had been." He says this like a warning, as if he's giving me reason to refuse the canine sniff-fest and thereby incriminate myself.

"Hell, that wouldn't make any difference, Tom. There's noth-ing to smell. If you wanna give the pooch a work-out, go right ahead."

Sure, Loni could have left behind miniscule traces of beloved "cop dope" – dope she says came from THC in the first place – but I'm more concerned about the suitcase full of cash.

Carter walks around the back of the Volvo, looking in the windows.

"Been out of town, have you?"

He notices the suitcase and my black Bugatti bag.

"Yeah, I was in Seattle being famous."

"Uh-huh," he mutters thoughtfully. "Isn't that your Buick out at the airport?'

"Yep. It has a battery problem, or maybe the starter. I'll get AAA to take care of it – of course I'd get faster help calling AA."

He awaits an explanation. Good. I've hooked him.

"I'll just call AA and yell, `my car broke down! I want a drink!' I'll have five recovering alcoholics on their way faster than you can say `I'm a friend of Bill W.' and, " I pause for dramatic emphasis, "not only will I get my car fixed, they'll take me out for coffee!"

There's nothing like a well-delivered punch line to diffuse a potentially dangerous situation. Shrimp chortles, and THC stifles a spontaneous laugh.

"Okay," says Carter, "seriously, if you have a drug problem, I want you to know that you can always call me. I'll be there for you. Anytime."

My skin crawls.

"Thanks, Carter. That's kind of you. Have you made the same offer to Loni?

This irks him. Sometimes I don't know when to keep my mouth shut, okay?

"I suggest you stay away from her. Maybe you're doing as you say – using her for one of your `little mystery stories,'"

Ouch.

"but I'll tell you this and I'll tell you straight – if I bust Loni for dope and you're with her, I'll do what I have to do."

What does he have to do, shoot me?

"That's understandable," I concur, "you've got a job to do."

Again, we all stand there.

"Speaking of Loni," I offer, "she was in a swell cat fight at the Pastime…"

Shrimp spontaneously interrupts.

"Yeah, I saw that one..."

Hell, now I know. He was the guy sitting at the bar when Loni whacked Verna's noggin – the fellow who took his soup with him.

THC looks pained, then approaches me.

He's dangerously close.

"Whatever you're doing, step back. Cool it. You don't know what you're getting into, and you don't want to know. Trust me. Just stay home and write your books, and don't be going places good people don't go – especially not alone, and not at night."

Weird.

"Okay," I say, "and I won't rip my clothes or..."

I've already slept in a graveyard.

He looks at me as if I'm an idiot, a facial expression becoming uncomfortably common.

"C'mon," he motions to shrimp, and they head back towards their car.

"Come back anytime, fellas," I call out, "always nice to see ya."

They're gone.

Whew.

Your respectable citizen drags the fruits of his illegal activities into the house, still thinking about a Peanut Buster Parfait. I think it's the Spanish peanuts – cocktail peanuts, some people call them – cute little things with red skins, that make those parfaits so damn delicious. The hot fudge doesn't hurt either.

Well, no parfait for your hero today. See how my mind works? I'm sitting here with a fortune in confiscated currency spread out on my table, I was just hassled by the city's resident corrupt drug cop, my life may be in serious danger from Dickhead, and I'm obsessing on red skin cocktail peanuts.

Go figure.

Another engine idles outside, and I lift the drapery's edge. It's the mail. I'd requested a little something from the State of Washington after my first meeting with Richard – the Gambling Commission's handbook on punchboards.

It's arrived along with a postcard from China. My daughter is refusing to learn Chinese because she's afraid that by doing so, she'll forget English and she won't understand me when she get's back.

When she gets back.

Someday.

I miss her terribly, never open the door to what was once her bedroom, and pray for her every day.

Ah, the joys of fatherhood.

There's a postscript to the postcard: "Started your new book yet?"

Right. Rub it in.

I haven't written anything beyond proposals since I kissed the kid goodbye.

I toyed half-heartedly with writing more fact crime books, but my agent refused to submit my most recent proposals.

"Too regional, not high-profile enough. Unless you're Ann Rule or O.J.'s lawyer, fact crime is a soft market," he insists, "even if it's a true story, make it fiction."

Moment of truth, folks. I haven't had a book come out since *#10 Drowning Street*, and that was a year ago April. I desperately needed a plot, a victim, a culprit.

You always get what you need, and now I've got Richard, Dickhead, Verna, Faron, and the ever lovin' Phineas Priesthood. Getting what I want is another matter. It's hell writing on spec. I'd love a contract and a deadline.

I told you from the get-go why I agreed to meet Richard Tibbit that first time at the Red Apple, I just didn't tell you how much it mattered.

As for the Washington State Gambling Commission's Rules Manual, I'm a little busy right now, but I'm sure it's fascinating reading.

Loading Faron's correspondence and the digital photos onto my computer, I call Richard.

"Hey, why would Dickhead be in Dayton?"

"Well, maybe he has relatives there."

Duh. Oh.

I grab the Telfax phone book. Sure enough, there's a Livesay in Dayton.

"He knows I'm back, knows I was with Loni last night, and I know he's gonna get hold of me anytime now."

He clears his throat.

"What you want me to do, Jeff?"

"The same thing you've been doing for fifteen years, but don't bother being paranoid, I've got enough jitters for both of us."

Hell, I'm jumpier than a bag full of cats. Call the cops?

Nope.

Richard warned me not to go to the police. Police, of course, is rather a broad term. The current Chief of Police is, to the best of my knowledge, one hundred percent ethical. Sure, he deals with inter-departmental realities, but his concerns are more operational, budgetary, and public relations. Besides, I know exactly where he is everyday between noon and 1pm – home having sex with his wife.

How do I know this? Hey, this is Walla Walla. His wife and mine served together on some PTA Committee a few years ago, and she confided the secret of their joyous union: everyday, ever since the kids were in school, he comes home at noon for hot sex.

It's almost lunchtime. I bet his gun belt's getting tight. Of course, If I break the mood with my allegations, both he and his wife will resent me. Besides, it could just stir things up worse. I could come off as nutty as Richard, and wind up marginalized or a suicide victim in Rooks Park.

Not a good idea.

Let's scan Derek's email for domain names. As I mentioned, the bulk of his cyberbuddies use anonymous remailers, but you never know when you'll find an exception.

Here's one: *topcat@bmi.net*, which I find on a forwarded message from a remailer who carelessly neglected to remove the headers.

"20 @ 10 confirmed"

The server, bmi, is Walla Walla's premier Internet provider. Topcat. TC

Tom Carter?

Oh, this is too tempting.

If I can figure out topcat's password, I can configure my computer to pick up his email.

Dare I?

I dare. I'm not Travis Webb, but he's taught me a few tricks.

Figuring out passwords can be absurdly easy or impossible, depending upon the individual's personality. Some folks select random numbers or letters; others choose names or numbers of inherent significance. Even if I can't figure out his password, there are backdoor methods for unraveling any Internet mystery.

Derek made his easy, but not intentionally. Let's hope topcat does the same.

I log on bmi as myself, start Eudora Pro, then select "options" from the Eudora menu. I change my name to topcat@bmi.net and attempt retrieving mail.

"Please enter your password."

Hmmmm.

I try his badge number, initials, and various combinations of both.

Nope. None work. This may be a waste of time.

Maybe I should call him on the phone and ask for it, that would surprise him.

I type in the last four digits of the police department's non-emergency phone number.

"You have Mail!"

I certainly do.

Someone calling himself "xident" sent a message entitled "Keys to Paradise." It's a very short message: "ready when you are." Then xident adds an intriguing post-script: "one way or another, they stay slaves."

They stay slaves.

Xident isn't hard to decipher, it stands for "Christian Identity" – the malignant form of a theological tumor termed "Anglo/British Israelisim."

In case the term is unfamiliar, allow your favorite private eye to elucidate. I know this stuff inside and out. Why? Because manifestly absurd beliefs fascinate me, and Anglo/British Israelism meets the criteria.

Ready? Here, in a nutshell, is Anglo/British Israelism: British, Americans, and Canadians are the *literal descendants* of the ancient Israelites.

Now, you don't need a degree in anthropology to know that's absurd, but it sure made manifest sense in 1840 to John Wilson, author of "Lectures on our Israelitish Origin," who first proclaimed the British were the actual descendants of God's "chosen people."

If there were ever a doctrine born of ethnocentrism, and ripe for a swift transformation into white supremacist polemic, this was it. The appeal was obvious and instant – as the British Empire ascended, so did this self-exalting doctrine. After all, one look at the Bible lands of the early 1800's confirmed the place with crawling with dark skinned, uncivilized Moslems and Jews under Turkish domination. How could these be God's chosen people when the Almighty had so blatantly blessed the British Empire?

Wilson and his supporters developed the belief that the "Lost

Tribes" of Israel wandered far from the Middle East to Merry Old England.

This hodge-podge of UK exaltation faded from popularity in England when the once great British Empire disbanded. As with many failed domestic products, if found new life in export. In the early years of the 20th century, Charles Parham and John Allen were the main promoters of Anglo/British Israelism in the United States. Parham later went on to found the Pentecostal movement; Allen spread the concept through America's Adventist churches where, only mildly mutated by merger with anti-Catholicism retained from the mid-1800's nativist movement and Irish immigration "threat", it survives with virus-like resilience.

If Great Britain and America have replaced Israel, what about the Jews?

Read Derek's email and you have the malignant answer:

"The `Jews' of Judaism today are NOT Israelites but are impostors and are indeed Christ's and Christian Israel's principal enemies. The white peoples are the true descendants of Abraham, Isaac, and Jacob/Israel."

God in a boxcar, indeed. 1840's British nationalistic theology cross bred with National Socialists rants of the 1940's gives birth to America's latest crop of racist anti-Semites – the Christian Identity Movement and their armed associates, the Phineas Priesthood.

Race War Coming – R U Ready?
Xident is ready for Tom Carter.
20 X10.
What's the math?
200,000.
Dollars?
"Keys to Paradise"
Keys. Kilos. Carter's the drug cop. Kilos for sure.
20 kilos at $10,000 each would be $200,000.
Cop dope for sale. Makes sense.
With all those bank robberies and other criminal activities, the Priesthood has the loot. Drugs are a good investment for white supremacists –they turn a profit and enslave minorities.
"They remain slaves."
Sure. Those darkies can't resist crack, right?
Well, that's the idea.
Looks like ol' THC is going for the big score. He pulls in a

quick $200,000, takes early retirement, and joins Jake in Arizona or Nevada or one of those "uh" sounding states.

Am I in over my head?

No doubt.

Shall I call the cops?

Ha.

Sometimes it pays to be more oblique, utilize a less direct route to ultimate justice.

First I return my email settings to normal, then pick up the phone and dial a museum in Southern California. I love museums, and I have an acquaintance from a few years back that works in research and acquisitions.

"Hi, is Rick there?"

"Yes, may I ask who's calling?"

"Tell him its Jeff Reynolds, Brilliant Author, in Walla Walla."

A moment later, Rick's on the line. He's not law enforcement, he's not a private eye, and he simply works for a museum. He does, however, have a pre-occupation with certain aspect of contemporary American culture.

"Hi, Jeff. What do you need."

Predictably impersonal, Rick is Rick. You could pull him out of a burning building and he'd still talk to you as if you were a customer in an auto parts store.

"Numbers 25:7-8, Rick, Numbers 25:7-8"

"Phineas."

"Hey, it could be the Cozbi Show,"

He doesn't laugh.

"So?"

"Shreveport, Tulsa, Spokane, Wenatchee, Yakima – bank robberies, pipe-bombings, counterfeiting..."

"And?"

"Not only is there a connection, I found the template."

If I expected an emotional response, I'd be disappointed. I didn't, so I wasn't.

"How, what, where...details."

"Not telling you how, Rick, I'm just telling you to have your computer call my computer in five minutes and download everything in the file named `Phineas.' Once you get it, read my accompanying explanation. Study it carefully."

"Will do. What your computer's number?"

I tell him, and give him my home number as well.

"I'm an anonymous source, okay Rick?"

"No problem."

"And promise me you'll take appropriate action ASAP, and I mean ASAP."

"For real?"

"Yep. Urgent."

"Hey, if you can't turn to a museum in times of need, who can you turn to?"

That's his humor. Not dry, brittle.

I quickly compose a point by point expose and append it to the file. In exactly five minutes my computer takes Rick's call. File transfer in progress. Done deal. That takes care of that.

I'm surprised Dickhead hasn't called. He will.

Phone rings. This could be him. I check caller ID. Better.

"Hiya Randy!"

"Hi, how's my favorite author?"

"I hear Jerry Ford's just fine, and so am I."

She giggles. Nice giggle, as giggles go.

"You're still serious about taking me to Palm Springs, aren't you?"

"Randy, I never joke about Palm Springs. Besides, when Ford sees us together again, the jokes will go on forever. I've already reserved a suite at the Hyatt on Palm Canyon Drive."

"I miss you, Jeff. Really. You're different than other guys..."

"A deformity?"

"Be serious for a minute. No, I mean I think I'm...you know..."

"Feeling romantic and lovey-dovey?"

"Well, yeah. Is that okay with you?"

It's perfect with me.

"More than okay, okay?"

"Okay!"

"O-Tay!"

"So," she asks, "whatcha been doing since I saw you?"

"Hanging out with drug addict hookers, burglarizing the hidden hide-out of a right wing fascist, interviewing a dead woman, and being accosted by a crooked drug cop."

"Yeah, my day's been slow, too," she replies breezily, "I'm going on an interview for a new job with a non-profit organization."

"If they don't make a profit, how can they pay you?"

"Ha, ha. Very funny. They get funding, or grants, or something. Anyway, I'll find out in about an hour. Gotta get ready, put on my face, all that."

"I like your face."

"You better, it's the only one I've got."

"Fine. Two faced women have never appealed to me."

"Everything going okay on your big case?"

"Hey, I wasn't kidding about what I've been doing today. That was all real."

Concerned silence.

"Be careful, okay? I don't want to lose you."

Should I tell her I love her? No. Too much, too soon. Maybe I do, maybe I don't. Maybe I will. Things take time.

"I'll call you later, Jeff. Think nice thoughts."

Agreed. Nice thoughts.

I set up my video 8 dubbing station and start a copy of Violet's confession. With tape rolling, I dial a number in Spokane.

"Yes, is Ted Olmstad in please"

"Ted Olmstad speaking."

"The *real* Ted Olmstad, partially balding Assistant Federal Prosecutor for the State of Washington?" I ask with mock awe.

"Oh, no, it's Jeff Reynolds!" he laughs, "how's the brilliant career going? Still hiding out in Walla Walla, reading palms and selling books to television?"

"Yeah, your life story. They're casting Courtney Cox in the lead role."

"Hey, no complaints from me. She's got nice legs."

"Calve implants."

"Really?"

"That's the rumor."

"Figures. What's up?"

"This is an unofficial phone call – just two buddies talking. Got me?"

"I didn't even hear the phone ring," he says.

"The bank robbery in Spokane. Do you have serial numbers for the bills? If they loot is passed, will you know?"

A sigh.

"I wish. Why?"

"Oh, working on a story."

"I bet." His voice takes on a professional edge. He's no dummy. "Listen if you've got something…"

"Ted, If I have something I'll make sure you get it. I'm just being Mr. Curious."

"So, you don't have *anything*? Can't you go into a trance and at least give me the perpetrators social security numbers and street address?"

"I gave up trances. Call the Psychic Pals Network."

"Tried that. They told me I'm going to meet a tall, dark, stranger."

"If his name's Phineas, they're right."

I love taking him by surprise.

"Jeez, when you're hot your hot. The FBI tossed that around too, and there was some guy here from the Department of Terrorism and Violent Crime, but we haven't seen anything to take us beyond speculation."

"You will."

"Damn it, Jeff. Are you screwing with me?" He's half-laughing, but I know he's serious.

"Nope. I'm your friendly unnamed source. Keep the Phineas concept in the heart of your cosmic consciousness. Also, keep in touch with your Oregon counterpart. If something happens in Pendleton or La Grande, don't be surprised."

"Yes, well, there's a crime upsurge throughout the region, and I don't mean the random stuff. The Feds are also looking into some new twist on the old `Protection Racket' over in the Seattle area. I have the distinct intuitive impression, Jeff, that you know more than you're saying, right?"

"This is an unofficial call, remember. We're just too pals talking."

"Okay. How ya holding up since..."

"Since the little woman became the ex?"

"Well, yeah..."

"Fine, really. In fact, I've got a new squeeze, a real knockout."

"Oh, a Boxer?"

"No dogs allowed. Bye!"

Click.

No serial numbers on the bills.

Convenient.

Now, you might wonder why I'd give everything to a museum and not to the Federal Prosecutor. It's not that I don't trust Ted, it's that I don't trust the law enforcement personnel he'd give it to, not unless I know them personally. If it goes through Ted, the authorities will know it came from me. I'll be in the loop, and that loop can be a noose.

It's a simple sad fact of life that right-wing fascists recruit cops, especially in this redneck of the woods, and it's also a fact of life that minority Caucasians such as myself don't trust the police.

Minority Caucasians is, for most folks, an unfamiliar term. Hispanics, for instance, are minority Caucasians in this part of America. So are Iranians, Russians, numerous other refugees, and religious minorities.

Remember the O.J. Simpson verdict? Television commentators portrayed reaction as divided along racial lines – blacks thought he was innocent, whites thought he was guilty. Not quite. Jews, Hispanics, and other Caucasian minorities were, for the most part, firmly on the defense side because, as one pundit put it, "minorities know better than to trust the cops."

Yes, that's a prejudice, and yes, there are individual exceptions, but let's be honest. Five white guys standing on Walla Walla's Main Street talking are just five guys; five Mexicans standing together is suspected gang activity, and five Blacks is a crime ring from the Tri-Cities.

This is, after all, a prison town. The Washington State Penitentiary is right here in Walla Walla, Washington. Big Indians go there. So do Mexicans, Blacks, and plenty of white guys. From small time hoods to serial killers, we stack them up in a 920-bed maximum-security unit, 588-bed medium security, 107-bed minimum restricted, and the all-important 48-bed intensive management unit. Intensive management means they might bite off your nose just to alleviate boredom.

We didn't get this prison by chance. The city could have snared the State College, but who wants those city boys coming here and knocking up our farm girls? If we're going to have men coming here from out of town, and minorities at that, we should make sure they are safely behind bars other than McFeely's.

The major industrial function of this fine penal institution is the production of auto, truck and trailer license plates for state motorists, and highway signs for city and state use. More than 2.5 million license plates are produced annually.

Imagine how that looks on your resume. The prison once offered career training for real jobs in agriculture or barbering, but the "tough on crime" policies now assure us that no prisoner upon release will be qualified for anything other than crime.

This is not all bad news. Where there's crime, there's matching Federal funds, more prisons, and more employment opportunities in law enforcement.

Speaking of cops, what are we going to do about Mr. Jake Livesay, aka Dickhead? I'll give him five minutes. If he doesn't call me, I'm calling that number in Dayton.

I grab the remote control and my old Quasar comes to life. I got it at a real bargain years ago, it still works fine, and despite my deep investment in high-tech gear, I've kept the Quasar in the wall unit opposite my desk. Happily, there's no wrestling this time of day. Instead, we have the animated equivalent – *Popeye the Sailor*. I'm not talking about the sanitized, white-suited chap with fine posture and cheerful demeanor, I mean the muttering, cranky, pipe smoking, gruff little guy who ritualistically beats the crap out of Bluto. Of course, Popeye is not the aggressor, he's just defending Olive Oyl's honor.

Violent as hell.

Never call Popeye a son of a bitch.

I love these old cartoons' predictability – Bluto grabs Olive, Popeye objects, Bluto pounds Popeye, Popeye eats spinach, Popeye wins and saves the day. "Oh, my hero!" croons Olive.

Cultural experts and accomplished theologians watch Popeye and hold him up as the essence of America's obsession with redemptive violence. No matter how often our well-drawn trio lives this scenario, they never learn a thing. Getting pounded didn't teach Bluto to treat Olive Oyl with respect, nor have repeated pummeling taught Popeye to eat his spinach *before* the fight.

Hell, it's only a cartoon. My favorite part is when that can of spinach pops out of Popeye's pocket and he gets an infusion of Divine Power – the Holy Ghost packed in an eight ounce can.

When all else fails, he turns to the transforming power of pre-packaged vegetables.

When all else fails.

Perhaps that old one-eyed sailor isn't any more comfortable with his gift than I am with mine – avoids it, but always knows it's there when he needs it.

Actually, it sounds more like Loni and her drugs.

It's been five minutes, Popeye just knocked Bluto through an astonishing series of heavy support beams; Olive melts in adoration.

HEADLOCK

I pick up the phone and dial that number in Dayton. This ought to blow his mind.

He answers.

"Good afternoon, Mr. Livesay, this is Jeff Reynolds calling."

"Uh…how did you…?"

"Just a guess. If I were you, I'd stick around and visit relatives for a day or two, so I played a hunch," I say pleasantly, "I came back earlier than I planned, so I decided to track you down."

"Wonderful," he replies enthusiastically, "I'm eager to get together."

Let's bait him.

"You're correct, of course, about Richard having some pretty far out ideas…"

"Delusions," he clarifies as if the very thought exhausts him, "pure delusions.".

"Well, you said you were here to warn me, and I always appreciate being warned, especially when I'm paid for the honor."

"Trust me, Mr. Reynolds, you'll be glad you did, and I'll save you a lot of time and trouble," says Jake, sounding as friendly and sincere as an up-scale BMW salesman.

"What's your schedule?" I ask, "are you available to come on into town, or did you want me to…"

"Oh, you don't need to drive out here," he interrupts affably, "I'll come in now if you like. It's a lovely day. How about if we meet outside, say at Rook's Park?"

Yeah, right: BYOL – Bring Your Own Luger.

"Actually, I feel more comfortable meeting clients in public, no offense. Plus, we can enjoy lunch or at least dessert together. How about I meet you in an hour at the Pastime?"

"The Pastime? Can we move a little more uptown?"

"We can do the Red Apple if you'd rather."

He thinks for a moment, perhaps longing for Rooks Park.

"Yeah, okay, the Red Apple is fine. We can sit in the back if we need privacy. I just want us to have a good talk."

"You do the talking, I'll do the listening. I know how to keep my mouth shut, okay?"

I'll listen to anything.

***

I meet Jake Livesay early afternoon at the Red Apple. He greets me with a well-polished veneer of social relaxation, hot-potato handshake, and predator smile.

Sometimes I take risks, other times I play it safe. If this is my last meal, I'm ordering the chicken fried steak. Dickhead orders a spinach salad.

When I take out my tape recorder, he's visibly uncomfortable.

"Relax, Mr. Livesay. You're my client, I work for you, and anything you say is like `patient-client,' understand? This give me the opportunity to confirm that I heard what I think I heard."

He smiles as if he never scowled.

"Of course. As a former law-enforcement officer, I'm used to speaking around those things. No problem. On another topic, I have a compliment for you."

Who can resist a compliment?

"Really?"

"Yes, I read *Finding Sarah,*" he says, "Excellent. I'm not much for fiction, so I can't say I've bought your other books, but that one was .."

"Gripping? Compelling? A page-turner?"

He croaks out a prefabricated chortle.

"All of the above," Jake confirms, "especially the procedural detail."

"Hey, thanks, I appreciate it. Of course much credit goes to the real investigators and law enforcement personnel – without them the book would have been about thirty pages. But you know about that sort of thing, having been a cop for so many years."

"Oh, very true," he concurs, "even in a small town like this you see it all. Now, I can't say I believe that entire amazing mind-power psychic nonsense…"

If he's trying to piss me off by casting dispersion upon "the gift," he's failing miserably.

"Oh, I took what we authors call `creative license,' you know we have to spice some things up."

"Is that common in true crime?" he asks.

Okay, the man wants to establish a positive rapport. I can do that. Let's loosen him up a bit with male ritual bonding.

"Sure. In fact, we don't call the genre `true crime' anymore, we all it `fact crime' – that means it has some facts in it, but the story may or may not be `true.'"

"So, you can't always believe what you read?" Jake asks.

"Nope, not in the paper; not in books. But before we get too serious, ominous, or whatever," I begin with a light laugh of amusement, "what's the deal with punchboards? Whacky Richard brags that he was a guaranteed winner. C'mon, Jake, you're out of uniform, retired, and in the Red Apple in good ol' Walla Walla. Did he have it down to a science or what?"

Jake, smiling and wagging his head back and forth like a puppy in paradise, pooh-poohs and interrupts.

"That's because that was then, not now," he explains, "back in the old days, punchboards and pull tabs were illegal in Walla Walla, but we had a tolerance policy. It used to be that tavern owners didn't even need to put the winning tabs in the board at all – winners were optional."

He laughs, smiles, and leans forward.

"That means that some yokel would sit there and plop down quarter after quarter with no chance of winning anything, ever. Well, you can't go without winners forever, so if the player got up to go to the can, the owner would quickly slip a winner or two into the board. No kidding."

"Amazing," I prompt. The waitress brings coffee and place settings.

"Now, years ago there was a guy who frequented McFeely's who had a ring with ten prongs on it – a most unusual design, right? Well, he would swivel it around so the prongs faced down, then when no one was looking, he'd slam it into the punchboard. The prongs were perfectly spaced so they punched out ten tabs. He'd scoop 'em up and take off for the men's room where he'd check 'em out for winners. See, he was playin' without payin'. If he found a winner, he'd come back and put down a quarter and then claim he's won. But where the jerk screwed up was one time he's in the crapper and he hears someone come in, so he tosses the tabs in the toilet and flushes. Well, those damn tabs don't flush! They float! Sure enough, it was the boss who'd walked in," he pauses for a silent eruption of mirth, "and the guy got thrown out on his ass!"

I laugh, too. We're bonding now, boys.

"Oh, hell," he goes on with measured enthusiasm, "McFeely's is a hoot and a half. One day a guy walks in and hands the bartender a two-party check, and says, `It's okay, I know McFeely.' Can you imagine that? `I know McFeely.' They threw him out faster than the other guy!"

"I know McFeely," I echo, and we both laugh so hard we're gasping for breath. Get out the Oscars.

"Hey," I interject while still chortling, "wasn't there some guy who used to run around town in a surgical mask?"

"Oh, yeah," laughs Jake, "ol' Rantin' Rodney. The poor geezer had one of those germ obsessions like Howard Hughes, so he always wore a surgical mask. He used to walk all over town with this big walking stick, babbling to himself. Think he finally dropped dead about four years ago."

That settles that. Here comes that chicken fried steak.

"Punchboards," I pull him back to the initial topic, "could a guy have a system?"

"By `guy' you mean Richard Tibbit?"

He said it, not me.

I shrug. I've shrugged more in the past thirty-six hours than I have in the past three years.

"Not any more," he says, "but back when Tibbit was playin' them you could learn a board and play that same board in another town. For example, he would devote himself to a particular model or style of board in Walla Walla, and then have a spotter tell him when the same model board showed up in Prescott. He'd run out there, you know, about a half-hour drive, while the board was fresh and clean it out *bam, bam, bam*, and maybe give his spotter a cut. Not uncommon shenanigans in those days, but it's different now, the State Gambling Commission made sure of that."

"Sounds like the old days were more colorful," I say with nostalgic appreciation.

"Well, more colorful perhaps, but more shady as well. The old police chief in those days, from what I hear, would go into the Pastime and warn them if the State authorities were comin' through so they could take down the pull tabs. When the coast was clear, he'd tell them to put 'em back up. Of course, the Chief always walked out with a freshly folded hundred dollar bill."

The chicken fried steak is perfect.

"Cops have always had a knack of making extra money," I comment dryly.

He doesn't warm to that comment, but lets it slide.

I take out my billfold and remove his hastily scrawled thousand-dollar check.

"Listen, Jake, I know you gave me this, but you may have been a bit hasty. I can't discuss the things Tibbit's shared with me, and I don't want a conflict of interest situation. If you've got a warning for me, I should be paying you, not the other way around."

I slide the check towards him; he slides it back.

"As long as you have the check, I'm your client, right?"

"Yeah…"

"And what I say is confidential, correct?"

"Yes."

"Then you keep the check for now. When this meeting is over, you can decide how much of that you want to keep."

Fair enough.

"Here's the deal," begins Livesay, "I've known Richard Tibbit and his family almost forever, at least since I came to Walla Walla. You couldn't be a cop here in those days and not know Tibbit. Now, I'm not a social scientist or a psychologist or a counselor – my career was law enforcement. It doesn't matter too much to me why people do the things they do, it was just my job to enforce the law and try to make Walla Walla a safer, more pleasant place to live."

"Makes sense," I concur evenly.

"My wife and I lived right across the street from Richard's dad and step-mom. In fact, my wife and Violet became rather close. Actually, Violet needed that friendship in a big way. I mean, here she was married to a fourth-stage alcoholic and on top of that, she's got a first-class troublemaker for a stepson."

"You mean Richard, of course."

"Exactly. His older brother, whatever the hell his name was, was out of the loop fairly early on, from what I understand. Anyway, Richard's real mom died when he was only about two years old and I guess he was shuffled around from relative to relative when he was growin' up. The guy never had anything resembling a stable upbringing, plus I hear he had some sort of accident when he was a kid – a head injury – plus he inherited his father's fondness for booze."

Jake shakes his head in an accurate imitation of sad dismay.

"Well, you put that all together and you have a time-proven recipe for trouble. I don't need to go into details, you might even know them already. Fights, jail breakouts, car thefts, and close association with all manner of riff-raff. I'd say if there were ever a guy destined to spend his life behind bars, it was Richard Tibbit. The only thing that saved him was that wife of his. Somehow he managed to hook up with one of the nicest, most levelheaded women in Walla Walla. I don't know how or why, but those things happen. But even a positive influence like her can only do so much. She toned him down, shall we say, but she didn't cool him off. He was still a hothead who always thought people were out to get him. The very fact that he and his wife are still living happily in their same little home pretty much shows that his `plotting enemies' were a figment of his imagination."

I spread more gravy on the steak.

"Because," I reason aloud, "had anyone been out to get him…"

"They would have got him long, long ago." Jake completes the sentence, punctuating it with an affirmative nod and a fork full of spinach.

"The long and short of it," he continues, "is that Richard despised his step-mom, thought she was the Wicked Witch of the West or something. She knew it too, and she gave up real early on trying to make peace with him. Hell, he even tried to convince his father that Violet was gonna bump him off – bump off the dad, I mean. She knew all about that, and used to whine about it to my wife. Bad enough she was married to a drunk without having to put up with that sort of nonsense from Richard."

"Did this Violet really love Mr. Tibbit?"

He swallows another mouthful of salad before speaking.

"Oh, maybe when she married him, I don't know. He wasn't an ugly man, had a good career, nice pension, and excellent benefits. Maybe it was security for her, companionship for him. Whatever it was, it worked fairly well. Of course, it was just a matter of time 'till the old guy drank himself to death. He was diabetic, as most alcoholics are, and he was committing suicide every time he took a drink. He finally died out at the V.A. Well, there was nothing to keep her here once he was gone – it wasn't like she had strong family ties to Richard, right?"

"Right."

"Anyway, she split and died of some heart problem I guess a few years later. But the bizarre part is that Richard believed then, and perhaps believes now, that not only did Violet murder his father, but that I was an accomplice."

184

He rolls his eyes for emphasis.

"Imagine that for a moment, and you see how the poor bastard's mind works. He'd convinced himself that the evil stepmother was out to kill his father, a cop lived across the street from them, so when dad died of natural causes, the fact that Violet wasn't arrested for murder `proved' that the cop was 'in on it'."

"For people who think that way," I remark, "that's the way they think." I'm not tipping my hand on anything.

"Well, Richard would make these allegations to anyone who'd buy him a drink or give him half an ear. It got back to me. Now, what am I supposed to do? Sue him for slander? He doesn't have anything anyway, and it would just cause a stink. But I did try, in a subtle way, let him know that he should stop spreading rumors."

"Subtle way?"

He sets down his fork.

"This is a small town, and Tibbit like to hang out in small taverns. I figured a well-placed word, not a threat, just a word, might…"

"Get him to keep his mouth shut?"

"But it only made it worse. You see for years my wife and I had taken in foster kids. I figure if you can get to kids while they're young, you can have an influence – after all, think how much different Richard would be if his childhood had been different. Well, damned if that nut case didn't start telling people that I was some sort of pervert. Oh, he didn't make any formal allegations, just rumor mongering among the tavern crowd. People are always willing to believe the worst about cops, no matter how many murders you solve, or people you help."

He's right about that.

"So?"

He sighs for dramatic emphasis.

"Then Richard really crossed the line and I figured he was finally going to keep his long awaited appointment with the State Pen stamping out license plates – he master…well, *I believe* he masterminded a local bank job. I was in charge of the investigation, and I'll be up-front with you. I don't know if he pulled the job himself, but every indication is that he planned it. If he did, he did it perfectly. Despite our suspicions, there was never one shred of evidence to connect him. In fact, we never had a suspect against whom we could even begin to press charges."

The waitress refills my coffee.

"Why did you suspect Richard?"

"It's no secret we have informants…"

"Snitches."

"We prefer to call them `informants'. As they're criminals themselves, we can't always trust 'em, but we do get some good information, and the word on the street was that Richard Tibbit did the bank job."

"And the `word on the street', " I offer, "was that you were a pervert. So, maybe you guys are even."

He toys with his salad fork, carefully considering my previous remark's manifest logic.

"So, Jake, what brought you back, and why are you so concerned about my well-being?"

He pushes away the plate, folds his hands, and leans forward.

"Allow me to be blunt," he states flatly.

"Please," I encourage.

"You're not exactly…how shall I say it…the most experienced PI on the planet. You are, I believe, primarily an author, right?"

"Well…"

"And Jeff Reynolds is not even your real name."

"It's a professional alias," I say in a most professional manner.

"Okay, so we both know you're not Mickey Spillane."

He means Mike Hammer.

"Mike Hammer, you mean."

"Or *Magnum* or *Mannix* or…"

"Richard Diamond."

That brings him up short.

"Richard Diamond? Ha. Haven't thought of him in years. That was…"

"David Jansen, and Mary Tyler Moore was the leggy secretary."

"No kidding?"

"No kidding. Now, you were saying?"

"I was saying that we both know you're not really much of a private eye. You don't have years of experience, and you basically got your license as a gimmick, as a thing to go along with your career as a mystery/crime writer."

"Well, I've worked a few cases…"

"Very few, mostly legwork for attorneys," he asserts accurately, "and if someone wanted the best, they wouldn't come to you."

I see where he's going, and I'm ahead of him.

"Someone would come to me if they thought there was a book deal in it."

"You got it, pal. That's what he wants."

"That isn't news, Jake. He told me that up-front."

"What?"

"Okay, I'll tell you straight out. Richard hopes there's a book."

He drums his fingers.

"You're not the first."

The first what?

"Meaning?"

Jake cracks his knuckles.

"You're not the first writer to get involved with Richard Tibbit. I take it he didn't tell you about Jim Schaefer."

I know the name. Schaefer, now deceased, was a reporter and feature writer for the Walla Walla Union-Bulletin. A quiet, bald man of short stature, he rode the morning bus everyday from Wildwood Park to downtown at 7:45, then back again at 4:45.

"Tibbit thought Schaefer was his ticket to financial independence and fifteen minutes of fame," Jake explains, "and I guess he concocted a fairly good adventure from his own troubled life and some rather entertaining delusions."

"So?"

"Well, the way it went down wasn't pleasant. Schaefer wrote it up and sold it to television, all right, but somehow managed to leave Tibbit out of the deal. "

"Not by accident."

"Right, not by accident."

"Tibbit got screwed?"

"Royally. Schaefer got the credit, the money, and Tibbit got nothing. Now, this was before his dad died, so the story wasn't any of this latest nonsense. Anyway, it's sort of interesting that Richard would, in time, turn to another writer for a second chance."

Hey, it's vindication or cash, but what the hell. Am I supposed to feel two-timed because Richard ran for media's brass ring once before?

"Perhaps Richard trusts me. Besides, I can always use a good plot, a victim, a culprit."

Dickhead pouts.

"See, this is where you have problems. One of those problems is me."

"That's not news either, considering our first encounter."

"I mean I could sue."

Oh, brother.

"Listen, Jake, I write *fiction*. Let me say that as clear as possible – I tell lies for a living. I gave up writing true crime after I read *Sleepers*."

"*Sleepers?*"

"Forgive me. That was author humor. I gave up true crime after *Finding Sarah*. If I wrote a novel based on every wild delusion Richard Tibbit has stored up in that injured head of his, I'd change the names of everyone involved, add make believe subplots, and give myself a drop-dead gorgeous ingenue to sleep with just of the hell of it. Also, I'd preface the book with `This is a work of fiction. The story is not based on a true case nor real people – just like *Law & Order*'."

He eyes me intently.

"There is another, more serious consideration," Jake says.

"Worse than you suing me over a book I haven't even written yet?"

"Tibbit's kept his mouth shut, amazingly enough, since the bank robbery. Now, that's smart of him. But I think his desire to make money off your writing talents has gotten the best of him."

"Please explain."

He leans in and gives me that cold eye cop look.

"This is the real warning, the one you better take to heart whether you write your damn book or not. Now, this is my best law-enforcement hunch, all right? I have far more experience with crime, criminals, and the way they think than you do, agreed?"

He gets no argument from me. Maybe he'll pick up the check.

"I believe that the element in with him on the bank job are not adverse to murder, especially if it endangers them. That job was almost five years ago. If Tibbit makes too big a stink, stirs stuff up, I doubt he could get much accomplished in terms of arrests, but he could get himself and maybe you killed."

"So you're saying my life could be in danger?"

"Yes. This is more than just you checking up on Richard Tibbit's delusions. You could be putting yourself in harm's way."

"Who would pull the trigger?"

"If I knew that for sure, I'd go to the police."

HEADLOCK

I'm so sure.

"So, what is your brilliant suggestion, Mr. Livesay?"

He smiles.

"You'll like this: you keep my thousand and just drop the whole thing at least for a year or two. You and Richard will both be much, much, safer. In time, you can go ahead and crank out your little mystery novel and maybe you guys will do real well with it. But I'm afraid that right now your smartest move would be to do absolutely nothing at all about anything."

I pretend to think it over, using my best mulling expression.

"I don't know, Jake."

"What don't you know?"

Sometimes I take risks, okay?

"This reminds me of our first conversation at McFeely's, the one where you said some things are best left dead and buried...."

He sighs, and attempts appearing apologetic.

"Hey, I'm sorry about..."

"No, that's okay," I interrupt, "it's just that the message is sort of the same – let it go. And that's all right with me, honest. But the thing you don't understand is that Richard doesn't care about you or the bank job."

A floodlight goes on behind his eyes. Oh boy. He wanted me to violate confidence, and it sure sounds like I'm about to do exactly that.

I look from left to right as if double-checking our privacy.

"In fact," I say softly, "he doesn't give a cartoon rat's ass that...." I allow my eyes to dart around a bit; he leans closer across the table as I slide both my hands down and under the booth.

"Yes? What?"

Here we go.

"That the bitch step-mom is up in that trailer dying of brain cancer, or that her son, Derek, is an old snitch acquaintance and your alleged ex-lover, or even that you or Derek blew that guy's brains out in Rooks Park and called it suicide. Nope, Richard doesn't care about any of that. Not now, now any more, not ever again."

Had we been in animation rather than the Red Apple, Jake' lower jaw would have clanged open with force sufficient to rend the table asunder.

"You'd think he'd be vindictive or something," I continue, "but he couldn't care less. Nope, for all that guy's been through, real or imagined, he really doesn't care one bit."

Jake lips move but nothing's coming out.

"So, you don't have a damn thing to worry about, Jake. I'm just an author with a silly PI license; Richard's only a well-known nut case."

He casually lifts a sleek ballpoint pen from his pocket. All in all, it's a bit too nonchalant for me.

"If that pen's loaded, I wouldn't click it if I were you, Mr. Livesay."

He grins and swivels it between his fingers.

"No?"

I can't tell if he's kidding.

"It's not the caliber of what's pointed at you under this table that should concern you, but the target. You might give me a heart attack, but I guarantee that you'll be chirping like a canary the rest of your unnatural life."

He can't tell if I'm kidding.

Hell, for all I know that's just a pen; for all he knows, I'm bluffing.

He puts away the pen; I bring my hands up above the table and toss my harmless ClassicWax ink stick down next to his salad bowl.

"It's only a pen." He says evenly.

"Mine or yours?"

He smiles.

"Both."

"Good. It's nice that we trust each other. Now tell me, where did you get that Classic Wax pen I took from you at McFeely's?"

He drums his fingers on the tabletop.

"I don't have the slightest idea," says Jake, "it was just a cheap pen I picked up somewhere."

Stalemate.

"Listen Jake, let's say we have a deal, okay? I know how to keep my mouth shut. I mean, I don't want any trouble. I already had Tom Carter pay me a visit."

"Carter? He's narcotics. Why would he pay you a visit?"

As if he doesn't know.

"What difference does it make? I also don't want a cross burnt on my lawn, " I add just to make him wonder how much I know, "so lets agree that I humor Richard, keep your money, and we'll both just let everything go."

He studies me in silence. The waitress offers coffee refills.

"Okay, Jake, listen. You need to trust me, right?"

He smirks.

"You've gotta trust me just as if we were wrestlers together in the ring."

This catches his interest. I bet he misses the Mountie.

"As proof of my cooperation, I'll give you the best proof you could imagine – a face to face apology from Richard Tibbit."

Livesay is stunned for the second time at one sitting.

"What?"

"I'll tell you straight out, Richard hired me to simply find out who all was involved in his father's death, and if it's over – if he can stop being paranoid. The answer, based on my expert investigation, is that there is nothing to suggest anything other than natural causes. But, if it *was* murder, Violet acted alone. In short, you're clean, deserve an apology, and a face to face reconciliation. I can arrange it. It's doable. I can convince Richard as long as part two is true – that from now on, it's safe. If Richard Tibbit never needs to look over his shoulder again, I'll have earned my pay and can get on with writing a true work of hometown fiction, with the emphasis on *fiction*. Richard gets the best of both worlds – comfort and cash; you get to rest easy knowing the bad-mouthing is over, and I can just sit in my basement hunched over a word processor. Hell, even my agent will be delighted."

The pretzel-logic sub-text is painfully obvious – if Jake assures me that it's safe, that it's over, he's admitting involvement and control. The signal from me is that I know how to keep my mouth shut. Besides, I'm prudent.

He has only one response. He can't turn it down.

"When do I get this...apology?"

"Oh, let's say tomorrow. For now, we'll agree on eleven in the morning, at McFeely's Tavern. Does that work for you?"

"McFeely's? Why..."

"Why McFeely's? Why not? I would suggest the Dacres, but McFeely's has more emotional resonance, plus it has punchboards."

"Eleven, you say?"

"If that doesn't work for some reason, I'll call you in delightful Dayton, home of the Jolly Green Giant."

True. There's a Green Giant plant in Dayton.

The waitress brings the bill; I slide it toward him.

"Thanks for lunch, Mr. Livesay."

"You're welcome. So, we do indeed have a deal."

191

I turn off the recorder and stand up.

"Absolutely. You'll never hear anti-Livesay nonsense from Mr. Tibbit nor myself the rest of your life."

And may it be short.

We part company, I return to Snob Hill, and call Richard. No answer. Even a recluse and his wife go out on occasion.

Up since early this morning, I need either a good nap or complete change of atmosphere. Too many McFeely moments mingled with portions of paranoia have besotted my mindset. I couldn't discern Jake's center of gravity right now if my life depended on it – and it probably does.

Either too wired or too cautious to sleep, I take another shower and change clothes for the second time. The clothes make the man, right? In that case, you can call me Georgio Armani. We're talking maroon double-breasted. Eat your heart out, David Letterman.

Next stop: the Walla Walla Country Club.

Despite my complete lack of proficiency in, or enthusiasm for, the game of golf, I retain a social membership in this decidedly upscale organization. The clubhouse, recently remodeled, is luxurious but comfortable. The lovely deck overlooking the greens is perfect for refined reflection and light reading. My Morroco bound briefcase contains the infamous three-by-five cards, Block's paperback, and *the Washington State Gambling Commission Rules Manual.*

I order a milk shake and open the Manual. Page one informs me that the commission was created pursuant to RCW 9.46.040 as the licensing and regulatory agency charged with the authority and duty to control statutorily authorized nonprofessional gambling.

I read several pages, softly intoning. Yes, sometimes my lips move when I read. Don't mock me. I'm not stupid; I'm recording it on my mental hard drive. It's not exactly compelling content, and were it not for my audiographic memory, I'd retain nothing.

Satiated with punchboard regulations, I put the green manual on the glass-top table. I'll read the rest later.

Strange thing, this audiographic memory. Twenty years ago I did an oral report on anti-Catholicism in America. To this day, I can detail Maria Monk's *Awful Disclosure's of the Hotel Dieu Nunnery of Montreal* – an 1836 diatribe against the Church published, and in large part written, by a consortium of New York anti-Catholics. Ms Monk, a prostitute, died in prison in 1849 after being busted in a whorehouse for picking a customer's pocket.

The book attributed to her sold over 300,000 copies by 1860, and stayed in print for another hundred years. A new edition was published in 1960.

She must have had one hell of an agent.

It could be worse.

There was a contestant on the old TV show, the $64,000 Question, who had both an audiographic and photographic memory. One catch: he couldn't forget anything. Everything stayed in his short-term memory forever. His brain was literally cluttered with information. Incapable of concentration, he couldn't hold a job. For every blessing, there is an equivalent curse.

Sitting outside in the mid-afternoon sun, I sip the frothy chocolate shake while watching two duffers consider their best approach to the green.

This is perfect. I can see for miles. No one can sneak up on me here. Oh, they could shoot me easily enough, but killers can kill anywhere. Here, in the Country Club's delightful surroundings, no one can sneak up on me.

I close my eyes and allow a slow wave of relaxation to flow slowly over my entire body, from my toes all the way to my head. I've got the bass line from an old Jefferson Airplane song playing over and over in my head.

Good thing I like the riff. The lyrics are *Alice in Wonderland* references.

"Excuse me, Mr. Reynolds..."

Damn. Someone sneaked up on me.

VIII

I don't know the voice, but I already don't like the sound of it.

Eyes open, I turn and look up at a dark suited gentleman in his early thirties. He looks more Van Heflin than Van Halen.

"May I talk with you for a moment?"

He's not asking, he's insisting.

"Pull up a chair," I tap the table and motion for him to join me.

"Sorry to interrupt your afternoon," he begins, not sounding sorry at all, "but it's rather important that I have a word with you."

"Word up," I encourage, "and who are you that you need a word with me?"

"I'm Agent Cosby with the local office of the D.E.A."

He shows me his card.

Cosby.

Right.

I'm supposed to believe this. He looks like a FBI extra from Twin Peaks sent by Central Casting.

"Is Agent Zimri out with a bad back?" I ask, flashing a warm smile.

He must be a masterful poker player, as he doesn't bat an eye.

"I'm not familiar with Agent Zimri. I'm rather new here."

He clears his throat and begins his spiel.

"I realize that you are a licensed private investigator in the City of Walla Walla," he says seriously, "and it's not unusual for people in your line of work in this town to cross…"

The line?

"…the border into Oregon without checking in with local law enforcement and letting them know you're working on a case."

"Sometimes I go to Oregon to buy cheap smokes."

He doesn't smile.

"Basically, Mr., uh, Reynolds, what I'm here to tell you is that we want you to back off, step down, or whatever you want to call it, regarding a particular fellow who owns a trailer and cabin in the Tollgate area above Weston."

Big surprise.

"What would I be doing up at Tollgate?"

"We're not sure, but we have photos of you there early this morning. I can't explain what we're doing, except to tell you that we have the location under surveillance. I was sent here in the interest of your personal safety, and to advise you that the DEA strongly urges you to stay away from that location and refrain from any contact with the resident."

"Because...?"

"Because you could inadvertently interfere with an ongoing investigation, endanger yourself, our agents, and innocent others."

"Oh."

Why doesn't he just shoot me right here and get it over with?

I give him my best thoughtful, pensive expression, and say nothing.

"It's not our intention to disrupt your business, Mr. Reynolds," he elaborates, "nor cause you problems. To be perfectly honest, were you not, shall we say, such a well-known and respected person, we may have simply taken you into custody just to keep you out of our hair."

He laughs as if I can take that as a joke or a fact.

"But...?"

I smile when I ask.

"Well, we figured your experience of working so closely with law enforcement personnel over the years had predisposed you to cooperation. Basically, we felt that if we simply asked you to help by staying out of it and keeping quiet about it, you would assuredly do so."

I raise my milkshake in a friendly toast.

"Assuredly. You have my word. Obviously, I would never do anything to interfere with an investigation."

We both watch two plaid attired duffers sink their putts.

He's not done.

"Mind if I ask a question?"

"Shoot."

"Why were you up there this morning?"

195

I wonder what those photos show.

"Don't your photos tell you?"

He shrugs.

"Photos provide images, not intentions. We can tell who drives in and who drives out – hardly anyone does either — and we have a clear view of the front of the trailer and a partial one of the cabin. We know you smoked a cigarette out front, and talked to the woman who stays there a few days a week. A house sitter, apparently. The two of you seemed....close."

He'll get neither details nor information from me, at least nothing beyond what I'm willing to share.

"I'm interviewing her for a chapter of my new book," I answer, "her life, her loves, her husbands, that sort of thing – a character study for a work in progress. There's no reason for me to return. I can chat with her another time in another place. As for the owner of the property, I don't believe I've ever met the fellow nor does he know I was there."

He sits in silence for a moment, looking out over the golf course. Even he is not immune to it's manifest calm.

I attempt hospitality.

"Would you like a chocolate shake?"

He smiles.

"No thanks, not while I'm on the job."

I wave away the approaching waiter.

"May I ask you something else, Mr. Reynolds?"

I can stop him?

"Sure."

"I've read about you in the paper, and in various...uh.."

"Tabloids?"

"*New York Times Review of Books*, actually," he clarifies or lies, "and I read *Finding Sarah* and the Prime Minister mystery…"

"*#10 Drowning Street*"

"Yes. I enjoyed that. Now that I hear you speak, I better understand your interest in English politics."

Not again.

"Yes, I'm as British as Garner Ted Armstrong and the Moody Blues."

He's never heard of Garner Ted Armstrong, former spokesman for the World Wide Church of God, the premier advocate of Anglo/British Israelism back in the 1960's, but he's heard of the Moodies.

HEADLOCK

"*Days of Future Past*, right? My older brother played that one all the time. I imagine only the Moody Blues heard it more often than he did."

I sip my shake.

"In reality," I offer helpfully, "your brother heard it more than the Moodies, especially the drummer."

He awaits explanation; I comply.

"There's a drumming error on side two. They can't listen without hearing it, so they don't listen. Artists don't experience music the way fans hear it. Same with authors."

"Do you read your own books?"

"Once, aloud."

"Why?"

"Once I read something aloud, I never forget it. I can't remember names, numbers, or dates, but I never forget anything I read aloud."

This guy, who I figure is as much a DEA agent as Violet Langness is a happy homemaker, seems to be warming to me. Hell, he should be delighted. I assured him I'd back off; I assured Jake I'd back off.

Damned if I'm gonna back off.

Here I am with neo-Nazis and corrupt drug cops circling me like sharks, and I'm going to back off? Not with a book in it, I'm not. I'm sure there's a book in it.

"What was the last book you read aloud?"

Is this a test?

"The Washington State Gambling Commission's Rules Manual."

He raises his eyebrows as a visual prompt.

Okay. I'll show off.

"No operator shall put out for play any punchboard," I recite, "wherin the winning punches or approximate location of any winning punches can be determined in advance of punching the punchboard in any manner or by any device, including, but not limited to, any patterns of manufacture, assembly, packaging or programming. Winning punches shall be randomly distributed and mixed among all other punches in the punchboards. The punchboard..."

"Okay, okay," he laughs, "you've convinced me. That's quite a trick, or a talent, or whatever."

"It's a whatever."

197

"You could be on Ed Sullivan," he says, standing. Agent Cosby smiles as if he means it, and extends his hand.

"The show, not the journalist, right?"

This momentarily throws him.

"You know, like the guy spinning plates or Señor Wences."

He lets it go. No one spun Señor Wences anyway.

"Thank you for your cooperation Mr. Reynolds," he replies, invoking the tone of officialdom, "the DEA appreciates it."

"My pleasure."

He walks away.

Well, well, well.

I open the briefcase and pull out my three by fives. I select a blank one and write Cosby's name on it.

DEA? Phineas Priesthood? Some Dayton relative of Jake seeking confirmation that I am, indeed, standing down as I promised?

What was it Marlon Brando called Martin Sheen in *Apocalypse Now*? *"...an errand boy sent by grocery clerks to collect a bill."*

I loose a long, slow, exhale, then stretch, signal the waiter, and request a cup of coffee.

As you've no doubt noticed, I'm not Mr. Deductive Reasoning. I love mysteries, but not puzzles. My mind works in circuitous routes.

Shaded clouds slowly roll in from the mountains; I smell the breath of a storm.

Leaning back, eyes closed, I meditate. Images and impressions flow behind my eyes in random patterns. I'm not accessing that damn gift, I'm just letting the mind sort and process.

At length, I pack the cards and the Gambling Commission's rule book in my briefcase and head for home. On the way, I stop at the County Court House and do a quick search on who owns the property at a certain Bonsella address, then scoot by Video Giant to rent Orson Welles' "Touch of Evil."

By noon tomorrow, Richard Tibbit's problems will all be resolved. Mine however, will take a bit longer. By the weekend, God willing, I'll have lived through the adventure's climax and be on my way to Palm Springs. Tonight, amidst my elaborate planning, deviant emailing, and innumerable phone calls, we'll admire Mercedes McCambridge.

HEADLOCK

"I want to kill him."

That's Richard talking, and he's emphatic.

"I mean, I'd wanna just come right across the little booth, wring his neck, and leave the body right there in McFeely's as part of their permanent collection."

Obviously, I've told Richard about his proposed face to face with Dickhead.

"I know you want to kill him, Richard, but what are you really going to do?"

Zippo click.

"Oh, I'll show up and be as polite, humble, and goddam contrite as you could imagine."

Really?

"Because?"

"Because I want it over. What good would it do to be hostile?"

I'm on the hand-held, walking downstairs to my basement office carrying the rented video in my other hand.

"You know he's going to say he had nothing to do with your father's murder."

"Yeah."

"And you're going to apologize for every nasty thing you ever said about him."

He sighs.

"Yeah, I know."

Between you and me, I'm worried.

"You're not going to lose it are you, Richard?"

"Naw. I mean, he'd really have to push my buttons for me to go ballistic."

"He's not coming to push buttons, remember. He's coming to make peace. "

Make peace.

Jake as Messiah; Zimri as atoning sacrifice.

Even peace may have a touch of evil.

In Welles' perverted little movie of similar title, Charlton Heston plays a Mexican, and does so without an accent. That's okay. Marlene Dietrich, her German accent thick as the plot, plays a Mexican gypsy, and Zsa Zsa Gabor portrays the owner of a strip joint. So much for type casting.

These absurd cinematic shenanigans illumine the Quasar while

I scheme away like the Maverick brothers on a con-job bender.

I figure Richard and Jake are pretty much a done deal. All resolved; it's safe. I hope.

Carter and his Phineas drug lords are another story. I've got big plans for those boys, and if this is going to be a first class production, I'll need more players than my current ensemble cast. No problem. Check my resume – I know people, okay?

I dial the Pastime, but I'm not looking for Verna.

"Pastime, Robert speaking."

"Hi, Robert. This is Jeff Reynolds."

"Hi. Hear you were in here last night for the big fight. Sorry I missed it."

Robert Fazzari, blessed with the perfect personality for his family's business, is outgoing, quick, honest, and tolerant. He and his dad own the Pastime, his uncle owns McFeely's. Robert's seen it all, done plenty, and never pretends he hasn't.

"It wasn't quite the Thrilla in Manilla, but that's what you get for working a day shift, Robert. Is Travis there?"

"Travis? Yeah. He's drinking 7-UP and teasing the waitresses. Hold on, I'll get him."

As I mentioned previously, Travis Webb is our mutual pal. Descended from three generations of Protestant Ministers, he's a former high-school football hero who returned to Walla Walla from Seattle following four highly publicized federal indictments for computer hacking. You ever see the movie *Sneakers*? Kid's stuff for Travis Webb.

So what if it was the Pentagon's computer system? Twice. Hell, he was just a kid, okay?

His effective defense was the absolute truth: he just wanted to know how good he really was. Travis' motive wasn't terrorism, only vindication. The let him off with harsh warnings and a tarnished reputation.

Had he not been with Robert, I'd have tracked him down soon enough. In Walla Walla, there are too few hiding places for a man of his proclivities. He's either on his computer, someone else's computer, reading science fiction, or digging through the historic archives of the new Bahá'í Library.

Travis will gladly discuss whether or not there are dogs in heaven, the metaphoric nature of physical reality, or Islamic contributions to civilization. Tonight, the topic is neither dogs nor metaphors. In fifteen minutes he'll be helping me read, route, interdict, and re-route communications between *topcat@bmi.net* and xident. Even with such programs as MegaCloak and MetaHide, email interception and forgery is tricky business. I'm good at it, but Travis is better. I can't afford to screw up. Once I explain the situation, his center of gravity pulls him eagerly into the loop.

Ah, criminal pride adapted for a moral cause. May God forgive me if I've led the boy astray.

By the time Mercedes McCambridge makes her leather wrapped appearance, Travis and I have consumed several cans of Pepsi and violated all manner of email security.

When the pizza arrives – an extra large because Travis eats like a moose – we've discerned that Tom Carter and xident are engrossed in heavy negotiations. Carter will deliver 21 kilos of cocaine in exchange for $200,000 cash — a simple exchange – the bone of contention is "where." Carter suggests the parking lot of the Rose Street Safeway at 12:00 Noon. Xident doesn't like that idea. It's too public and he's too paranoid. They wrestle back and forth because, underneath it all, they don't trust each other. There's always the chance one could rob and/or kill the other if the deal comes down in the dead of night in the middle of nowhere.

They do agree that xident, accompanied by Dirty White Boy or Ovrlrd11, will arrive with the loot in a briefcase. A 1985 Pontiac will be parked with the dope in the trunk. They'll give Carter the briefcase and one of them drives off with the coke.

But where?

It has to be daytime and public, but not too public.

Everyone's plotting.

What's that line in the Qur'an?

They plotted and God plotted, and verily God is the best of plotters.

When I told Randy I had this case solved, I wasn't far wrong. Sure, the Phineas business was a surprise, but it didn't change my basic approach – give the people want they want. And that includes me.

"This is really a weird flick," remarks Travis about `Touch of Evil' as we await Carter and xident's decision, "was it a book first?"

"Yeah, `Badge of Evil' by Whit Masterson. I met the author, or half of him being as he's two guys, in San Diego."

Whit Masterson is no more his real name than mine is Jeff Reynolds.

"The biker chick isn't even in the book," I explain further, "neither is the gypsy."

"She doesn't sound very Mexican," says Travis.

"Actually," I say, thumbing through my personal phone directory, "the Heston character isn't Mexican in the book, his wife is."

Travis pours another six ounces of Pepsi down his throat before posing another question.

"When they made a TV movie out of your book – the Sarah one — sorry I didn't see it – did they change much?"

"Yeah, I was played by a black woman, and I didn't even get to keep her outfits."

He looks at me as if I'm serious.

"Really?"

"You ever seen me wear clothes that would look good on a black woman?"

"Nope."

"Well, there's your proof."

I dial, my call goes through, and I wave Travis' attention back to my computer screen. There's nothing new, so he concentrates on Orson Welles's profuse padding and false nose.

"Hello."

"Mr. Ronald Faver, please."

"This is Mr. Faver speaking."

"Yeah," I bark into the phone "someone ought to arrest your ass, you pervert."

Stunned silence.

"Who's this?" demands Ron Faver.

"The man who knows what you did with that fourteen year old dwarf."

Faver erupts in gales of laughter, riding a wave of recognition.

"I'll be damned," he exclaims, "what rock did you crawl out from under, white boy? I thought you took all your big book money and TV movie loot and ran off to Bora Bora."

"That's Walla Walla, not Bora Bora."

"Sheeeeeeet," he says as if he's Wolfman Jack on XERB, "you be one sick muthafuka. Now, tell da Wufman why you callin'!"

He deserves an explanation, and he gets one. I also make him an offer he can't refuse – one that won't cost me a cent, but

202

make us both look like heroes.

"You shittin' me?" he asks.

"Never, Mr. Faver. You in?"

"Just like I was with the dwarf," he confirms, and one more professional eagerly joining the cast.

Travis, overhearing the dwarf references and other tasteless aspects of the conversation, looks at me as if I'm the most peculiar person he's ever met.

"Who's this Faver guy?"

"We used to work together back in the old days."

"What exactly are you up to, Mr. Reynolds?"

Read my resume, Mr. Webb. I have no secrets.

"Wrestling with my past, plotting for my future."

He gives me the same look I get from Verna. I'm getting used to it.

This has been a very busy day, my long distance bill keeps climbing, my email box is full, and the three-by-fives are crammed with notes and cross-references. Too bad I can't read my own writing. Richard, of course, is wound up tighter than a two-dollar watch. I told him to just relax, trust me, and watch Wheel of Fortune.

That Jefferson Airplane riff is still stuck in my head.

"Action!" calls out Travis, and his nose is pressed against the computer.

"What action?"

"They decided."

"What, where?"

Travis clicks the keyboard, laughs, and waves his arms.

"I love this clandestine computer stuff! I feel so, so…"

"Travis, calm down. Just give me the info."

"Tomorrow afternoon in the parking lot of the Whitman Mission."

That may be too soon. I re-dial Faver immediately, relaying word for word Travis' latest news.

"Can you move that fast, Ron?"

"Got gear or access?" he asks.

"Both. Just tell me what you need."

He does.

"Sure you can get here in time?"

"Hey, does the Pope shit in the woods? Is the bear Catholic? I be known for my speed and agility, besides this be hotter than the

203

Jamoomba Sisters' last three XXX-rated videos, you know, the ones where they have tennis balls duct taped to their gums."

"You've obviously been taking gentility lessons in your spare time."

"Who you callin' a gentile? I'll check the flights. We gotta have this planned out perfectly."

"Any problem getting this a green light?"

"I can get clearance on this baby in two seconds."

I give Faver my cell number, email, and all particulars. Short, sweet, and I help myself to a piece of pizza.

"Really, you should get a new computer, Mr. Reynolds," remarks Travis, "with a faster processor and a bigger hard drive."

"You don't have to call me `Mr. Reynolds,'" I tell him, "you can call me `Jeff.'"

"What difference does it make? You're not either one."

Smart ass.

Several more keyboard clicks, accompanied by devilish cackles of self-amusement, and Travis swivels from the computer.

"There! In and out and they never knew we were there."

Wonderful.

The cellular rings and I dig it out of my coat pocket.

Loni in tears.

My stomach goes into knot-mode.

"What is it? What's wrong. Where are you?"

"Here at the trailer, and I'm getting' out of here soon," she talks fast, then faster, "I called my friends to tell 'em to come get me in an hour 'cause Faron called and said he was on his way and they said they had a surprise for me and sure enough they put him, and I mean my husband, on the phone and it was him and I got all choked up and started crying and everything and tonight we'll be together."

"Congratulations, Loni, you just won the run-on-sentence award, and I'm happy for you, but listen. Tomorrow, eleven in the morning, be at McFeely's. This is important. I need you because I've got Richard coming race to face with Jake the dickhead."

"But my husband…"

"Hell, tell him he's invited if you want, just remember our deal."

"Uhhh…"

Swell.

"Be there, promise me."

HEADLOCK

"Well.."

Damn.

"We'll see, I mean…"

Orson Welles is stuck in a mud bog.

"Do what you can, Loni. Enjoy your reunion."

Travis pokes around in the empty pizza box, searching for errant pepperoni or overlooked mozzarella.

"If you don't need me for anything else," he says, "I've got a hot date with another hard drive."

"Sure, go ahead. Hope you enjoyed the film."

He stands and shakes the last few drops of Pepsi into his mouth.

"Yeah. I liked the fortune teller or gypsy or whatever that heavy-lidded German lady was supposed to be."

"Yep. She has the best lines in the film."

I walk Travis upstairs and outside. The night sky, crowded with clouds, allows no starlight.

Is it safe?

Travis drives away, the cats circle my shoes, and I stand on the porch smoking an Old Gold.

If there's book in this, I'm putting the advance towards a new car. Maybe that hot Volvo C-70 sports coupe – "Not the Volvo you need, the Volvo you want."

Yeah, I could get away with a Volvo sports coupe in Walla Walla without people thinking I'm showing off. If I buy a Porsche, folks will make rude remarks. In Walla Walla, they say the difference between a porcupine and a Porsche is that with a porcupine, the pricks are on the outside.

First things first.

Everything must be victoriously resolved.

"The white knight's talking backwards," I say seriously to the cat, remembering lyrics from that Jefferson Airplane song.

Angel meows, nagging.

She couldn't care less about the Airplane. Hot Tuna is another matter.

The phone rings, nagging.

Everybody wants something.

Center of gravity.

Everyone has a pull.

I'm going in.

The house, that is.

It's Richard. Again.

"I should tell you what I didn't tell you before."

"Does it involve a hookah smoking caterpillar?"

"What the hell does that mean?"

"Oh, just some old song lyrics I've got stuck in my head – I thought maybe you were broadcasting." I didn't think that at all, but it's a good excuse. Sometimes recurring songs are a message, other times they're simply nostalgia. "What didn't you tell me before."

"When the wife and I was out," he explains, "we were up at the supermarket looking for Bel-Airs, okay?"

Okay. Pooter is face first in the water dish, just like Orson Welles in the mud bog.

"Anyway, I'm just about ready to leave because they didn't have any. Seems they ran out."

"Due to the overwhelming public demand?"

"Hey, I'm tryin' to tell you something, alright? So, we're goin' to drive over to Safeway when this fellow I know, a very conservative survivalist sort, actually comes over and tells me that I shouldn't be talking to you."

"You know this guy?"

"Yeah, not that I've seen him much over the past years, but he knows who I am and I know who he is..."

Conservative survivalist. Anyone ever hear of a liberal survivalist?

"Is he some sort of Constitutional Patriot gun club anti-government black helicopter nut-case?" I ask.

"Well, let's just say he's conservative," answers Richard, accentuating each distinct syllable, "and he tells me I shouldn't be talking to you."

This is not good news.

"He actually said my name?"

"Well, he said `Jeff Reynolds,' the author."

That's me, the same guy scooping Mixed Grill onto a plastic plate.

"What did you say back?"

"I told him, `listen, you're not going to dictate to me who I talk to or what I talk about,' that's what I said back."

"Uh, mind if you tell me his name, Richard. That might be helpful to me."

Silence.

"No, I really can't do that."

"Yes, you really can do that."

Zippo click. He must have found those Bel-Airs.

"I choose not to do that, I don't think it would be prudent."

Prudent.

"So, why do you think he said that, and why are you telling me?"

"Because he must be tied in with the guys who did the old bank job, that's why. And I'm telling you because I figured you had a right to know."

"Yeah, I know my rights. Tell me his name."

I prepare two plates, otherwise the arthritic Pooter dominates the dish and Angel throws a fit.

"Naw, I'm not doing that. In fact, I didn't even tell ya what I told ya, okay?"

"Just be at McFeely's."

"You're serious about that, aren't you?" He sounds like he's looking for a way out. There is no way out.

"Dead serious. Think of it as a family reunion."

Wrong phrase.

"Hell," says Richard.

"See you at eleven. Remember, it's safe and it's over by noon."

The cats fed, I make a fresh pot of coffee and get back to work. I still have several phone calls to make, emails to answer, and details to take care of.

Faver calls back. Everything is go. Now, I'm going to spend a good hour on the phone just listening to Randy breath. Busy day tomorrow, kids. Eleven in the morning, a rather diverse group will be relaxing freely at the McFeely.

The leggy redhead lights another Doral and toys with the wine cooler bottle. Just my luck, Loni's hooched again. If she's serious about taking off for pot, my little scheme hits a serious snag.

The moment I hang up the bar's phone, I scoot back towards her. Leaning over as if reaching for the ashtray, I whisper in her ear.

"You're not taking off, Loni. C'mon, we made a deal. Maybe you won't have to do a thing, but don't split."

She stubs out the Doral as if it said something rude.

"My husband and I had a fight already," she says as if that

has anything to do with what I'm talking about, "no sooner do we get together than the slappin' and the swearin' starts."

"Who slapped and who swore?"

"Me. I did both!" She laughs too loud and pulls another Doral out of her purse. "Actually, we got into an argument while we were doin' it, ya know, doin' it."

"How romantic."

"Romantic? It wasn't romantic at all," she insists, taking me seriously, "I mean, he was on top of me, ya know, puttin' it to me, when we started arguin'.

The Fighting Missionary Position.

"So, anyway, I split when he got off. Verna and me toked up at her place and watched some wrestling videos, you know, to take my mind off him."

"Wrestling videos?"

"Yeah," she grins so wide I see green lines between her teeth and gums. She should date a periodontist, "She had a whole batch of 'em. You know, sort of `The Best of...' or I guess what you'd call like `Greatest Hits' or something. We really got into it, man. No shit."

"What about your recently released beloved? You two gonna make up?"

"Oh, I talked to him. It's just rough, you know, the first time together. He got all moral and shit since being in the joint. He's all reformed, like he's gonna be an alter boy," she says, awaiting a laugh she doesn't get, "plus he wanted to know who was givin' me rides to work, you know, like pulling a jealousy thing on me, right? Well, fuck him being jealous for God's sake, okay? So what if I'm not as tight as I was before he went to jail? What does he expect? He knows what I do, and he never bitched about the money I sent him when he was inside. But," she finally lights the new Doral she's been tapping on the bar, "we sort of worked it out."

Then she winks at me, and I have no idea why.

I glance towards the tavern's back entrance. Verna's stationed by the Lethal Weapon pinball machine, beyond the pool table. Perfect. I've more plants in this place than a flower shop. Once again, I check my watch. Almost showtime.

"Did you also tell hubby that Jake was coming here this morning?"

She drags a needle marked hand across her nose, then wipes it on her pants.

208

"Oh, screw Jake and screw my husband...."

Before she completes the thought, or perhaps before she forms it, Jake Livesay walks into McFeely's.

"Put my purse back behind the bar, Shiela" says Loni to the efficient barkeep, "I'll get it later."

The man informally known as Dickhead greets me with his best impersonation of interpersonal warmth, and we move to the back booth closest to the pool table.

Did I say booth? These things are tiny little benches on either side of an itsy-bitsy table.

I sit facing the rear; Verna is directly past Jake's left shoulder. At the bar is a heavy-set woman in oversized Pendlelton shirt talking head-to-head with a younger blond whose hair is unceremoniously stuffed into a baseball cap.

Being hospitable, I offer Jake a drink.

"Beer's fine for me," he says, forcing a smile.

There's a sign on the wall: "For faster booth service, approach the center of the bar."

I obey they sign, order two beers and one Squirt, and sit back down. The other beer is for Richard, and he damn well better show up.

Bingo.

"Here he is," says Jake.

I turn and look. That's him, all right. Richard Tibbit, former recluse, out in public. He's actually shaved and buttoned his shirt. Damn, he looks almost respectable and positively rational. In fact, Jake, Richard, and I are the three best-dressed men in McFeely's.

I wave him over, my adrenaline pumping.

"I already got you a beer, Richard, join us."

Richard Tibbit saunters through McFeely's Tavern with all the grace and confidence of Fred Astaire dancing down a staircase. If this is a performance, it's nothing short of astonishing.

"Good morning, gentleman," intones Richard pleasantly as he sits down, "nice we could all get together."

"Uh, hi, Richard," chokes out Jake, and he extends his hand.

Richard doesn't falter for a second. He grasps Dickhead's paw in a firm, manly grip, and gives it a good shake.

My heart's pounding so hard my shirt shakes.

Both men take a gulp of beer; I clutch my Squirt.

Before the silence becomes awkward, Richard speaks. He sounds authentically humble.

"Listen, Jake, I owe you an apology and I know it. So, just let me speak here so I can get what I've gotta say off my chest all at once without having to drag it out, okay?"

Jake nods, opens his mouth to answer, but Richard just plows ahead. Good.

"I've said some things about you that I never should have said, and the only excuse I can offer is that I believed 'em when I said 'em. But, Jeff here – and I trust this guy, okay – Jeff says he's checked into everything, and that despite appearances – what I thought was happening — and inferences on my part, you're clean of any involvement with my father's death, you didn't cover anything up, or do anything illegal or immoral. So, that means that I've been a paranoid, suspicious, asshole, right?"

Jake doesn't answer.

"Anyway," Richard continues, "I regret talking about you like you were a pervert, or a murderer, or any other ideas I had about you that cast you in a negative light. I give you my solemn vow, and this is the God's own truth, that I take it all back, that I am truly sorry, and that I will never, ever, say a bad word about you again. There, I said it, and I can only hope that you can understand how a guy like me – you know, head injured and all – can get his thinking twisted sometimes, and that you can find it in your heart to forgive me. I've found God in these past few years, and my past is my past. I hold no grudges, and I don't want folks holding any against me."

Had this really been Jack Nicholson, the Academy would be polishing his Oscar. This is as good as it gets.

Okay, Jake, you're on.

"Well, Richard, it takes a big man to admit a mistake," Jake says, grasping at cliches, "and I want you to know that I accept your apology. I say that we should just forget all about those things. I don't see any reason to dwell on the past, especially the painful parts. You know I never had a thing against your dad. In fact, I thought he was a fine man...."

Jake should have shut up after the first sentence. Richard's ear-tips are turning red, and his eyes are losing focus. Please God, don't let him lose it.

"...so let's just let bygones be bygones, Richard. We'll enjoy this beer together and I'll be on my way."

"Yeah," says Richard, and it has too many syllables. His vibes are changing. It's subtle, but I can feel it. Richard's fighting to stay in character, his friendly smile smeared across that face like bad make-up.

Damn.

Everything went fine until Jake opened his mouth. Now, Tibbit has one hand on his beer, the other forming into a fist.

Jake lifts his beer, and proposes a toast.

"To letting the past stay buried," offers the dickhead.

What an idiot.

Richard rotates his neck, and it's as if all suppressed hostilities rise from his shoulders directly into his eyes. If Milton Layden saw this, he'd have a seizure. If Jake sees this, were screwed. If Richard loses it, we're doomed.

I lock eyes with Verna and give an emphatic nod.

"You stupid, ugly whore!" Verna screams at Loni from across the room. All attention immediately rivets on the heavy hooker with the big hair.

"Bitch!" counters Loni, and they race towards each other in heated rage.

The entire tavern is dumbstruck. Even Mr. GPC turns to look.

WHAM!

Verna clotheslines Loni with a strong arm across the chest. The red head flails wildly backward, her well-formed derriere slamming into our booth. The impact launches Jake's beer out of the bottle and into his lap.

"Jesus Christ!" he yells, scrambling to his feet while Loni pitches herself at Verna.

"This is incredible," Richard exclaims, his voice resonating with joyous surprise.

The McFeely crowd cheers.

"Cat fight! Cat fight!"

Assorted human out cries augmented by rapid metallic whirring and clicking accompanies this action-packed floorshow.

The bartender, drop-jawed, watches Loni leap like a flyboy and grab Verna by the throat. The screaming whores topple onto the pool table, kicking and yelping.

The bartender, initially slow on the uptake, now pushes her way past the customers, shouting for Loni and Verna to break it up. The battling hookers roll from the table, whacking away at each other with intoxicated enthusiasm.

Verna grabs Loni by the left arm and swings her towards the wall. The redhead bounces off, turns, and receives a solid kick to her midsection. Only momentarily dismayed, Loni grabs a metal folding chair from against the wall – the ultimate illegal object – and begins circling.

The bartender, surprisingly, does not come between them, but rather approaches Loni from the rear.

Wait a second. I know this match. This is the final moments of the classic battle between Irwin R. Schiester and Rick "The Model" Martel from the late 1980's. Schiester accidentally beaned the referee...

Loni, to increase impact on Verna's skull, throws the chair behind her head.

WHUMP!

Down goes the bartender, supposedly stunned but not seriously damaged. She sits, head in hands, moaning on the sidelines.

Richard can hardly contain himself, Jake is speechless, I'm increasingly giddy, and Loni now has Verna in a headlock.

In the original televised fracas, just when Irwin had Martel at his mercy, Tatanka, "The Undefeated Native American," rushed out from the dressing room and disrupted the match.

The rear door bursts open, and running down the back hall comes the biggest Indian I've ever seen in my life. Even though he's fully clothed, I recognize him immediately. So do Richard and Jake.

Loni, meanwhile, has modified the headlock into in a bizarre variation on the so-called "sleeper hold." When she notices the enormous Native American looming larger than life, she releases Verna. Then, in classic form, raises her palms pleadingly and backs away shaking her head from side to side.

I've got tears in my eyes.

Then Loni turns, bolts, and runs like hell down the hall and out the back door. Verna does likewise, as if chasing after her.

The Indian, however, stands his ground, leans down, and helps the bartender to her feet.

They both smile.

No one knows quite what to make of all this, but the McFeely's crowd never quite knows what to make of anything.

Someone asks for another beer; and someone else requests hard-boiled eggs. The bartender hustles back to work as if nothing unusual has transpired.

Still standing by the pool table, the Indian's pin-point pupils aim directly at us – or maybe for Richard, or maybe for Jake. His arms are so damn long he could probably reach out and throttle any of us.

He moves.

He's coming this way.

We stand, as curious as we are timorous.

As he gets closer, the big woman in the Pendleton shirt swivels around on her stool, leans out and puts her hand on the Indian's arm. He turns, looking directly at her.

As the last smoke stream vanishes up her nose in elaborate French inhale, Rikki says, "That one guy used to be a professional wrestler, remember?"

"Yeah, I remember." he replies flatly, and nods courteously at a flabbergasted Richard before looking into the eyes of Jake Livesay.

Jake gulps.

"You're the man who sent me to prison, aren't you?"

Livesay sets his jaw.

"Yes, I did. I was doing my job."

The Indian nods. He's thinking it over.

"Well, in a way I want to thank you. Best thing that ever happened. While I was in prison, I found God there."

I didn't know God was serving time.

"Oh." That's all Jake can come up with.

"Yes," the Indian explains, offering his massive grip, "I became a Catholic. I was raised Episcopalian, but now I'm Catholic."

Jake forces a smile and shakes the big fellow's hand.

"I'm trying to work things out with my wife," says the Indian awkwardly, "that was the redhead that ran out."

A peculiar grin tugs at his lips.

"Anyway, I say let the past be dead and buried. No hard feelings about anything."

And he looks at Richard when he says it, as if seeking consensus.

We all agree, the past is best left dead and buried.

With that, the big Indian turns and walks away.

The three of us look at each other, laugh a laugh of released tension, and shake our heads in bemusement.

"Well, we better be goin' I guess," I say, "besides Jake here looks like he could use a change of pants."

"No kidding. I almost wet them myself when Tonto there

came towards us. Shit, he's bigger than that guy in `One Flew Over the Cuckoo's Nest'."

We all exit gracefully. Jake' maroon car is parked directly in front of 1-2-3 Pawn, where fast cash is still a fact of life.

"Well, I guess everything is settled then, isn't it?" he asks.

I'll answer for both of us.

"Yes. Everything is settled for good."

He pauses after pulling out his keys. He's got something on his mind.

"That was really weird back there," he says, jabbing a thumb towards the tavern, "all of us together, the Indian..."

I can't resist.

"Forget it, Jake, it's McFeely's."

"Yeah," he concurs, "it's McFeely's."

If this were an episode of *Fury*, the horse would whinny.

With that, he's gone. Not for good, but gone.

I intentionally parked down the block, closer to the alley running between McFeely's and Blue Mountain Cable. Richard, as instructed, parked past the corner. I didn't want the three of us parked together.

As Richard and I pass the alley, out pops Loni, Verna, the Indian, and Rikki "Supertongue."

Verna races up, all effusive and enthusiastic.

"Wasn't that sumpthin'? Weren't we just fucking fantastic?"

"Perfect, absolutely perfect," I assure them, "but how did you get the bartender into the act?"

"Easy," says Verna, "she's my cousin Shiela, and she'll do any stunt for a good laugh. We was good, huh?"

Richard beams like a proud papa.

"Hey," he says, "you were as good as anything I've seen in the squared circle. Tell me," he says to Rikki, "where the hell did you come from?"

She allows that massive tongue of hers to loll out of her mouth simply for the sake of impressive visuals.

I'm impressed.

"Oh, Jeff tracked me down in Seattle. I own property here that's got some problems, so to speak," she says, and Loni looks around uncomfortably. It's her crash pad Rikki's talking about. "I needed to come here anyway, and Jeff just made it easier and more fun. Besides I had some catching up to do with the old friend I was sittin' with at the bar."

HEADLOCK

The Indian, towering in stature, steps forward.

"I don't think we've been introduced," he says politely, "my name is Jacob."

"The man who wrestles with angels," I remark, referencing the Biblical personage after whom he was named.

"Yes, and this is my angel right here," says Jacob, and he gives Loni a squeeze.

Oh, brother.

He may have found God, but at five o'clock, Loni is finding heroine. As *Redbook* would ask, "Can this Marriage be Saved?"

"Loni," I ask, "did Faron come back alone?"

"No, I meant to tell ya 'bout that. He came back with a couple of guys, and from what I heard, one of them is staying to watch the old lady while the other two come into town. The one guy gave me the creeps with a capitol K."

Spelling isn't Loni's forte.

"I mean, he's real weird, with veins stickin' out all over."

She's one to talk about veins.

"Well, we're off," says I, "Thanks for your help."

They all smile, and Rikki gives me a direct look.

"See ya later," she says, and anyone can take that as simple social expression or a direct promise.

They trot back into the alley, probably returning to McFeely's for Loni's purse and a round of drinks. I walk Richard to his perfectly restored Borgward Isabella.

Halfway there, he breaks into gales of laughter.

"That was one hell of a show. One hell of a show. Why did you go through all that trouble, I mean, to set it up?"

"Because I believe in putting an upbeat button on the end of every episode," I answer, "It's not enough for me that's `it's over,' it has to be over with an ending, something to leave you laughing or smiling when you walk out."

He stops and looks at me like he's not sure he's seen me before.

"You a private eye or a Broadway producer?"

He fishes out a Bel-Air and I dig out an Old Gold.

We share the Zippo.

"The last Broadway production I saw involved a drive-by dog shooting," I say. "It's just the way I do things, Richard. Maybe a bit over the top, but that's the style I grew up with."

We're at his car now, and we haven't said a word for a while.

I can tell he's thinking, and thinking hard.

"Listen, Jeff," says Richard, searching for words, "I asked you to find out...you know...and now it's supposed to be over. At least, over in that I don't have to worry anymore about somethin' happening to me or the wife."

"True."

"But I can't help thinking that Violet's still alive..."

"And out of her mind with brain cancer," I add helpfully.

"Yeah, and that ass-hole Jake we both know was in on it..."

I put my hand on his shoulder.

"Listen, Richard. We made a deal – a deal with Jake, a deal with ourselves – the past is past. Let it go. This part of the story, your part, is over. Understand?"

He's wrestling with it.

"It's over for you, Richard. Period. After all these years, it's over. Done deal."

He glances up at the dusty-brown storm clouds.

"Is it over for you, Jeff?"

No. Not by a long shot.

"To tell the truth, Richard, it's not over for me. But you're not me, and I'm not you. Everybody wants' something. Some want vindication, others want cash, some want both."

He averts his eyes. He's not going to ask if there's a book, not now.

"I want something too," I admit, "and it may be selfish or self-serving, or maybe not. Part of it is justice, the other...well, maybe good ol' American Retribution, but I want it, and I have every intention of getting it."

He leans against the Borgward and holds up a palm, feeling for raindrops.

"Mind if I ask..."

"Yes, I mind," I interrupt, but not rudely. "But you'll like it, I promise you that. Trust me, Richard. You do trust me, don't you?"

He looks at me as if his eyes can read my very soul. He smiles.

"Yeah, damn it," he says, "I trust you."

He unlocks the car and swings open the door.

"Richard, I have one last question for you, if you don't mind."

"Go ahead."

"Why is it that you get so tweaked if someone calls you a son of a bitch?'

He gives me that Verna look.

"Because," he says softly, "it's an insult to my natural mother."

"You're right. It is. I don't blame you a bit for feeling that way."

He nods. We are in perfect agreement.

A few prefatory raindrops splash on the windshield.

"Better go," says Richard, and he does.

I stand there for a minute, watching the Borgward make it's way up Poplar Street. Inside my head, the Jefferson Airplane's big hit from *Surrealistic Pillow* plays louder and louder.

I bring the first three fingers of my right hand together. What's the deal with this song?

Bunny rabbits. Little cartoon pink-eyed fluffy bunnies.

"Go ask Alice," Grace Slick sings in my head. I don't know anyone named Alice.

According to my watch, everything is on schedule. Walking back towards McFeely's, my cell phone rings.

"Yes?"

"Hey, it's me," says Ron Faver, "I'm in position and everything is wired, connected, and ready to roll."

"Don't worry Mr. Faver," I answer cheerfully, "I'm on my way."

"You bringing a gun?"

"I'm not the kind to carry a weapon, Ron, you know that."

"You liable to be one very dead author if you don't," says Faver seriously, "if you got one, bring it. You know, it may just be prudent."

Prudent. That word's sure making a comeback.

"Yeah, well if I get killed, I'll get rich via posthumous sales."

"Can't spend it in the grave, pal," insists Ron, "take my advice. Bring a weapon. Not that I have a weapon, mind you. In fact, none of my crew has anything more lethal than an F connector or a BNC plug. But you, you crazy-ass bastard — with the stunt you're trying to pull, someone's gonna wind up dead."

'You're very encouraging, Mr. Favor," I say as I approach my car.

"Hey, you seen that new Jewish Kosher Satellite Network?" he asks.

"No, what's the punchline?"

"You need two sets of dishes."

"Very funny. I thought they could only get transponder space for ten seconds on Friday before sundown – you know, just enough time to say `Don't touch that dial.'"

Conversation concluded.

Leaning against the Buick is the scruffy blond in the baseball cap. She puts her arms around me and kisses me on the lips.

"What happens now?" she asks.

We go chasing rabbits.

"Meeting Ron Faver near the Whitman Mission."

"Who's Ron Faver?"

"We worked together years ago producing irritating TV commercials," I explain as we get in, "Faver's his real name, but no one calls him that except old pals."

"What do new pals call him?" Randy asks.

"Chet Rogers, segment producer for America's number one tabloid TV show, *Hot Story*."

IX

"You really want to nail this bastard," states Chet Rogers flatly, "and nailed he's gonna get."

"Well, there's nothing like exposing a crooked cop on national television," I insist, "not that Mrs. Escarrega needs any more vindication. It's just my way of..."

My way of what?

"Getting even?"

No. No one ever gets even. I got the idea of exposing Carter on TV from the old movie, *Champagne for Caesar*. Ronald Coleman plays a know-it-all who decides to "get" despicable soap tycoon and game-show sponsor, Vincent Price, by bankrupting him live on Price's nationally televised quiz show.

Cute film, downright inspirational, and even Art Linkletter is in it.

Ron Faver, alias Chet Rogers, looks nothing like Art Linkletter, but exactly like Sylvester Stallone in *Night Hawks*. He also seems to have "gone Hollywood."

"You know, Chet, you don't need those sunglasses. In fact, it looks like rain."

"You be one smart ass small town rube," snaps Chet humorously, "wearing these makes me feel like a cross between Robert Evans and Doc Brown in *Back to the Future II*."

We're seven miles West of Walla Walla, stationed beyond the Whitman Mission, telescopic video lenses targeting the parking lot next to the Visitors' Center. I've already walked the site, following the path leading from the Visitor Center to the mission grounds, the Oregon Trail, and the bridge over the irrigation ditch. I even made the long climb up the high hill to the Whitman Memorial Monument and back again to pause for prayer at the Great Grave – final resting-place of the massacre victims.

Now, I'm wired for sound.

"The wind's not helping much, as far as the audio goes," remarks Chet to one of his crew, and the engineer makes adjustments.

Randy, her lovely face lined with concern tugs my sleeve.

"Jeff, are you doing something crazy or dangerous?"

"Both. In not too long, right in that parking lot down there, Detective Tom Carter is going to sell $200,000 worth of drugs to the Phineas Priesthood. We're gonna bust em on national television and let the chips fall where they may. Mayhem will reign supreme."

She doesn't seem enthused.

"What if they shoot you?"

"They won't commit murder on television. Hell, Carter would lose his job for sure, and no pension. Besides, not even the Phineas Priesthood runs around shooting nice, white, all-American tourists at a National Historic Site."

Looking up at the sky, she scowls. She's not convinced.

"Listen," I say reassuringly, "this is the perfect place for them to meet. It's public, yet not crowded. Neither one can `get the drop' on the other, and it would be almost impossible for one of em to rip off the other. It's open, safe, self-contained, and relaxed."

"Yeah, well, the weather sucks, and we all may get hit by lightning."

"Lightning hit me at the J&M," is my smart reply, but she doesn't laugh.

An unpleasant wind swirls dust towards us, and we briefly shield our eyes. The dark clouds appear a peculiar blue. This is Walla Walla storm weather, all right.

Randy turns her attention back to the Whitman Mission. "Is this where you have your climax?" asks Randy, forcing a double entendre.

"Hopefully," I murmur, "did you know there's a real mysteries at the mission?"

"Like what? I mean, they know who did the massacre way back when, right?"

I sit down beside her on the hard ground.

"Yeah, sure they know that. That's not it. The mystery concerns the little daughter of Marcus and Narcissa Whitman. She was born right there," I point towards the location, "in 1837. She was just past two years old when she left the dinner table, taking a little cup and saucer down to the stream. She never came back."

"Kidnapped?"

This isn't Sarah.

"They found the cup first, then the body. She drowned."

"How sad," says Randy.

"The mystery is: where's the body buried?"

She squints.

"Whadya mean?"

"When the massacre occurred in 1847, the bodies of Marcus, Narcissa and the others were buried in a mass grave next to the child. But, here's the problem: the first gravesite, hastily dug, was only two or three feet deep. The mass grave was ravaged by coyotes or wolves, so The Oregon Volunters had to re-bury the victims, searching all over the mission grounds for body parts."

She shudders. So do I. The scenario reminds me of Issaquah.

"Anyway, the remains were gathered together, reburied, a wagon box turned over them and a large mound of dirt put on top to protect the grave site. This action helped identify the location of the mass grave in later years. Then, in 1897 when that granite tomb you see down there was placed over the site, and the remains were placed in a coffin, the site may have been moved slightly again."

"Which means?"

"The mass grave's been moved from where it was in the first place, and the first place was next to the little girl. Hence, to this day, no one knows where she's buried."

There's a long pause of meditative silence before Randy speaks.

"You could find her, couldn't you? You could ask."

I stare out over the Mission.

"You said when you want to know something, you ask. Can't you ask? Maybe ask the little girl to tell you?"

For a man who'll listen patiently to anything, it seems to me that Randy doesn't know when to shut up.

I stand up and dig out a smoke. My discomfort is obvious, but Randy ignores it.

"Jeff, what was her name? The little girl."

Had she asked me any other day, I wouldn't know. Having just walked the site and read the kiosks, I know her name in full.

"Alice Clarissa Whitman." I always liked the name Clarissa.

Chet Rogers, more wired than his gear, approaches us with professional enthusiasm

"We've got video from two...no, three angles," he explains,

pointing towards an on-site camera-toting tourist, who's no tourist at all, "that's number three. Not that we need him, but he's good to have. Actually, we got the park covered no matter what happens, plus a powerful pin-point microphone will be pointed directly at the star players. When they exchange loot for drugs, we'll have it all documented. That would really be enough," he says to Randy, "but your boyfriend here wants to make it personal."

"Personal?" She looks to me, but I change the subject.

"Hey Ron, anyone mention that you look exactly like Sylvester Stallone in *Night Hawks*?"

"Yeah," he confirms, "it's the beard and the leather coat."

A few more cars drift into the Mission parking lot. For a lousy day, they're doing a surprisingly good business.

"Look," I call out, pointing, "here comes the drive-away car – the one with the dope in the trunk."

Sure enough. Here comes a 1985 Pontiac exactly as Carter described on-line. It pulls into the parking lot, and Chet has all cameras rolling. I've got an earpiece allowing me to hear everything via the super-sensitive shotgun microphone, plus Chet's closed-circuit directorial patter.

I peek through the viewfinder.

Yep, that's Carter himself, in Nike gear, getting out of the driver's side. He glances around, pulls out a cell phone, makes a quick call, and repockets it.

I check my watch.

He's fashionably early.

I turn to Randy.

"The next time we're in a record store," I say off-handedly, "remind me to pick up *Surrealistic Pillow* by the Jefferson Airplane."

"Yeah, *White Rabbit* was playing when we were in Classic Wax," she recalls, "you never mentioned you were an Airplane fan."

An airplane fan? How aeronautical.

"I can't get the song out of my head."

"Hey, it could be worse – how 'bout *Rice is Nice* by the Lemon Pipers?"

"You're right, it could be worse."

"Here comes a red Monte Carlo," barks Ron, "is that the one?"

That's the one, all right.

"Have a shot of courage," says Randy, offering me a bottle.

Pepto-Bismal

Cute.

There's a distant rumble of unwelcome thunder, I'm working my way towards the Mission, and damned if I'm not thinking about twitchy-nosed bunnies as I move through the high rye grass bordering the parking lot.

The Chevy approaches the highway 12 turnoff to the Mission, I'm in position, crouching in the rye, heart pounding, dangerously close to the Pontiac. The air is electric humidity.

The Monte Carlo drives in, and pulls to a stop at the other end of the parking lot. Two men sit in front. The driver kills the engine.

This is it.

Roll tape.

Derek Bane Faron, all legs and elbows in faded jeans and gray sweatshirt, exits the passenger side carrying a briefcase. The walk from his Monte Carlo towards Carter takes forever.

"Everything all right?" he asks Carter, and Carter nods. I can't make out the face of the guy in the Monte Carlo's driver's seat. They walk towards the Pontiac.

"You're gonna love this," enthuses Carter under his breath, his voice tinny in my ear piece, "Incredible stuff. You can step on it more than once, cut it 25%, and still get no complaints."

"I don't care if a buncha niggers complain," remarks Faron softly, "the idea is to enslave 'em and OD 'em, not entertain 'em." He laughs like that's really funny, and Carter laughs too. Two travel pals sharing a joke at a National Historic Site. Carter opens the Pontiac's trunk. Yes, a couple tourist buddies yukking it up and talking car talk.

"Whoop, there it is. The best damn cocaine available." insists Carter.

He ought to know.

"No shit," comments Faron. From my vantagepoint in the high rye grass, I can see his butt as he leans over. "That's good looking stuff. Let me check it out."

They both lean over.

Soon, they both raise up, slam the trunk, and I'm almost ready to make my move.

THC stands there, twirling the Pontiac's key on a rabbit's foot key-fob. Faron reaches for it, but Carter snaps it behind his back.

"First, the loot. You know my shit's real. Let's see yours."

I love it when cops talk scatological.

Faron looks around casually, smiles as if Carter made a light comment, then turns and props the briefcase on the Pontiac's closed trunk, snaps the release, and pops it open. Carter takes a look-see.

Pleased, THC shuts the briefcase, takes it, and hands Faron the key fob.

"Give me a ride back into the city, OK?" Carter asks, and Faron nods.

This is it, kids. The exchange has been made.

I'm in the open now, walking towards them, Chet Rogers snapping directions into my ear.

"Your right in frame, perfect!"

"Yes," I intone, "whether drugs or skin color, if it's all white, it's all right…"

A magnificent lightning fork slices the southern sky, followed by a quadraphonic thunderclap.

"Jesus H. Christ," exclaims Chet, "thank God for special effects. Keep going, this is gonna be classic."

Classic like Classic Rock. The Moodie Blues and the Jefferson Airplane.

Both men, staring at the lightning's last gleaming, turn at the sound of my voice.

"Ladies and gentleman," I announce as if the warm-up for Ed Sullivan, "here we see narcotics detective Tom Carter delivering $200,000 worth of cocaine to Derek Bane Faron of the Phineas Priesthood."

Faron and Carter are momentarily stunned, each looking at the other for signs of betrayal. Carter holds the briefcase full of cash; Faron stands stupidly clutching the rabbit's foot key fob.

Rabbit's foot.

White Rabbit.

White rabbits are white …

Oh my God.

In one horrid self-abasing epiphany, I realize my incredible blunder.

…because they are albino.

The man in the Monte Carlo.

Verna's been right all along – I am stupid. I see clearly now. The other man in the Monte Carlo is Arvid Armstad.

With brazen, willful bravado, I've blundered into a classic

reverse sting.

Carter isn't making a sale; he's setting up a bust. The takedown comes when they hit the city limits – Carter's jurisdiction. The Pontiac gets pulled over, Faron gets busted for 2 kilos, $200,000 goes toward the city's bottom line, and THC gets the glory, vindication, and career redemption.

Faron turns his gaze from my face to Carter's, and reality is written all over it.

The Monte Carlo's door kicks open, and out steps Arvid Armstad brandishing a .45 automatic. Suddenly, as they say in the paperbacks, the jig is up, and everyone knows it. Faron reacts, catching Carter off-guard, smashing his fist into the cop's throat and spinning him into the line of fire. Arvid pulls up short, Faron drops to one knee and fires a hastily drawn handgun.

Arvid's white right cheek explodes in red wetness, his weapon clattering to the pavement as he falls backwards, clutching his mouth.

"Holy shit!" yells Chet, but the blood pounding in my ears almost drowns him out.

In a thunderclap of synchronicity, all hell breaks loose. A drenching downpour of near-Biblical proportions hits us with horrific intensity.

Carter, gasping, goes for his gun; Faron sweeps his firearm in a wild arc, unsure if to fire at the cop or your nerve-wracked narrator. In that adrenaline fueled microsecond, another mind-numbing crack of lightning blinds us, the earth trembles, and a scorched, flaming tree limb rip through the power lines sending seven thousand volts snaking across the rain-soaked pavement like an enraged electric anaconda.

We all run like hell.

I dive towards the tall grass, splashing face first into slimy mud. Filthy, drenched, and personally humiliated, I don't need Marlene Dietrich's crystal ball to see that my future is all used up. The bust went badly, an undercover cop is seriously wounded, and the blame belongs to author/private eye Jeff Reynolds. And it's all captured on videotape for *Hot Story*.

I can see it now: Chet gets an Emmy; I get prison.

Only a moment's passed since my mud-bog belly flop, and I peek out at the insanity surrounding me. Terrified tourists racing for shelter in the Visitor Center, Armstad writhing on the ground, his face and hands covered in blood, and a wild-eyed Derek Bane

Faron not far from me — a scare-crow crouching in a hurricane, looking for a way out.

There is no way out.

Or maybe there is.

I must be out of my mind.

"Faron," I call to him, "take me. I'll be your hostage and we'll both get the hell out of here!"

He whirls, pointing his handgun at my head.

"What?"

He doesn't know who I am or why I showed up, and in all this chaos, it doesn't much matter.

"Listen," I yell over the storm, "I'm from *Hot Story* – we did that feature on the Phineas Priesthood, remember?"

He remembers; he's confused. We're both soaked.

"If I hadn't stopped Carter, they would have busted your ass big time the minute you drove away."

He looks at me, rattled, desperate, and drenched.

"You're on national TV right now," I lie, hoping I live long enough to rationalize my dishonesty – at this point I really don't care about Sissela Bok, no matter how charming the name. "The Feds know all about the Priesthood, the bank robberies," I figure I'll toss out everything and see what works, "even the one in Walla Walla you pulled yourself, Jake, your mother, even the AWA and NWA schedules."

He grabs me by the collar and shakes me like a rag.

"I don't care what they know," he yells, "this is war, I'm proud of every thing I've done, and I'll die before I let those pigs get me."

Mental note: when this becomes a book, never let his character say *that*.

He repeats it for emphasis, adding, "fucking" before "die" and "pigs".

"Fine with me," I offer honestly, "but if you shoot me," here's where I get forceful, "we kill the camera. That means you're sunk – no air time, no glory, no dogs in heaven, get it?"

He doesn't get the bit about dogs in heaven, but I think he grasps the concept – better a TV martyr than just another gunned down punk.

"Let's go!" That's him making like he's in charge, pressing his gun against my head, pushing me against the pelting rain towards the Great Grave. Carter's already called for backup; scream-

226

ing sirens are only minutes away.

"This is incredible shit," Chet exclaims, "and we're getting it all. Stay alive man, just stay alive! Carter's comin' 'round from the side! Hot damn! We'll get the climax on camera!"

I love exciting rescues, but Carter saving my life makes me want to puke

Faron suddenly stops and spins me around.

"You said *Hot Story* didn't ya?" He doesn't sound happy. "You're some television guy, a media person, right?"

"Well..."

"I know who fuckin' controls television, you asshole!" he yells, pushing me back around, "You know too!"

If this is my last line, I'll make it punch.

"The person who holds the remote?"

"The goddam Jews!"

WHAM!

My brains explode in blazing multi-colored light shards. The son of a bitch – and she *is* a bitch – whacked my head with the gun butt.

Sloshy mud and wind whipped grass rise up and slap my face. I'm sinking in cold ooze.

Head injured.

Hurkos.

Pain-throbs trigger red flash bulbs behind my eyes. These same heart-hammered throbs become repetitive bass lines.

Jefferson Airplane.

Sixteenth century mystic Isaac Luria believed it was beneficial to meditate while lying prostrate on the grave of a saint...

"Go ask Alice..."

...souls bound together, thusly fused, ascend together.

She's here, beneath me.

Radiant maiden

Glorious child

Alice Clarissa Whitman.

The red sea parts behind my eyes and I see only light upon light.

I have made death a messenger of joy to thee, why dost thou grieve? To visions of light I hail thee..

Death?

Swell. Dying is the last thing I want to do.

I am filled with an astonishing sense of hope – hope that this is a near-death experience and not the real thing.

I am entering a sea of light. It is a singing, exuberant sea, moved by waves of unspeakable love in a cosmic, melodic dance.

This is not good news.

If I come back, will I wear crystals and buy John Tesh albums? If so, I refuse to go.

I can't be dead; I'm still sarcastic.

Okay, this is all shock, trauma, and a gun butt to the head. You can say that if you want, and I don't blame you. But I'll tell you one thing, it sure looks real to me – especially the vision of little Alice Whitman holding her teacup and saucer. Suspended between earth and heaven, enveloped in shimmering opalescence, she clutches a corncob pipe between her teeth. Her massive forearms adorned with dual anchors, she offers two simple directives.

"Always eats your spinach," and "tell him to look to the left, now."

At a moment like this, I'll take all the advice I can get.

SPLAT!

I'm back, face first in the mud, my head pain-wracked, Faron standing Goliath-like over me screaming down about kikes, niggers, and media. Someone needs a nap.

I yank my face up from the muck, interrupting his diatribe with an absolutely authoritative command.

"Look to your left, now!"

He does.

Thwap!

A perfectly pitched hard glass bottle of Pepto-Bismal strikes him right between the eyes, breaking his nose. He stumbles backwards, stunned and blinded. God bless Randy Nussbaum.

"Freeze, Faron!"

That's Carter's voice.

I roll over and sit up.

Detective Tom Carter is in 100% Serve and Protect mode, his massive weapon pointed directly at Faron. Randy, red-cheeked and panting, stands off to the side, her camera hanging around her neck. She looks like she's been having hot sex. Must be from running in the rain. Why am I thinking like this? I'm in shock, okay?

"Drop the weapon, Derek," requests Carter, sounding every bit the professional negotiator. "There's no reason to die over two kilos of cocaine. Let the hostages go, and we'll talk this out."

Faron stares unmoved and unresponsive. I hear the metallic

HEADLOCK

click and whir of Randy's autowinder.

"Besides," continues Carter conversationally, "maybe our friend here," he gestures towards me, "screwed things up so much a good lawyer will get you off the drug charge, let you plead self defense for the shooting. Hey, it could happen. Who the hell knows anymore, right? " He throws me a look harder than Faron's gun butt.

He has every right to be pissed, but I'm in no mood for guilt. I hurt, I'm tired, and I want to go home. If I live, I think I'll have sex with Randy until I'm dehydrated

"He's right," I add helpfully, stumbling to my feet, "and I ought to know. I represented the Hell's Demon's in their dispute over the tag team belt."

"Fuck the Hell's Demons," snaps Faron.

Carter seems tempted to shoot me himself.

Sometimes I'm relentless.

"Just do what your fat-ass murdering mother did – hire a Jew-boy lawyer."

Faron whips that gun around, and points it right at me. Carter blows him away. Or tries to. The big gun doesn't fire.

"Shit!" Carter spits a reflexive expletive, Faron catches himself in mid murder, and THC is the new target.

"Drop it, and drop it now."

Carter drops it.

"Where's the camera," Faron barks at me, "where's the mother-fucking camera?"

Randy holds up her Pentax, snapping off more shots.

"Not that camera, the TV camera!"

"You jerk," yells Randy, "you...you...you have no real friends and...and...and everybody hates you!"

That'll fix him.

"Who says I got no friends?" he counters.

Oh, spare me.

"What is this," mutters Chet dispassionately, "*Jerry Springer* in the woods?" There's a professional media man for you.

Sirens scream down highway 12 — an ambulance, police, and probably a fire engine. We don't have much time.

"I'm gonna kill a goddam cop," declares Faron to the air, imagining a camera location, "and then I'm gonna kill this Jew."

"I never said I was Jewish," I insist, "Mom wanted me to be a Rabbi, but Uncle Kalib wanted me to be a Mulla."

229

He pays me no mind, and looks at Randy.

"You throw a mean bottle, bitch. What's your name?"

"Don't do this, Derek, please," begs Carter, but his influence is less than minimal.

"Nussbaum," she answers, "Randy Denise Nussbaum."

"Another Jew," he sneers, raises his weapon, and points in back and forth between Randy and Carter.

"Welcome to Ruby Ridge II, the Sequel," declares Faron, "first to die is one lying traitor cop."

He advances two steps towards Carter, his arm extended, pointing the gun barrel directly at the cop's chest.

I look into THC's eyes, and see only defiant resignation before he closes them, perhaps forever.

Randy screams.

A single shot echoes through the wet woods.

Carter opens his eyes. Only Randy and I are standing.

Faron, dead, is face first in bloody grass.

"What happened?" stammers Carter.

"You saved our lives," I explain, approaching him, "it was a fight to the death, and you won."

I hand him the Luger. Yeah, I kept it.

Reinforcements, fire trucks, and ambulances pull into the parking lot. Sirens wail, lights flash. He looks back at the arriving cavalry before asserting one inarguable observation.

"This is the only weapon Faron had, right?"

A little corruption and a dollop of practicality go a long way. We can all still get what we want.

X

I killed Derek Faron and lied about it.

Had Milton Layden been there, he would have shot Faron too. That (A+Ob) stuff only goes so far.

Make that double for Sissela Bok – she would have lied through her scholarly teeth.

The Talmud says a person may lie for the sake of peace, and Bok wrote that acute, life-threatening crises justify lies.

My lie gave Carter the peace he deserved. I was wrong about him, okay? He carefully cultivated that corrupt cop image for a long-term, well-plotted reverse sting on Faron and the Phineas Priesthood. In truth, Carter completely atoned for the Escarrega incident. With heartfelt professional dedication, he earned his redemption.

Yep, it all comes out in the wash, it's just the spin cycle that makes you crazy.

While I was getting my skull whacked during the deluge, DEA Agent Cosby and the Oregon Drug Task Force, accompanied by the FBI and the BATF, raided Faron's place at Tollgate. Violet Langness, carried out of the trailer on a makeshift stretcher, broke her neck when accidentally dropped in the mud. It's understandable — she was huge and hard to negotiate through the doorway. They pretended she was dead when they got there, and that doesn't bother me at all.

The Tollgate raid was only the beginning. Federal agents swiftly arrested suspected Phineas Priesthood operatives in Tampa, Shreveport, Yakima, Wenatchee, Portland, Moses Lake, Spokane and Seattle.

By the time Feds arrived in Dayton for Dickhead, he'd seen it all unravel on TV — Carter and I were the lead feature on *Hot Story*, and every network newscast. Jake supposedly suffered a heart attack or stroke right in front of the tube. I asked if he died with a pen in his hand, and someone seemed to think he did.

The spin on the Whitman Mission adventure, coupled with the largest number of neo-Nazis arrested in United States' history, made Detective Carter and me America's number one anti-domestic-terrorist tag team. In addition to television, we were all over the tabloids and *USA Today*. The following week, a R. Nussbaum action photo made the cover of *Time*.

All three Palm Springs television stations met me at the airport when I arrived for Left Coast Crime, and Jan Curran of the Desert Sun did an in-depth interview complete with full-color photos. I loved the headline: "Hostage Author's Reward: Big Book Deal."

Seven figures, in fact, and that doesn't include movie rights or licensing little plastic Richard Tibbit action figures with realistic HO scale Zippos.

As G. M. Ford said, "For God's sake, Reynolds, you're bigger than Tony Fennelly's tits. "

Albino Arvid was kept out of everything, as usual, allowing him to go back undercover. At least they have him busting Nazis instead of housewives at AA meetings.

I wasn't wrong about everything. Remember Jesus the dog and my impromptu explanation of drive-by dog shootings? Turns out that was the skewed 'Protection Racket' Tim Olmstad mentioned. It was the old-fashioned panhandler shakedown. Street beggars either paid up or suffered the consequences.

Amazing.

Randy's career in photojournalism, triggered by those still shots, took off like a rocket. In addition, she sold a collection of photographic character studies to a major publisher. Entitled *Relax Freely,* it's glorious black and white picture portraits of McFeely regulars. Very atmospheric and evocative, or so says the press release. Loni and Verna are in it, along with Mr. GPC, Rikki, the bartender, and Jacob, the big Indian.

Loni and Jacob's marriage was doomed the moment the big guy got out of prison. She found another job in home care, and when her kidney's started to collapse, she cut back the hard drugs. With the money she saved not buying heroin, she purchased a new set of teeth.

Randy also secured lucrative assignments from several international newsmagazines, and now travels quite a bit.

She called last week from London. She might move there for

good. Randy Nussbaum in the UK is Anglo/British Israelism at its finest. We don't see each other as much as we'd like, I guess. Not as often as we used to, for sure.

Hardly at all, anymore, actually.

Richard and his wife sold their house to Rikki. Turns out she's a real estate mogul with numerous local rentals to her name. Inherited them, I guess, from that aunt on Bonsella.

The Tibbits left town for a round-the-world cruise the minute I forked over Richard's chunk of the advance money.

"We're going to circumvent the earth," he declared happily, and I didn't bother correcting him.

THC is not in Walla Walla anymore either. We had those television appearances together – *Good Morning, America*, *Nightline*, and a few others. We got along, but never became close. He made an excellent career move, joining the U.S. Department of Terrorism and Violent Crime back in D.C.

Of course, there was one slightly sticky issue: fifty-seven thousand dollars of Faron's drug money was counterfeit; I had fifty-seven thousand dollars in my basement. I couldn't keep it, Carter sure as hell couldn't take it, and we couldn't figure out a way to turn it in without raising too many questions. Easy solution: an anonymous donation to the Museum of Tolerance in Los Angeles where my pal Rick is resident expert on hate groups.

Carter's diminutive partner gave up his career in law enforcement to tend bar at a disco in Kennewick, Washington. The police department replaced him with a handsome, young, Hispanic. I guess they wanted someone who could arrest Mexicans in their own language.

Lightning Rod Sullivan passed away recently, I hear, of natural causes. In other words, he died drunk.

I'm still here, still alive, still in Walla Walla, Washington.

I love this town. Always have, always will. Everyone has lovely lawns, and I can leave my car unlocked all night long. It's a new car, by the way. A sharp blue Volvo C-70 coupe replaced the '83 Buick.

The book is selling briskly, and the movie deal looks solid. Either Jason Patrick or Whitney Houston will play me, Nick Nolte or William Shatner will play Richard. I guess Jack Nicholson was unavailable.

Except for an occasional breakfast, I seldom frequent the Pastime, and I never go into McFeely's. Why should I? I don't drink, don't shoot pool, and never did play the punchboards.

The Dacres Saloon, where Richard Tibbit beat up a guy for calling him a son of a bitch, is empty and for lease.

When Tibbit insisted there was a book, he talked plots and conspiracies. Books aren't about plots; they're about vindication and cash, sin and redemption.

I still smoke – either Old Golds or Lucky Filters — ignore the occasional swastikas in my mailbox, the midnight phone calls, and the cars that follow a half-block behind when I drive to the store for Friskies. If someone really wanted me dead, I'd be sleeping in a graveyard fulltime by now. Maybe I'll force myself to move away to some exotic paradise. Maybe "Mukilteo by the Sea." Yes, there is such a place. Trust me.

My daughter returns from China soon, and I get her for an entire month. I'll strap her in the C-70's passenger seat and we'll blast down the highway, listening to whatever she wants, as loud as she wants. We'll rent a comfy cabin, and a small aluminum fishing boat, at Loon Lake's Granite Point Park. It's only 26 miles North from Spokane, and the perfect place to "treat yourself and treat the kiddies."

As the sun sets, we'll pilot that 6-hp outboard over to Cedar Beau Bay for our ritualistic, near-mythic experience of night fishing. I'll almost set myself on fire lighting up the old Coleman lantern, probably drop my tackle box in the lake, and jab numerous #10 glo-hooks into my thumb. She'll have a giggle fit, and I'll feel like William Bendix in 'The Life of Riley" – the bumbling dad you can't help but love.

On the mirror-clear lake, illumined by an oversize moon, we stay up past her bedtime talking, joking, reeling in good-size rainbows, and throwing back undersize catfish. I demonstrate the catfish's uncanny resemblance to Edward G. Robinson by sticking a cigarette between its lips. She doesn't know Edward G. Robinson, but the visual is vastly amusing. Her laughter bounces back from the hillside, accompanied by the soft creak of old wooden docks. At length, tired yawns replace giddy jocularity. Before pulling up the concrete-filled coffee can anchors and pointing the bow towards our cabin's distant light, we'll softly speak of serious matters, unresolved issues, and eternal questions.

"Papa," she'll ask, as she always does, "are there dogs in heaven?"

Burl Barer is an Edgar Award winner, and two-time Anthony Award nominee, born and raised in Walla Walla, Washington. In addition to the Jeff Reynolds series, Barer writes true crime, popular culture, and the new adventures of Leslie Charteris' The Saint. He is remarkably handsome and exceptionally entertaining.